TRAP

TERRAWAY
BOOK EIGHT

MARY E. TWOMEY

MARY E. TWOMEY, LLC

TRAP

BOOK EIGHT IN THE TERRAWAY SERIES

By

Mary E. Twomey

COPYRIGHT

ACKNOWLEDGMENTS

This series wouldn't have been possible without the help
of several people, each of whom deserve like, a whole
bucket of candy
(the good candy, not like, Necco or something).

The Write Club – for your critiques, your kindness, and
your infinite patience. I can't believe you're not sick of this
series yet. Kudos to you on keeping your groans internal.

Ruth Gross – friend and editor to the extreme. Thank you
for not letting me sound like a dummy.

Brian Androsian – the best assistant a girl could ask for.
You're not a bad brother, either.

Powerhouse – for your insight and team spirit.

Kim Saks McManaway – for being the coolest Political
Science professor in the universe.
Thank you for letting me pick your brain, so this series
could be stronger.

My ARC Team – Wow. You guys blew my mind this time around. Your emails, your typo-checking, and your encouragement have made this series far stronger than it would've been without your kindness. This string of pornographic twerks I'm about to do is dedicated to you. (You can't see it, but I just popped-and-locked in your honor. You're welcome).

DEDICATION

For Bruce Campbell,

*Not many are heroic enough to warrant
a ridiculous girl make-believing you're her own personal
superhero.*

*Thanks for being mine this time around.
Mine, all mine.*

1

MARIANG'S FUNERAL

Though I'd seen an avalanche of deaths in the past year, I'd only been to one funeral in my life. It was for Mrs. Kitsa, when I was young. I could still smell the thick pancake makeup on her, marring the cookie smell she'd always traveled with. Mrs. Kitsa had been one of our neighbors a few trailers down. She loved to bake, and always had a smile for Ollie, Allie and me. When she'd passed at eighty-two, I'd been only nine. Ollie and Allie took me to the funeral, clothes washed, faces scrubbed and somber. We sat in the back, and I watched with fascination the ritual of a funeral. The praying, the hopeful message, and the mournful family who had never once come to the trailer park to visit their mother, grandmother or great-grandmother. Yet they all cried quietly into handkerchiefs and sleeves, swearing they thought they'd have more time.

Mama McCray's funeral was when I was seven, but I hadn't been allowed to go.

Omen funerals in Terraway were... different. The grand affair was held at Kabayo's enormous stone castle. It somehow felt drafty and cold, despite the sunny ninety-degree weather that beat down on the expanse of grass covering the field. Last time I'd been in Silo, everything had been bone dry due to the drought, with barely a patch of green in sight. Now with regular rain coming, there were traces of emerald, jade and olive brushed through the woods, dotting the ground and filling out the mountains. It was beautiful, but I couldn't really appreciate it, being that we were there for Mariang's funeral. All six nations were gathered outside the castle. People from the furthest corners of Terraway came out to pay their respects to the woman who'd given everything to make sure they had a chance at survival. Mariang's body had been magically preserved somehow, making her look like she was merely sleeping, though she'd been dead an entire month now. Each day felt like heaviness in my breast that I couldn't escape. Every passing hour that Mariang remained dead, I grew more weighted, the youth gone from me completely.

The council and kings had been given ornate chairs to sit on, facing the crowd above the stone steps of the castle. The casket was before us, resting on the expansive dais between the royals and the people. I was on the council, and Mason as well, since he was the delegate from Sombi, so we were given chairs, but Von was made to stand behind me as my sentry, staring out at the crowd with a hollow expression.

The members of the council were dressed in their royal robes or their decorated military gear. I didn't put up a fuss about being given a long Renaissance-style dress to wear, but I couldn't stop fidgeting with the revealing neckline, the capped sleeves, or the heavy black and gold material that made me feel like I was wearing curtains or something. The black felt appropriate for a funeral, but the gold swirls that started at the hemline and crawled up like vines to cup and brush over my breasts did not. It wasn't until I saw Ezra's matching tie and Ana's black and gold baby gown that I realized the design must be a family thing. Ezra was seated at my left, his eyes bloodshot and expression vacant as he stared ahead at the millions his daughter had been sacrificed for over and over again. After all of it, she'd survived. It hadn't been Terraway that killed her, but our world, or nature perhaps. No one had expected her to die in childbirth – except Sama, perhaps, who had warned me in my dream back when I was pregnant that Omens had a higher mortality rate during pregnancy than other women. The shock of Mariang's death was still hitting us in waves. The world had left us bereft of her grace and kindness that only death itself could silence.

Von was behind me, wearing a fitted black suit, with a gold and black tie to match Ezra's. He was holding Anastasia Grace with bags under his eyes and a fatherly protective air to the way he cradled her. We hadn't slept much in the past month. Of course, no one slept well after Mariang passed, but we had been gifted the extra responsibility of taking care of Baby Ana. Danny could barely put one foot in front of the other, and couldn't comprehend that Ana was very much alive and in need of her parent. Von, Danny, Ana, Ollie and I had been living at my house, with the Vandershot boys rotating to pull for Danny as needed, which was often.

"Motherhood suits you," Finn whispered from his throne-like chair on my right. "You look lovely."

I responded with a polite, "Thank you, Captain." Everything I did was being scrutinized by the residents of Terraway, who were all sitting just a stone's throw away on the grass at the foot of the steps. I didn't feel the guilty thrill I usually did at being near Finn. My focus was on Von, Ezra, Danny and Anastasia. I hadn't even been to visit Allie in her coma in days. Ana had a penchant for screaming from midnight until around four in the morning, and intermittently throughout the day, so Von and I weren't sleeping much. Ollie had even bailed to spend a couple nights at Gabby's just to catch up on his rest. Apparently braving the "where is this going" talk with his on-again off-again girlfriend was less horrible than a nonstop screaming baby.

Mason was on the clear other end, sitting next to a man that could've been his twin. While the people were still milling about and finding their space on the grass, I got up from my chair and made my way over to my other Reaper, knowing he was afraid to get too near the baby – though Ana was now a month old, and supposedly in the safety zone to escape stirring the fetus hunger of Matruculans.

I knew I was supposed to be some queen or whatever, but I didn't care about decorum when it came to my Pullers. When Mason stood to greet me, I jogged forward after I passed the casket I didn't want to look at too closely. I threw my arms around him, squeezing tighter than anyone would have the tolerance for, were he not part The Hulk. Mason possessed a super strength that had a way of making me feel safe. Perched above the whole of Terraway for everyone to observe and comment on, I needed that feeling he instilled in me just by being there.

I could feel his smile against my cheek, his quarter-inch beard scratching my skin in a way that felt like home. "I missed you, *hani*. I know you've been busy taking care of Anastasia, but I'm worried about you. You're well? You're in one functioning piece?"

"I'm much better, now that you're here. This whole thing is horrible, and I'm sorry you're dealing with it all alone. I don't want that."

"Alton said he'd get me a phone, so I was thinking I'd start calling you every night just to check in and make sure you're alive. We're not meant to be apart this long."

I could feel him pulling for me, and I breathed for the first time in a while. "Mason, I missed you."

"You're a ball of anxiety. Haven't Von and his brothers been pulling for you?" He ignored the millions of onlookers that were shifting around on the grass. He held me around the waist, moving his head back to examine my face. "You look exhausted."

"Aw, you say the sweetest things. You look beautiful, too," I crooned.

"I didn't mean it like that. You're lovely, as you always are. But you need more pulling than this."

I shook my head, making sure to keep my tears sucked back behind my eyeballs. "Danny's a wreck still, and Anastasia…" I gulped, fishing for the right way to word the issue. "Ana needs her mother. She's colicky, so she screams a lot. Von's pulling for her now just so we make it through the funeral. I don't want to overtax the guys, making them pull for me, on top of all that. I can deal the old-fashioned way."

"I see. Well, let's see what I can do while I have you in my arms." Mason hugged me tighter, kissing the top of my head and tucking me under his chin. Waves of peace shot through me, making my eyes flutter shut as I burrowed my cheek into his burly chest. I stiffened when I heard the "aw" and the whispers that broke out from the residents of Terraway, reminding me that I had an audience of millions. Mason was a feared and respected zombie killer, and I was cozying up to him like he was a precious bunny. Or maybe I was his bunny. It was hard to tell who took care of whom on any given day. "Better?" he asked, leaning down to peck my lips. He dropped his arms so he could offer me his elbow to hold like a gentleman.

"Much."

"Would you like to meet my younger brother? This is Carter, King of Hayop. Carter, allow me to introduce Lady October."

Mason's double stood, showing off his midnight-colored royal robe overtop his black tunic, and matching fitted pants that were tucked into his sturdy boots. He had dreads tied back with a leather string, looking like Mason used to, back when I first met him. Carter tilted his head to me and dipped his chin, and I did the same to him, thinking that was probably the right thing to do. I really had no idea about the proper politics of Terraway, and now was a bad time to ask Ezra at what times I was expected to bow. "Pleased to meet you, Lady October," Carter offered kindly. Carter had a boyish light to his slate eyes that Mason just plain didn't. Mason had been all Viking from the get-go. Carter had the same build, but looked like he preferred the hard work being done from his throne. "My brother speaks very highly of you."

"Oh, well now I know you're lying. Mason hates me. I mean, one look at me and he starts ralphing." In hindsight, making jokes about puking the first time I met Mason's only living relative was probably not the queenly thing to do. But you know, whatever. It was either make playful banter or burst into tears. I batted my hand at Carter's grin. "But don't worry, the feeling's mutual. I mean, would you look at this guy? Barfalicious."

"Hey!" Mason bumped me with his hip, narrowing one eye down at me before his smile got the better of him.

Carter started to laugh, but then covered his mouth with his hand and faked a cough. "Excuse me. I didn't realize anyone on the council knew how to make a joke."

"Who said I was joking?" I motioned to Mason's perfect physique that shone even beneath his outfit that matched his brother's, but included gold cuffs around his wrists. "I mean, hit the gym once in a while, am I right?" The gold on his cuffs made it look like Mason belonged with me, with my family. It was a sweet assurance in the midst of the bleakness. I fished around for shtick, so I didn't plunge back into despair.

Carter's eyes were dancing with the light he seemed to travel with. "Oh, Mason. You said she was beautiful, but I didn't realize she was witty, too. Perhaps I won't avoid the council as much anymore."

"Yes, well." Mason smiled down at me, and I could feel the love beaming from him that I was making nice with his brother. "If you're finished bewitching Carter, perhaps you'd like to meet the other kings of Terraway who've been too busy to show up for council meetings."

I curtsied like I'd seen people do in movies and moved on down the line, shaking hands, bowing and making as pleasant of chitchat as I could.

Mason gave me one more solid pull in his parting hug when we reached the midpoint of the stage. "This is as far as I can take you. Anastasia's still too young for me to be near."

"Oh, sorry. I'll talk to you after." I leaned up and blessed his lips with a closed-mouth kiss. "Love you, Mason."

"Love you, too. Now go shake hands, and tell Von not to listen to you when you say you don't need more pulling."

It was just my luck that Aranya's was the next throne I came to. Aranya was the jaggoff who'd helped his father, King Geon, lock me in their dungeon in Sakuna, trying to keep me as a prize for Sama. I wanted to punch him, but knew that would probably not be good politics. Lang rose to his feet beside Aranya, along with their sinister sister, Luna. They were dressed in matching brown royal outfits, and a smattering of bees circled almost pleasantly around Aranya's head. Lang was no doubt anxious I might throttle his tool of a brother right there with a whole sea of witnesses. The three bowed, but I refused to tilt my head to Aranya or Luna. Luna noticed the affront, but Aranya brushed aside the offense, extending his hand to me instead.

Boy, do I wish I would've passed on shaking it. I couldn't stifle the anger that flared in me. I gripped Aranya's hand and jerked him close, leaning up on my toes to whisper a threat to him and Luna. "Don't you think I've forgotten the stink of your daddy's dungeon. Make no mistake, as soon as things settle down for me, I'll make it my life's mission to make sure you're taken off that throne and hurled into your own prison. Then we'll have some real fun."

Luna was snide, not bothering to conceal her snarl. "Step foot in Sakuna again, and you'll see how fun things can really get when father's not holding me back."

Aranya's black eyes widened. His brown skin had been scrubbed of mud, but he still felt dirty to me. He kept his voice low, but I moved on after I heard, "Listen you little..."

I wasn't little, and I didn't have to listen.

Kabayo rose, his left hand on the small of my back as he shook Aranya's with his right, leaning in to whisper a threat of his own. He released Aranya with a look of horror on the man's face that matched his sister's. "Leave him to me," Kabayo whispered in my ear, releasing me with a light push away from the man who'd helped abduct me, and the woman who'd delighted in my degradation.

I gave a slight nod to Lang, which he returned. I tried to appear professional, and not like I wanted to hug him. It was important to his family that he remain loyal to their cause. It could make things sticky for him if they knew we were friends. My upper lip curled at Luna's pinched nose and waist-length curly brown hair, but I moved on down the line without further incident.

In the front row of the millions sat Ollie, Lynna, Boston, Graham, Alton and Ms. Vandershot. It was the first time I'd ever seen Von's mother. I was afraid to look at her directly, though my eyes felt tethered to her face, bouncing back whenever they wandered too far. She'd come in for the funeral, and to meet her first grandchild. There was much of Von in her face, the angular cheekbones, the black hair that was thick and did what it felt like. Her long, dark waves were pulled back and pinned elegantly, making her look like a model for hairspray or something. She was beautiful, and second only to Sama was my fear of her.

The ceremony finally started a few minutes later. Some guy I didn't know gave the eulogy in a long black wizard's robe, performing several herb-centric rituals over Mariang's body. She lay like Sleeping Beauty inside her clear casket for all to admire, palms open and feet bare – as was the tradition in Terraway. Even in death, she was beautiful. I hated how lifelike she appeared, and gripped my fingers in my lap to keep them from clawing at my arms. I wanted to be there for Ezra and Danny, and knew I couldn't do that if I fell apart.

Danny was in a world unto himself, unable to speak, eat or make a decision unless someone helped him. The only time he slept was in my arms after Von pulled so hard, Danny had no choice but to go limp. I alternated between rocking Ana and holding Danny all the hours of the day I wasn't reaping. Now he stood at the head of Mariang's casket, facing the people with soulless eyes in a tailored black suit with gold cuffs that I knew he'd never wear again.

The service lasted two hours. Two whole hours I prayed Ana would sleep through. I didn't want her seeing any of this, and since she was a colicky baby, I worried about Von having to miss the funeral if she woke. Two whole hours I willed with everything in me that Mason and Ezra would have the strength not to shapeshift with a new baby so near them. Ezra was more controlled, his years giving me a little solace that he wouldn't lion out and try to eat my niece (I really hope that was the weirdest sentence I'd ever thought). Mason and Carter's chairs had been strategically placed at the far end by Kabayo, keeping as much distance as possible between the fresh newborn and my favorite Viking.

Finn had been assigned to watch Ana and me for the duration of my time in Terraway that day. The council worried that Sama's spirit or his whole friggin' army might make an appearance, since I was in Terraway, ripe for the abducting. It made for a tense funeral, as if we didn't have enough to stress about. Had I a solid two hours of consecutive sleep in the past month, I might've been able to be worried about Sama, but lucky for my sanity, I couldn't feel much.

I didn't understand the different steps of the ritual, but I managed to stand when the other council members did, and murmur the things I was told to say. Finn was my coach at my side, making sure I didn't embarrass Ezra or the council.

I was pretty sure I was blending in until the grand wizard in charge announced the procession of the *hiya*. I didn't know what that was, but I knew I was not all that comfortable around the silver-haired guy doing the funeral. Von had informed me he was Mangkukulam, which I knew was what Sama was. While this guy seemed on the up and up, I was positive I'd never be comfortable around any of the few warlocks of Terraway.

The Grand Mangkukulam in charge of the funeral raised his arms, allowing the last row of civilians to make their way past the casket to pay their respects first. I bowed my head and paced myself for the first of millions to make their way past Mariang in all of her sleeping ballerina beauty. What made my chin jerk up with sudden rage was when I heard the distinct sound of spitting in Danny's direction as they walked by.

2

OVER MY DEAD BODY

"What the..." I whispered when I saw residents with brown skin and muddy clothes from Sakuna bowing their heads to Mariang, and spitting on Danny as they crossed the stone dais. Danny stood at the head of the casket like a soulless sentry, not reacting to the disgraceful affront. My head jerked to Finn for an explanation, or I don't know, a spare knife so I could threaten those jerks right good.

Von placed his hand on my shoulder while Finn touched my arm. It was like they were both trying to anchor me to the fancy carved seat that was much too big and grand for me. "This is all part of burying an Omen," Finn explained. "Respect for the Omen and cursing the Reaper who let her fall. Danny's being shamed now. It's part of the ceremony."

My mouth dropped open in horror. Poor Ms. Vandershot was weeping softly into her hand in the front row on the grass, her eyes closed against the painful sight. Ceremony or not, I wouldn't sit back like a cold queen and let something so horrible happen to my brother. When I bit it someday, this would all be happening to Mason and Von, who didn't deserve that. Over my dead body would that happen to my guys, and I sure as Sunday wasn't about to sit back and let it happen to Danny, who'd been through enough.

When a woman my age who should've known better spat into Danny's face while he just took it, I knew I couldn't endure another second. "Dad, can I borrow your handkerchief?" I asked Ezra quietly.

"Of course, dear." It was already in Ezra's hands, wet from his own tears. He handed it to me, and I stood from my throne, ignoring Finn, who barked a whisper at me to come back and sit down.

Without a word, I stopped the procession of respect and mockery. Sliding in front of Danny, I wiped his face with Ezra's handkerchief and dabbed at the few gobs of spit on his beautiful black suit. The gold cuffs that matched Ezra's, Von's and Mason's united us as a family, and I knew I couldn't do nothing while someone I loved was being bullied.

"Go sit down," Danny whispered, his eyes meeting mine. When my face filled his vision, he was finally able to focus on anything other than his perpetual misery. "It's what's supposed to happen. I let her f-fall."

"This stupid tradition stops today." I wrapped my arms around Danny, proud of myself for so many things with that simple hug. He was spattered in germs, for one, and I didn't shy away from the mess. Secondly, I was publicly hugging someone while standing up for what I knew was right, without apology. Without turning around to check, I knew Ollie was proud of me.

Danny kept his stiff position while I turned to face the next person in line with an "I friggin' dare you" face, my chin raised defiantly. The man who easily could've been Ezra's age paused, unsure what to do. He couldn't spit on Danny without getting me, which I knew wasn't kosher. His confused bronze face looked to the Grand Mangkukulam Wizard for direction.

The Grand Mangkukulam made his way to the foot of the casket, whispering over Mariang to me. "You're to sit in your seat of honor, Lady October. They can't curse the Reaper if you're in the way."

I raised my voice, not bothering to hide my anger. "Anyone who curses Danny, curses me. He's my brother, and your fallen Omen would cry for a hundred years if she could see how you're treating him. Danny gave up his life for Terraway, too. This tradition is terrible, and it ends right now. You'll show my brother the respect he deserves, or I stop reaping today!"

Scared and confused murmurs rippled through the

crowd. The millions of faces gaped at me like I'd just stolen their puppy. I heard one common thread rise above the din. "Can she really do that?"

I pressed my fist to my chest. "You'd best believe I'll make good on my word. I'll go on strike before I sacrifice myself to save a world who treats their heroes like this. No one spits on my family!" Though I was standing up for Danny, that one truth rang through me like the reverberations from a gong. I met Ollie's eyes, allowing his proud nod to fuel me. I wasn't just standing for Danny. I was declaring my unswerving loyalty to the whole Vandershot clan, the Reeses (those dead and alive), and the Manauls. Somehow we'd become one family, and I knew better than to throw something valuable away.

Before I knew it, Von was at my side, holding Ana and standing in front of Danny with me to form a wall of protection between his brother and the people. He yelled out so everyone could hear his defiance of tradition. "This is Lady Mariang's daughter – a future Omen! This is Terraway's daughter – your daughter. If you spit near Danny, you'll be cursing Lady October, *and* Lady Anastasia! I dare you to see how well that goes over with the council."

Mason stood and moved forward on his side of the stage, still too afraid to come near the baby, but unwilling to stand down and let us face the whole of Terraway without him. He pounded his fist to his barreled chest. "I belong to Lady October, so I would think twice before spitting near her and facing my wrath."

I turned my chin to look at Mason, meeting his eyes and tapping my chest to show him where his home truly was. He nodded solemnly, fists still clenched in a dare for anyone to test him.

That was all it took for the Vandershot brothers, Ms. Vandershot, Lynna and Ollie, who were front and center on the grass, to run up to stand in front of Von, Ana and me to form a more solid wall to protect Danny. Ms. Vandershot wept quietly at the display of her family standing together as a united front, her chin raised and eyes fierce with defiance. She reached behind her and gripped my hand tight in a silent thanks that both scared and humbled me. I didn't have much experience getting moms to like me, and hoped this was a good sign.

Seeing the brothers all lined up in their black fitted suits, staring out at the millions with jaws and fists clenched made my heart swell. I knew Mariang would be proud of the family who loved her even after death.

Finn and Ezra stood to unite themselves with us. Finn and Mason directed the line on the left of the stage to bypass our family after paying their somber respects to Mariang. Ezra stood behind Von and me, wrapping his arms tight around Danny, who I could hear sobbing in his gentle father's arms.

"Thank you. Thank you for standing up for my brother. I'm furious I didn't think to do it," Von said out of the side of his mouth, glancing at me from the corner of his eyes as he faced the masses. "I love you, you know."

I ventured a smirk on the dark, awful day, as I looped my hand to clutch the crook of his elbow. "I don't blame you."

3

EVIL LITTLE GHOUL

The funeral procession lasted hours. I don't know how long it was that I stood in front of Danny, but my whole body was yelling at me to go to sleep when the line continued long after the suns went down.

I nearly jumped when Ezra placed his hand on my shoulder. "Darling, can you take Anastasia Grace for a walk? My self-control is waning."

It was only then I realized he was breathing through his teeth, and no doubt holding onto his human side for dear life. "Of course. You guys got Danny?"

"Keep walking, old man. That's right." Boston's fists clenched as he snarled at a man who walked by with a glare aimed at Danny. "Not a problem. I could do this all night."

Von and I moved into the castle, gusting out a deep breath

when we were finally hidden from the public eye. I fished through the diaper bag that I'd stashed just inside the heavy wooden doors. "I've got you, baby doll," I offered as I shook some formula up with the bottled water I'd brought for her.

Ana had just started fussing, so I sunk to sit on the floor and held my hands out for her to give Von a break. He'd been the one ducking into the castle to feed and change her today, since I couldn't leave my post. "I'm sorry. Your arms must be so tired. Let me have a turn."

"Thanks, love. Easy with her. I know we said we wouldn't use pulling on her, but I couldn't very well let her scream throughout the entire service."

"You've been pulling this entire time?" My eyes went wide as I cradled the sweetest sweetness in my arms, feeding her the bottle I knew she was hungry for. She was pleasantly staring up at me, making precious cooing noises that erased the memory of the hours of screaming she'd done all night long. She was magic incarnate, bewitching me at every turn; Von and I were completely enamored of her.

"I wasn't pulling the entire time. Just when she starts to go on about the sodden state of the union."

"You must be starving. Do you need to refuel? I stashed a blood pouch in the diaper bag."

Von's gold and blue eyes softened as they fell on my face, which held no condemnation of all that he was. "You love me."

"Can you blame me? You're doing that suit all sorts of favors."

Von offered up a silent snort, trying to hold onto a sense of humor that had served him so well until today. Today was simply bleak, and there was no painting a happy face on the frown. "I can't believe we're here, that this is happening. It doesn't feel real."

"If only it wasn't real. What happens after the *hiya* procession?"

"Terraway watches while the Mangkukulam burns her body. Then Kabayo gives an address, and that's that."

My mouth gaped. "Burns her body? Why can't Kabayo just bury her in his crypt?"

Von swallowed hard, running his hand through his short hair. "It keeps her body from reanimating. So much goes on in an awakened Omen's body. It's not safe to simply bury her. Omens who've been awakened have a lot in them that regular Terraway citizens don't. We can't take the risk of her turning."

I chewed on my lower lip, forcing out the image of my sis coming at me with skin patches missing and jaw slack, like the residents of Terraway did when they weren't buried properly. "Oh. Well, I guess we don't want Mariang reanimating. That wouldn't be good. We wouldn't want her walking to Sombi."

"She has too much magic to turn into a zombie." Von waved his hand like this was all no big deal to be discussing. "That's for the commoners like me and the rest of Terraway. She wouldn't do that. She'd turn into a Woman in White."

"Huh? Like a bride?"

"Not exactly." Von sunk down next to me, his back against the stone wall as his knee rested against mine. Not to oversell the Omen-Reaper bond, but I could practically feel his exhaustion through the small contact of his knee on mine. I kissed his cheek as he explained. "A Woman in White is a sort of apparition. She appears to desperate men and beckons them to her. Eventually they succumb, and usually they die." He unscrewed the cap on the blood bag, wrapping his free arm around my shoulders to bring both of us closer. "You have to burn her whole body, other-wise her spirit will cling to her remnants. Then she'll turn into a Woman in White who roams near where her body remains. Utter havoc."

My mouth fell open. "Bruce Campbell never had to deal with crap like this. He got to shoot demons and call it a day. Take 'em out with his boomstick, and that's that. Now we're all burning bodies and dealing with ghost-zombie nonsense."

"I'm pretty sure none of this would've thrown your first love. Bruce's got a chin that could conquer anything."

I leaned my temple to his shoulder and sighed in the quiet of our little huddle. "You're so sexy when you talk like that. When you love Bruce Campbell, it only makes me want you more."

Von chuckled, draining the last of the blood bag. He

crossed his arm over me to stroke Ana's cheek. "It'll be alright, yeah? You've both got me to watch over you until Bruce's schedule frees up and he can guard you nice and proper, as he should."

I closed my eyes and kissed Anastasia's forehead, wishing she would never know anything about Terraway. "I don't want Ana to ever have to be awakened. To think of her withering away like Mariang did? It's eating at my guts just thinking about it. She's so tiny."

"*You're* so tiny," he commented, his arm tightening around my shoulders in protection.

"I was thinking maybe we should up the daily count of souls we reap. I mean, now that Mason's back, I think that'll help me be able to reap more. Six a day isn't cutting it."

"Slow down, speedy. We need *one* soul per day. The six a day we're doing is more than plenty. We've got a nice stock of souls built up for the occasional day away. Nice jaunt for holiday here, soul-crushing funeral there. We don't need to do more than that."

Ana felt so small and fragile in my arms. "But if I do enough for years, maybe even decades, then no other Omen has to be awakened in our lifetime. Anastasia can enjoy a normal life Topside. She's only a month old, and she's already had a rough life."

"No," Von ruled. His usually relaxed tone was resolute as he planted his stake in the ground to show me how little he was willing to compromise on this. "I won't sacrifice you like that. Danny had no choice in the matter. Mariang couldn't keep up, no matter how hard she worked. I want you to be the first Omen to see her forties. I mean it, Peach. I know how you get when you're jonesing to work, but this isn't an option. Anastasia will be awakened when she's an adult and can handle such things. She'll have to reap one person a day, which means that both of you could live to be old women." He kissed my temple. "I want to see you with white hair all done up in a sexy librarian bun someday. I want you to take up knitting tea cozies and carry around sweets in your purse."

"Well, I've got blood bags and formula in my purse now. Does that count?" I don't know why I tried to make a joke out of his sincerity. It was such a beautiful thing for him to say – I didn't feel worthy of so grand a compliment.

Von narrowed one eye at me, seeing right through my deflection. "I love you, no matter how you try to make jokes to deal with that reality. Let's just get through this, yeah? One day at a time."

I nodded, but couldn't help voicing the thing that had only just begun to plague me. "They're going to burn my body."

Von stiffened, his eyebrows tenting in the center of his forehead. "What? Who?"

"When I die someday. You're going to stand at my casket with Mason, and they're going to burn me, so I don't come back and haunt you." I pursed my lips, unsure how to feel about it all. "I had big plans for haunting you, too."

"Then I'll steal you away, and you can haunt me until I'm mad in my obsession for you. I'm near enough to the edge of sanity as it is. I'd love nothing more than a lifetime of your hijinks, you evil little ghoul." Von gave me a light kiss that softened both of our dismal moods, but didn't take us fully under with hallucinations. When we blinked away the trickling of blue and gold, the music that usually started lulling us blasted in our ears, making us jump. Anastasia startled and began wailing that we'd jostled her when she was trying to drink her bottle in peace. "What is that?" I shouted to Von, who stood to peer through the heavy wooden doors.

His eyes turned to saucers, and he backed up when Finn and Mason crashed through to join us in the safety of the stone castle. "The four of you are porting right now," Finn declared with no room for argument, and no explanation. "Up you get." He held his hand flat to Mason, who kept his distance from Ana as if her life depended on it, which it did.

"What's going on? What's wrong?" I stood with Ana in my arms and the diaper bag slung over my shoulder. "What are the trumpets for?"

Mason looked at Ana with fear that was mixed with longing and self-loathing. "I'm porting Von and Danny to Ezra's mansion now! I can't be around the baby yet. She's too fresh! Take October to her house so I don't turn and... Just take her and the baby to her house and wait for Von there."

Von opened his mouth to protest at our parting, but Mason was running out of self-control. He dragged Von out of the castle toward Danny, so the three could port together.

"What's happening, Finn? What's going on out there?"

"There's no time. We have to go now." Finn's arms went around me, keeping the wailing baby sandwiched between us with great care. He gripped my waist, while his other hand touched Ana's head tenderly.

When the wooden door burst open again, Ezra shouted a frantic, "Go! Get them out of here!"

Then Ezra tripped forward, pelted with something from behind that hit him with too much force. A large stone followed up the assault, missing Ezra and smacking Finn in the head. Ezra's intake of breath and the sudden surprise on his face scared me more than the thrumming I could hear coming from outside, mingling with the whirring in my ears. Ezra's cry felt ominous and made my heart race as I ran toward him. My dad's jaw went slack in a pained moan as he toppled forward, smacking his face on the stone to reveal an arrow sticking out of his back.

FATHER ON THE FLOOR

I don't know how Finn ported all of us out at once, but when the four of us arrived in my living room, my favorite captain blacked clean out and collapsed on the carpet. I nearly dropped Anastasia, but managed to hold onto her, clutching the tiny baby for dear life as I tried to make sense of what had just happened, so I could form a plan.

Finn was a warrior; he would be fine dealing with a fainting spell and a blow to the head. He would be priority number two after Ezra.

Ana was pissed, but she was alright. I needed both hands to tend to Ezra, who was busy bleeding as he lay face-down on my beige living room carpet. Though she screamed operatically, I ran Anastasia to my bedroom and laid her in the bassinet. I knew she wanted to be held, but breathed through my panic when I reasoned she would be at least physically okay in the bassinet. I shut the door to keep the smell of her baby skin away from Ezra, hoping with everything in me that Ezra didn't shift and turn into a lion in my house. I shoved the throw that had been folded over the arm of the couch under the door, to stem the baby smell from tempting fate.

I raced to the bathroom and yanked my first aid kit from the counter under the sink. I dove headfirst into nurse-mode as I ran to kneel between the two men, checking Finn's pulse and then turning my focus to Ezra. I didn't have time take him to the hospital or even to wash my hands. I'd only just gotten the brace off my wrist from my run-in with some monsters in Sombi, so my dexterity wasn't all that reassuring. Using the scissors in my kit, I clumsily cut a slit from the hem of the back of Ezra's shirt and suit jacket up past the arrow, folding the material out of the way so I could see his back and his side fully exposed. I counted his ribs to make sure the arrow hadn't punctured anything vital, praying that my shaking hands wouldn't make more of a mess than what was currently painting his body red.

Treating inmates was different than trying to save your surrogate father. I didn't blink twice when someone came in with a shiv sticking out of their leg. Ezra was the man who'd done everything he could to save me from my life and myself. I couldn't let him die on the day of his daughter's funeral. It was too awful.

I blew on my hands and then took in a deep breath as I

gripped the arrow where the steel married with crude wood. Anastasia screamed in time with her grandfather when the jagged tip slid slowly out. More blood bubbled out from Ezra, trickling down over his side as he bit down into the carpet to take his pain out on the soft fibers. "It's out. It's okay. I know it hurts, but I don't think it got anything vital." I ignored his groans as I pressed my fingers around the area, making sure I wasn't speaking my hopes as if they were fact. My shoulders drooped in relief. "No, your organs are intact. Let me clean this and sew it up. Then we'll take you to the hospital so they can give you a second look to be sure."

Ezra was sweating, and I wasn't sure he could even hear me. I set to work disinfecting, apologizing for every cry he uttered at my hands. When he was cleaned, stitched, and bandaged, his body went limp on the floor. Ezra's eyes closed as the pain mixed with his grief, and took him to a place where no one could reach him. Where *I* couldn't reach him.

I hadn't cried at the funeral. Blame it on shock, or blame it on the millions of people watching my every move, but there it was. I was a robot. I hadn't been able to feel the awful sting of the girl I'd regarded as my sister dying since they'd placed Anastasia Grace in my arms. Since then, the world had revolved around Ana: her feeding schedule, babyproofing the house, moving the baby stuff in and setting everything up (if you ever want to see your fiancé talk in only a string of swears, let him set up the crib without the directions he promises he doesn't need), her sleeping schedule, and a litany of other things I was still trying to figure out. I couldn't cry. There wasn't any time.

Anastasia had no problem telling everyone and their mailman how unhappy she was. The pediatrician had assured me that colicky babies are just like this, and that time is the only thing that helps, though I was welcome to spin my wheels trying everything under the sun. The super nutritional allergen-free fortified formula was no help. Girlfriend had lost her mother, and was grieving the way she should – the way *I* should, but couldn't.

"I have to go back down to Terraway. They need my help down there." Ezra tried to get up on all fours, but didn't make it halfway to kneeling before I laid him face-down again on the floor. "Easy, now. You're not going anywhere."

"But I'm on the council. I have to help the people."

"You won't help anybody if you bleed out. Just rest. There's nothing you can do right now."

Ezra exhaled, tears coming to him even more, now that he had mountains of physical and emotional pain to surround him. I placed a kiss to the back of Ezra's head, holding his hand when he reached for me in his haze of never-ending sadness. "She's gone," he whispered, his eyes shut tight. "My little girl. I did everything I could, but she still... I never expected Terraway wouldn't be the thing what brought her down. I didn't think to safeguard her from motherhood."

He was still lying on his stomach, so I didn't know how to comfort him without moving him, which I didn't think he was ready for yet. I brushed his blond hair back with gentle fingers around his temples while he clutched my other hand. I didn't have words of solace to offer him. I mean, what was there to say? Dude had lost his wife, his fiancée, and now his daughter. I reached into my heart and produced the only thing I could think to give him. "Ezra, we're all here for you. The Vandershots, Ollie and me, Anastasia – we all love you. I'm so sorry I can't fix this."

"My little girl," he moaned, cupping my palm to his face so he could weep into my skin. He winced when his breathing was so erratic that his wound made him gasp in pain.

My free hand ghosted over his back, landing on the center and slowly rubbing the ache in his heart. "Easy, now. The more worked up you get, the worse your injury's going to hurt."

Ezra seemed to come to himself marginally, sucking in the tears I could see he was embarrassed by, though I couldn't tell you why he thought I'd judge him for breaking down. "I'm sorry, dear. How dreadful, me lying on your floor, bleeding and weeping all over. Help an old man up?"

"No. You lie down and take it easy. I don't want you moving for anything, understand? I don't think the arrow hit your vitals, but I can't be sure nothing got nicked. That means you're not moving." I stood, clumsy in my too-long dress, and took a throw pillow from the couch, working it under his head. "There. That's gotta be a step up from your face on the floor."

"Indeed. Thank you."

I slid the second throw pillow under Finn's knees. Then I pulled Ollie's comforter off his mattress to cover Finn with it. I checked his steady pulse again, his pupils to make sure they dilated properly, and placed a kiss to his forehead before digging in my diaper bag and pulling out the balisong blade Finn had given me. I didn't know who had shot at Ezra, but I was certain we weren't out of the woods yet. I had a baby, a king and a friend I cared deeply for to protect. With Ana shut in the bedroom, I positioned myself between the two men, my knife drawn as I waited to kill whatever came through the front door to get at my family.

5

SAMA'S USEFUL PILLOW TALK

Von was not thrilled that I had the knife out, aimed and ready to stab him when he stepped into the house using his key. "Will you put that thing away? He's not coming here to attack you."

"Who?"

Von looked at me like I was playing around. "The Easter Bunny." He gasped when his eyes fell on Ezra, and the drips of blood that stained the living room carpet. "Is he..."

"He's alright, just not moving for now. The arrow was in deep, but it's out."

Ezra raised his arm. "I'm alright, son. Mason and you are well?"

"I don't think any of us will be well after today. But no arrows in my bum, if that's what you're wondering." He made his way to the bedroom, unable to let Ana cry for more than a minute without intervening. He came out with the red-faced angel, and I knew from the way her operatic cries slowly lessened in waves that he was pulling a small amount to get her to calm down.

I narrowed my eyes at him and pointed with the knife. "We agreed we wouldn't use pulling. She has to learn to self-soothe. It's in the book, Von."

"I can't think when she's screaming. I can see myself throwing whole cars out of the way when she gets going, just so I can get to her and calm her down. She's already been through so much. Baby's first war – and me without my camera to capture it on film for the baby book."

"Huh? What happened down there?"

Von looked up to assess my serious tone. "You truly don't know?"

"Of course not. Finn passed out from porting three people at once and getting hit in the head with a rock, and Ezra's been resting. What happened?"

Ezra reached up to paw at Von's pant leg, silently asking for help to stand. Von lay Anastasia on the carpet and took one arm of Ezra's while I took the other. "Slowly," I cautioned. "Try not to move your back so much." We carefully lifted Ezra and lowered him onto a chair in the kitchen, taking in his "oof" to mean he would not be leaving the house for a while. When he was situated, I poured him a glass of water and set it on the table before him. "Now tell me what happened in Terraway. Who shot Ezra?"

Von came back into the kitchen with Anastasia holding onto his finger. "Take your pick. I don't know how Sama got his hands on so many live soldiers, but they were all wearing a mark – an X burned into their foreheads."

The blood drained from my face as I sat down, my head in my hands. "What did he want? Just the general mayhem and dominance?"

Ezra was pale, but he managed to sit mostly upright at the kitchen table. "I didn't stick around to find out. I knew he would want you, so Finn and I ran to port the both of you out. I need to go back down there." He tried to stand on his own, but Von and I were firm on him not going anywhere. "Our people were ambushed! The nations were grieving together, finally united in something, and Sama shows up to attack. What for? What could he possibly want? The more people he kills, the less potential clients he has for selling rations to. And some of those mourners could've already been his clients. It makes no sense!"

"More deaths could mean more soldiers for him," I suggested.

"Sure, but he would have sacrificed many of his own, waging a war like that. I don't buy that he'd be so reckless. Sama is a man of many plans. I'm missing something, and I've learned that underestimating Sama is a danger to us all."

Von's jaw was set in a tight line. "Maybe he wanted to slaughter the council. They sunk an arrow in you easy enough."

I shook my head, wishing I didn't know Sama better than most. "He wants you to know *he can*. That's what this is about. It's the largest gathering Terraway's seen in ages, right? There's usually always fighting between the nations. Now everyone's in one spot, united in their sadness, so Sama shows up to let everyone know he can dominate without the council, with an undead army, and do it all at any moment." I rubbed my forehead. "He's punishing Terraway for coming together. He wants them only united under him."

"How can you possibly know all that?" Von gaped, bouncing his knees slightly to soothe Ana as he stood between Ezra and me.

I shrugged, wishing for a different answer. "Pillow talk. Sama told me way more about himself than he ever got outta me. Like it or not, I know him. He needs people to know he's in charge." I thought back to all of our conversations about his "management" job, and the subsequent ones about him ruling with me by his side. "So yeah, he might go after the council, but he prefers people come to him on their own, not as a last resort. His pride runs deep. It's not all that complicated. He likes trophies and respect. If he killed Ezra, that would be his trophy. With the army he brought, that gets him the respect. Simple as that." A wave of dread washed over me, and I realized my brain had been sorting things in the wrong order of priorities this whole time. "Ollie! Ollie's down there! Your mother,

Von! And your brothers. We have to go back. Where's Mason?"

"He's still at the mansion, love. And you're not going back down there. You're staying in this house, where the guys and I have reinforced the charms too many times to count. This is your fortress, so you don't step a toe outside, understood?"

"I can't leave Ollie there!"

"Ollie will be alright."

I stood, indignant, rolling my shoulders back and staring up at Von defiantly. "I don't need anyone to patronize me. We're talking zombie army, here." I stalked out to the living room, kneeling down beside Finn and running my knuckle down his cheek. "Finn? Finn?" I tried to rouse him, but he only responded with a weak groan.

Von strolled out from the kitchen with Ana in his arms and a cold smile on his face. "Really? That's your plan? Ask Finn to take you to Terraway? The one thing I trust Finn with is your safety. Next time you probably should pick someone who isn't mad about you to help you throw your-self to the wolves."

"Wolves! Thanks, babe." I retrieved my cell from my bedroom on the nightstand, and trotted back into the kitchen. I called the mansion, requesting Mason when Lynna answered in a fretful tone. "Ezra's alright. He's just resting. I've got Ana, Von, Finn and Ezra at my house, and we're all safe. May I speak to Mason, please?"

When Mason came on the phone, I could hear the

relief in his voice at my confirmation that we were all safe. "I was worried. I need you to stay inside your house, *hani*. I mean it. Stay with Von, and in the house. Don't open the door for anyone but us."

I cringed at Von's cocky look that didn't have an ounce of understanding to it. "What's that? Is Mason telling you to run your quick little legs back to Terraway?" He clicked his tongue. "Oh, is he telling you to stay put? Oh, dear. How embarrassing for you. It's almost like you're wrong. Now, I forget. Do you *like* being wrong?"

I palmed Von's face to get it away from mine. "Mason, Ollie's still in Terraway. You have to take me back down there so we can yank him out. Sama's already messed up Allie and me. I don't want him anywhere near Ollie."

I bit my lip through Mason's pause. I wanted to yell at him to just get over here already. When he finally spoke, it was slowly, as if he thought I was stupid. "You can't honestly think I'd take you back down to Silo smack in the middle of a war. I know we've had our differences, but do you really think I'd gamble with your life like that? I love you."

I hung my head while Von gloated. "I love you, too. Doggone." I harrumphed when Von started turning in a slow circle, shaking his booty while he whisper-sang a song he made up on the fly about how I loved to be wrong. I swatted at his butt and tried to focus on Mason. "Are you alright over there?"

"I'm fine. I'm heading back down in a second. If I see Ollie, I'll try to get him to safety."

Dread clutched me around the throat, making my voice come out a pathetic squeak. "Mason, no! You can't do that. Not without me. There's no way you can go down into a war without backup. I can help you!"

"I have to try. My brother's down there, too."

"No. I'm putting my foot down."

Mason chuckled with a honey-like sweetness that warmed me. "Is that so? Mighty big threat, that is. You're allowed to be scared for your brother, but I'm not allowed to be worried for mine? You forget my brother was in the chaos, too. I'll port down, but you know the landing spot's a couple days' journey from the castle. It's the best I can do, though. Have Ezra summon me if the battle ends before I get there, and I'll come home."

"Just stay where you are. You'll never make it there in time anyway. Best be safe Topside."

I could hear his indulgent smile. "Oh, you know me better than that by now, I hope. I'll wolf out and run most of the way, so it won't take me all that long. Plus I've got to help port Von's brothers back. See you soon, *hani*." He hung up the phone before I could try to talk him out of going there without me to help him fight. I'd wanted him to just port down and bring back Ollie, but I'd forgotten about only being able to land in the porting spot when you go down. Stupid magical rules.

Von had slowed his rump shaking. His brief break from

the reality that our families were stuck in the middle of a war came to a crest. "I hate that I'm up here instead of helping my brothers. It doesn't feel right."

Ezra tapped his fingers on the kitchen table. "It'll take a week to get our families all out. Finn ported the three of us, and it severely compromised him." He shifted uncomfortably, and I wished I had some pain meds to give him. "Though, that could be the blow to the head, as well."

Finn's voice greeted us from the entryway to the kitchen, where he stood with his arms crossed over his chest. "I'd like to know when everyone lost their faith in my abilities. I closed my eyes for a few minutes. I think that's allowed."

Relief spread over me that Finn was upright and seemed to be moving without much hesitation. "Oh, you're okay! Sit down. Let me take a look at you. Here, let me get you some water."

Finn quirked his eyebrow at me and clicked his fingers, flicking water onto my face. "Save yourself the glass." He sat in the chair next to Ezra at our quaint round table. "Are you alright?" he asked Ezra.

"Never better, old friend. You missed the round of jumping jacks I did just before you came in." Ezra cleared his throat and lowered his voice to speak to Von. "Son, could you take my granddaughter into the next room? I fear my self-control isn't what it needs to be."

Von didn't need to be told twice. He ran into our

bedroom and grabbed Ana's blanket. "I'm going to take Ana for a walk. Be back in half an hour."

"Is that safe? What if Sama sends his spies Topside to attack? Mason just told me not to step a toe outside the house."

"Darling, it's either a Matruculan *for sure* eats Anastasia, or Sama's spies *might* attack her. There's no safe place right now, so I'll take the lesser threat." Von ran her out of the house to the garage, where the stroller waited for her. I think we all breathed a little easier when Von made his way down the street with our collective treasure.

6

SCOTCH AND MY BAD DECISIONS

I ignored the blood on the carpet as best I could and opened the window to air out the kitchen of any baby smells that were tempting Ezra. I watched my father's shoulders droop at the relief and the shame that followed. "Never do I loathe myself more than when my Matruculan tendencies come about."

I draped my arm around his shoulders as he remained in his seat at the kitchen table. "Well I love you, no matter what shape you come in. Lion or king or dad or friend, I wouldn't trade you for anything." I planted a kiss atop his head. "Except a really good apple pie. Then it's a tossup."

Ezra clutched my fingers, and I could tell he was doing his best to smile through the pain. "I adore you, my girl. You're all the medicine I need."

I squeezed his fingers, then moved over to the fridge, dragging a chair and standing atop it to reach the small cupboard over the fridge. I frowned at the thin layer of dust I'd permitted to accumulate atop the new major appliance, knowing I'd come far from my days of dusting regularly. I pulled out the McClelland's Scotch I reserved for my most sleepless nights, jumping when I felt Finn's strong, but unsteady hands on my hips. "I could've gotten that down for you, you know."

"Oh, thanks." I sucked in my stomach when Finn lifted me off the chair and hugged me to him, letting my body slide down his front until my bare toes touched down. "You need to sit down, though. You just got hit in the head."

Finn complied while I poured Ezra a glass of Scotch and glided it over to him. "For the pain you won't admit to. I don't have any pills in the house to help you."

"Thank you, darling. This is just the ticket."

I managed a smirk for him. "I have a feeling I could've given you expired orange juice, and you would've said the exact same thing."

Ezra's phone rang, and I knew it would be the first of many phone calls that wouldn't allow him to rest. He cast me an apologetic glance before pulling his phone from his pocket. "Might I use one of the bedrooms to answer this?"

"Of course." I motioned to Ollie's room, which didn't smell as much like baby, since it was furthest away from mine and Von's. "Make yourself at home." Finn and I helped him up, and acted like two crutches to guide him into Ollie's bedroom. I fished around in my brother's dresser for a change of clothes to lay on the bed, coming up with a business outfit and cozy pajamas, since I wasn't sure which would make Ezra more comfortable. Ezra gave me too profuse a thanks, which meant he was starting to get himself back. Finn brought him his Scotch, and we shut him in the bedroom so he could go about his kingly duties.

I turned my attention to Finn, who sat back down at the kitchen table, leaning heavily on the surface. I cupped his chin and tilted his head upward so I could see once more how his pupils reacted to the light. Then I tested his reflexes and gave him various small tasks to ensure he was on the road to recovery. I tried not to feel his eyes on me, but it was impossible. "You're so serious when you're a nurse," Finn commented. "I'm not sure I like seeing you go so long without smiling."

I straightened and looked down on him, working up a decent calm expression, since I couldn't manage a smile. "My brother's in the middle of a war."

Finn tugged on my wrists, bringing me down to sit on his thigh, my legs draped between his. I knew I should protest for too many reasons, but it was all too much. I wanted comfort. Comfort, a bed, and the rest of that Scotch. I hadn't slept even half a night through in so very long. Finn wrapped his arm around my back and leaned me to his chest, thumbing my cheek slowly. "I'll find Ollie. I'll port back down and run the whole way. It'll make our trek to deliver the stone through Silo seem like a joke with how fast I'll go. Just give me a few minutes to get my bearings back."

"No. I don't want to keep losing people. You'll stay here. Mason going back down was stupid, but makes sense because he can run faster as a wolf. You can't exactly swim the whole way. Stay."

Finn's fingers trailed down and lifted my hand, studying my ring with an unfathomable expression that made him seem like he was very far away. "You're getting married. I don't know why even after a councilmember's funeral and a war, this makes me saddest." We both swallowed together. While I debated getting up to have some distance, Finn placed my hand back in my lap and held me tighter. "Is he good to you finally?"

I nodded into Finn's neck. "Better than I deserve some days. It took us a while, but we're getting better at the basics. It all feels so far away – the engagement, normal life. It's been a steady stream of chaos lately."

"Talk to me about the chaos. You look exhausted."

"Well, Anastasia cries all night long, and then when she's bored of that, she screams most of the day. Von and I haven't slept in about a month. Then if it's not her that cries through the night, it's Danny waking me up with his nightmares. They're not normal bad dreams. He doesn't know where he is for a solid few minutes. He's not used to dreaming on his own. He and Mariang have been dreamwalking for like, almost a decade. His mind's all messed up at night. Not much better during the day, either."

"I can't imagine. Can you stay at the mansion for a few nights? Let Danny stay up with his daughter so you don't have to hear her in his room?"

My nose crinkled. "Anastasia doesn't sleep in Danny's room. He's never even held her. He's sleeping in my spare bedroom, which is where Von and I end up when we finally get an hour or two to rest. Then I wake up to either Anastasia screaming, or Danny fighting who knows what in his sleep. Then Von and I have to calm him back down, remind him where he is, that we're here." I shook my head. "I'm happy to do it, of course. I didn't mean it to all spill out like that."

"You can talk to me, you know."

I stood from Finn's lap and took down a glass, pouring myself a finger of Scotch. I sat next to Finn this time, feeling a little less whorish in my own chair. I shifted my black and gold dress, feeling like I was all dressed up for prom or something. I'd not gone to my own prom, so I'd never had need for a legit princess dress before. My breasts felt on display and my posture stayed straight of its own accord.

I took a drink, hoping anything would soothe me at this point. "Danny's beside himself. He can barely put one foot in front of the other. He can't take care of himself, much less a newborn. Ana sleeps in my room with Von and me. We've taken care of her from day one. It's been good for us. You know, after losing September." I drank more than a mouthful, wincing at the burn. "We get to pretend to do the parent thing until Danny gets back on his feet. Not sleeping is a small price to pay for getting to love my niece like a daughter."

"But you've got enough on your plate without this keeping you up." Finn brushed a stray curl away from my forehead with a gentle finger. I tried not to lose myself in his touch. He was only delicate with me, and after the funeral, the attack, and raising someone else's baby, I was so very fragile.

I rubbed my eyes. "That's only the half of it. I can't actually go to sleep without Von anymore."

Finn's face soured. "Spare me the sonnets about how much your love for him has grown since he put the world's most ridiculous diamond on your finger. People were talking about it all the way up to the casket."

"Ha, ha. No, it's that Sama will try to get into my dreams if I'm not with Von in my mind while I sleep. Sama can't find me there if we're dreamwalking."

Finn's shoulders lowered. "Oh. I forgot about that. So Von can't even take the baby for a few hours to let you sleep."

I took another drink, grimacing at the burn. "It's all fine. I'm happy to do it. I love Anastasia. I'm just not as battle-ready as I used to be."

"The whole point of being near me is that you never have to be battle-ready if I'm around."

We gazed at each other for several beats, not saying the things that would only get us into trouble, and would do nothing but mess up the lives we'd both established for ourselves.

I finished my drink and moved to the cabinet under the sink, fishing around for the necessary supplies for cleaning blood out of the living room's carpet. Finn stood and caught my arm, bringing me to stand in his embrace that quickly swallowed me. My bottle of cleanser and the paper towel roll fell to the tile floor when too many emotions swelled in my breast. "Send me away," he whispered with a note of pained begging. "I won't be able to leave if you don't make me."

"I live here with Von now. You and I don't have a world we can live in together. You know that."

He nodded. "You're good here? With him?"

"I am. Beneath the grieving, sleep-deprivation and whatnot, I am."

"Then I'll be off. I'll look for Ollie and send him back first thing for you."

I sunk into the hard chest I'd spent too much time tracing the muscular curves of. "No, Finn. You can't go back there. You'll never get there in time, and I don't want you involved in any war."

"How sweet that you think you can tell me not to fight. It'd be like me telling you not to fight. We were born for it." He leaned back, looking down at my face so he could study each slope of my tired and worn features. "Look, *hani*, I've tried being your friend, but it's not enough. I want more of you," he admitted, lowering his voice like he was telling both of us a secret. He thumbed the lower lip of my mouth that had dropped open. His other hand cupped my waist with his firm grip, his thumb stroking the dip in my hip through my dress. His touch had a note of possession to it, like he wanted to plant his flag and own my body with a single touch.

"Finn, we..." My protest was weak. *I* was weak, and we both knew it.

He spoke in a whisper that made me lean closer to hear the lusty words. His low growl made me press my chest to his, just so I could feel the rumble. "*Sinta*, you can't wear dresses around me if you don't want me to untie your stays with my teeth." Then he lightly bit my earlobe, tugging gently as his fingers fondled my throat.

I shivered, my eyes fluttering shut as I lost myself in a moment I had no right to be in. "Don't tempt me," I begged, afraid the empty house might see us and tattle. "I'm too tired and emotionally wrecked to think clearly."

Apparently, that was the wrong thing to say. "If you can be tempted, then I want your dress in a pile on the floor." Before I could protest, Finn scooped me up in his arms, carrying me out of the kitchen and into the living room like a bride, heading for my bedroom.

That sure knocked the sense back into me. "Finn, wait! No. This can't happen. I'm engaged to Von. Put me down."

Finn stopped his beeline to the bedroom and slowly

lowered my legs until my feet touched the carpet. "You're driving me crazy! One minute we're so close, and the next you're a married woman. Tell me, did I ever have a shot?"

I touched my forehead as I tried to center myself. The alcohol was doing its trick to make me just stupid enough to engage in this conversation. "Don't put this on me. You know I'm engaged. I told you as much. You're the one saying things you know are going to make me melt. You're the one trying when I told you not to. You think I'm jerking you around? You're the one jerking me around! I was clear as crystal that I'm with Von, and you're still... So stop it! It's confusing me, and I don't want to be confused. I want a normal life, dammit! Just let me have my Mr. Brady!"

Finn's eyebrow rose at the last reference. "Fine. If what you want is staying up for weeks with a kid who isn't yours, necking with a vampire who, make no mistake, *will* kill you someday, then fine. I can't imagine how much you must love him if this is your idea of bliss." He motioned around my quaint house, and then crossed his arms over his chest. "If you can look me in the eye and tell me that you want nothing more than this here with him, then I'll leave you to your happiness."

I looked up at him, utterly lost in my blur of Scotch and sleep-deprivation. "You think I'm happy? You think on the day of my sister's funeral that happy's even a thing I'm familiar with? You think it doesn't rip me up inside to take care of a baby girl who isn't mine because her dad's too out of his mind to care?" I forgot myself and shoved Finn backwards. His eyes widened that I was so distraught, I'd resorted to pushing him around. "I wanted *my* daughter! I want to actually get married without Terraway pulling me in so many directions that we can't even set a date! I want peace and quiet and a whole mess of big fat nothing to fill my days with. I want Allie to wake up. I want..." Embarrassing tears sprang to my eyes, so I shoved Finn again out of sheer frustration. "I want to sleep! I want to be able to decide when and where and who with I fall asleep, but Terraway took that from me, too! And now you want me to bring my chaos to your doorstep? You want to be with me when I'm this wrecked? Von's already in it, but you can save yourself. Can't you tell that's what I'm trying to do every time I push you away? Go, Finn! Go far away and be happy with someone who isn't such a train wreck."

I don't know when it was that Finn's mouth crashed onto mine, but when the living room disappeared from my vision, his lips and a crush of guilt were all I felt.

7

SO MUCH YES… AND ONE NO

Finn's lips had the taste of the ocean to them, plump and delicious, just as I remembered. I hated that I knew how good kissing Finn felt. If it was all in my mind, I could talk the hype down, but he was an amazing kisser.

Finn's passion pushed me to the living room wall next to my bedroom door, as green and silver started taunting my blurred vision. He pinned my arms next to my head, not bothering to be gentle or waste time with romance. It was all animal, and I was lost in the wild tangles of his appetite that only seemed to grow hungrier over time. The trumpet music of our psychedelic kiss started playing a frenzied tune of warning. My heart raced with confusion and a thrill I had no way to wrestle into submission.

"I want you to say it," he ordered between kisses, moving his lips to my neck and then my shoulder, pushing the capped sleeve of my dress out of the way so he could suck on my vulnerable skin. "Tell me you want me to take you into the bedroom."

I couldn't find words – at least not the right ones. I let out a breathy moan when his large hand gathered up my wrists and pinned them over my head against the wall, making me his willing prisoner through my haze of Scotch, grief and exhaustion.

"Tell me!" he demanded, reaching behind me with his other hand and tugging at the black ribbon that cinched my dress tighter and kept the whole heavy garment from falling down.

There were too many things racing through my head, but one truth surfaced above the others: I didn't want to lose my virginity like this. Not cheating on my fiancé. Not with coitus interruptus being imminent. Not on my way to drunk and half out of my mind from sleep deprivation. "No, Finn!" I cried as he pulled the ribbon cinching my dress loose. My arms above my head kept my dress in place, but only just. I clutched it to my chest as Finn slowly let my arms down, hitting his decrescendo like a dying star. "We can't. Not like this. Not ever. I'm engaged. I just... I can't." I hung my head, blinking the silver and green glitter from my vision. I had to raise my voice to be heard above the last of the trumpets that blasted through my insanity. "I'm sorry. I'm so sorry."

Finn's eyes were still glazed over, and I could tell he was stuck in his hallucination. I hadn't had a vision, so I knew that no matter how overpowering my feelings for Finn were, I wasn't in love with him. I suspected as much, but it was nice to have it confirmed.

Or it was horrible, being that the only way to confirm it was to cheat on the man who was currently helping me raise my sister's baby. Finn put his hand out and leaned heavily on the wall, his chest moving in and out as his pupils finally started to shrink to normal size. "I saw it all. Tell me you saw it, too!"

I couldn't bring myself to say the words, so I chickened out and shook my head, keeping my eyes on the floor so he didn't see that I was on the verge of debasing myself by bursting into tears all over again.

Finn let out a solitary growl of pain, slapping the wall behind me and making me jump. "I'm sorry, Finn! I shouldn't have... I got caught up and I... It can't happen. You know it can't!"

Finn reassembled his bearings and glared at me, whirling me around with rough hands and pressing my front to the wall. He pulled the ribbon angrily as a sob escaped my lips. He worked quickly to tie my dress up again, so I wasn't a breath away from being topless. Then he pressed his body to my back, smooshing me to the wall as he twined his fingers through mine and squeezed them above my head angrily. "I don't ever want you to apologize to me for a kiss *I* wanted. Of all the things I want from you, an apology isn't one of them." He all but growled at me as he held me to the wall, making it difficult to breathe. "Say it. Say, 'I kissed Finn, and I couldn't get enough.'"

Humiliation engulfed me when I knew that he was right. My words came out choked, every syllable stuffed with shame. "I kissed you, and I couldn't get enough." My chin was quivering, but I knew I couldn't let that be the parting message. "But it's not enough. I'm marrying Von, and that's not going to change just because I got confused when I was exhausted and had been drinking. It's not enough to build a life on, and you know it." I struggled against him, but he held me tight to the wall. "Let me go, Finn."

He kept me there, but his tone turned to take on a note of pleading. "But I've seen that life. I see it so clearly when we kiss. You live in Dagat with me." He mashed his nose to my cheek, closing his eyes in desperation. I didn't just hear his words, I felt them permeating my very being, soaking into my skin and clutching me around the throat. He hiked up the layers of my dress so he could grip my thigh, his fingers digging into the tender inner flesh to give my leg a rough massage. "I see our life together. We go swimming and laugh during the day, and read together before bed. We make love for hours. I've seen it all, *sinta*. You're happy with me."

"I belong to Terraway, Finn. I can't be without my Reapers, and without me doing my job, you die!"

"But I love you. I die without you either way."

A tear drooled out of the corner of my eye and landed

on the bridge of his nose that was ground into my face. It was too much. All of it was too much. "Let me go!" I cried, struggling with more conviction this time.

After a few seconds of internal debate, Finn released me, stepping backward so I could pull in a full breath again. "If that's what you want, then that's what I'll do." He shook his head as he wiped a tear from my face and smeared it over his heart in an X. "I'll let you go. I love you too much to watch you be with him, to see you play house with someone else's kid." He studied my features as I faced him, trying to hold myself together.

Maybe I should've expected him to lean in for another kiss, but when my hand flew out and smacked him across the jaw with a loud "No!" the shock on both our faces was real. I stared at my hand, examining the oddity with horror. "Finn, I..."

Finn held his cheek, blinking in surprise that our relationship was capable of stooping to these depths. Neither of us moved for several weighted seconds while the uncertain waves shifted around us. Then Finn cleared his throat and stood at attention, transforming before my eyes from wayward lover to stiff soldier. "I'll port down to Silo and make my way to the battle to see what assistance I can offer. Good evening, Lady October." He bowed slightly, and before I could register the verbal slap he delivered me with his formal address, he vanished in front of my eyes.

8

LAVINIA VANDERSHOT

I blinked at the spot where Finn had been standing until enough tears were blinked away that I could move from the wall. I picked up the spot remover and the roll of paper towels, dragging my feet to Ezra's blood on the carpet. I felt chained to the drips, bonded to them until they were expunged from the carpet that hadn't asked for any of this. This carpet was new to my home, and most likely new to the world. Now it was spattered in my father's blood. This was the despondent life I could provide my new carpet, and the worst part of it was that this was the best I could do. Anastasia screamed too many hours to count, and my best efforts did nothing. I'd overreaped so Mariang could have a longer life, making myself sick to the point of unconsciousness, and she still ended up dying a young woman. Allie was still frozen in her slumber, my nursing degree failing her every single day I couldn't find a way to wake her. And now my carpet was subject to my failures, paying for my shortcomings, and the hard truth that I might never be able to truly save the people I loved. I started scrubbing, taking no victory when one of the drops came up in the first few swipes.

After five minutes, the carpet was clean, but I was still dirty inside. I grabbed a rag instead of the paper towel, scrubbing the same spot over and over again, digging the material into the fibers. They called out to me in mocking after having witnessed the awful woman I was.

I don't know how long I scrubbed the carpet for no reason, but when the front door opened after a courtesy knock, I knew it had been too long – and still somehow not long enough. I didn't even look up when Graham came in with several accompanying shuffles of feet. "Hey, love. We made it safely home. Kabayo had a few of his men port us out after Sama's army retreated. It's all calming down. Pretty anticlimactic battle, if you ask me."

"Is everyone alright? Did Ollie make it back?" My voice caught on the last sentence, and I knew it was obvious I'd been crying. I kept my head down and scrubbed at the spot more vigorously.

"I think so. I requested we be brought here. I know Danny was taken to the mansion. Alton, too. Darling, are you alright?" Graham was always considerate, but I wished he was less observant this time around.

Boston chimed in with, "She's doing her touched in the

head cleaning thing. Of course she's not alright." He walked into the kitchen, opened my fridge and pulled out a beer, using the bottle opener on his key ring. I knew he wasn't capable of drinking without spilling a few drops. "You want I should put on a pot of tea for you, Mum?"

"Sure, sweetie. Thank you. Lady October, let me get that for you. It's not right for you to be cleaning the floor like a commoner."

I froze, my eyes still on the carpet. I hadn't realized Von's mother had come in with them. Here I was, splotchy-faced and kneeling on the floor, cleaning a spot that didn't exist. I cleared my throat a few times before answering. "It's okay, Ms. Vandershot. I'm almost finished."

"No, she's not," Boston corrected me, making me cringe. "When she gets worked up, this one cleans the whole house from top to bottom."

Of course Von would walk in through the garage door right then when I was the lowest of the low in front of his mama. "The first person to talk above this level suffers my interminable wrath." Von's voice was just above a whisper. "Anastasia just fell asleep, so if you're even thinking about breathing loudly, sod off." He went into our bedroom and lay Ana down in her bassinet, coming out with a loud harrumph as he rolled back his shoulders to shake out his arms. "She's a beauty, that one, but boy, can she scream. I'm thinking opera singer for her future career."

Boston reached over me and handed Von a beer. "I see

an angry protester in her. 'No more naps! No more naps!'"
He pumped his fist in the air to pretend like he was at a
rally.

Ezra poked his head out of Ollie's bedroom. "Lavinia
Vandershot, as I live and breathe. How do you keep getting
younger each time I see you?" He strolled out, rolling up
the sleeves of Ollie's blue dress shirt I'd given him to wear.
It was slightly tighter than his usual clothes, showing off
the tones lines of his physique. I noticed Ms. Vandershot
observing his form with appreciation.

Ms. Vandershot batted her hand at Ezra's compliment,
and I noticed a slight blush climb in her cheeks. "Your
eyesight's failing you, old man." She moved over to him,
and I watched as the two kissed on both cheeks like old
friends. "I heard rumor you took an arrow out there. Come
now, let me see."

I scrubbed at the carpet as Ms. Vandershot inspected
the wound I'd sutured shut. Ezra was actually blushing at
being on display, and I wondered errantly if they'd ever
had a thing together.

Ezra cleared his throat after he'd been ruled fit to live,
and tucked his shirt back in. "It's lovely to see you again,
Lavinia. Your smile can brighten the darkest of days. Do
stop by the mansion during your visit. My room is always
open to you." He caught himself too late. "Rooms! Many
separate rooms for you to take up in, should you like."

Von's gaze met mine in excitement that was mingled

with horror. We shared a shocked, silent gag as we visualized our parents hooking up.

"Thank you for the invitation. It's most kind of you."

"Yes, well. I must be off. I'm not ready to stay with my granddaughter just yet, I'm afraid. October Grace, might I borrow Oliver's car?"

"Sure, Dad. Keys should be on his dresser." I scrubbed at the carpet, hoping to lose myself in the fibers as Ezra left.

Von set his beer on the coffee table and knelt in front of me, lifting my chin so I couldn't hide in plain sight anymore. "I'm here now, so you're going to sit on the couch while I clean the carpet."

Graham sighed. "But it's clean. Not a spot on it."

"Then I'll clean it until November tells me it's good enough." Von removed his suit jacket and folded it over the side of the couch, draping his tie overtop. He rolled up the crisp, black sleeves of his dress shirt, not taking his eyes off the scrubbing I couldn't stop doing. He carefully took the rag from my unsteady hand with no judgment in his kind eyes. Then the man I loved got down on his hands and knees in front of me, and started swiping at the carpet. "Go sit on the couch, Peach. You haven't slept in ages."

"Neither have you. Don't clean the floor. You don't need to do that just because I'm..." I was going to say "crazy," but bit my lip, afraid of tipping my hand too soon to his mama.

"Because you're a beautiful woman in a dress? Because you're an Omen, and this isn't your job? I'm here to make sure nothing bothers you. If this carpet's bothering you, then I'll fix it." He scrubbed at the carpet, unperturbed that there was no stain.

I sat back on my heels on the floor and watched my boyfriend prove that he loved me just the way I was. Von knew me, and despite his knowledge, he loved me, down to the sick and unstable bones. I watched him work, marveling at the striking man I was lucky enough to be stuck with. "It's clean," I ruled, not even looking at the carpet.

"Well, fancy that. I think you're right." Von put the rag and the cleaner aside, kneeling before me and gathering me in his embrace, so my weary head could rest on his chest. Our thighs were touching, so I knew he could feel the tremble in my unsteady body. "What else is troubling you, lovely girl?"

"My sister's dead, and my other sister's in a coma," I whispered, my hand bunching in his shirt as more tears cascaded down my cheeks. "Can you fix that?"

"No, but I can draw you a bath. Let's get you cleaned up before Ana wakes, and then we can figure out this parenting thing together. Start fresh."

I wanted to sob at the thought that Ana never slept more than an hour or so at a time before she'd wake up screaming. I sagged in Von's arms, closing my eyes and wishing the world would just leave us the crap alone for one whole day.

Ms. Vandershot spoke up in an authoritative tone,

making my spine straighten. "I'll be watching my granddaughter tonight. I was thinking of checking into a hotel nearby. I'll take her and the boys. Give you two a night to sleep."

I opened my mouth to protest, but Von spoke first. "Thanks, Mum. That's all we need. Just one night to sleep a solid eight."

"Von, I'm not going to make your mama sleep in a hotel. You can stay here, Ms. Vandershot. It's no problem. We're happy to have you and your family here."

"Nonsense, dear. You're barely upright. I won't take no for an answer. When Anastasia wakes up, we'll take her to the nearest hotel. Is that alright?"

I wanted to protest, but all that tumbled out of my mouth was a grateful, "Thank you. Thank you so much. I promise I can handle it. Just one night of sleep would be so helpful."

"You've been looking after my granddaughter. It's the least I can do, and while I'm here, I hope you'll let me do more. You reap to save Terraway, and you've been given the future Omen to care for? How many ways are you being expected to save a world that wasn't yours to begin with? It's absurd you've had to do this much. Both Von and Ezra have told me how gracious you've been about the whole thing. I'm here now, so I can take at least one responsibility off your plate for a while." She turned to her youngest son. "Boston, could you show me to Anastasia's things? Let's pack her a bag. Graham, why don't you pack up you and your brother for a night or two away." She shot me a flicker of a smile. "In fact, pack enough for a whole week, just in case."

9

THE NIGHTGOWN AND THE NIGHT

When I got out of the bathtub, I finally felt clean enough to lay in my white sheets. Von had helped his mama with Ana, giving her directions to the hotel five minutes away. I took my time brushing my hair and changing into a nightgown Mariang had bought for me, and Von had laid out on the counter next to the sink. I caught occasional glimpses of Von's toned silhouette through the shower curtain as I brushed my teeth, and he washed the horrible day off himself.

I poured myself another finger of Scotch, drinking quietly by myself at the kitchen table when Von came out in his boxer briefs, freshly shaved and smelling like the kind of man you want to see in nothing but his underwear. "Where'd you get the good stuff? I thought you only kept beer and vodka around the house."

"Wouldn't you like to know?" I wasn't actually

supposed to drink much on my medication, and knew I'd already surpassed what my doctor would've deemed acceptable. I had no justifications; only grief and poor choices.

He poured himself a glass and sat down across from me. "I heard from Ezra while you were in the bath. Ollie, Alton, Lynna, Danny and Mason are safe at the mansion. The council's convening as soon as they sort out what's what. Ezra's going back down to Silo to help Kabayo sort out the damage. There were limited casualties, however, the councilmembers were all wounded, except for you, Kabayo and Mason. It's like Sama was sending a message."

"Message received. I almost want to go to sleep without you just once so I can thrash him right good for everything." I rubbed my forehead while Von stilled.

"If that's your idea of a joke, you have a terrible sense of humor. You can never, never sleep without me as long as Sama's alive. I mean it. He could put you in a coma, just like Allie. Once he has you, he'll never let you go."

I was quiet for a second as I let that thought settle over me. "For a second tonight, I thought Ezra might bleed out and die in my arms on the day of his daughter's funeral. I'm just... I'm barely holding on anymore." I finished my drink faster than my throat was comfortable with, but I managed to swallow the last mouthful with only a minor wince. I ran my hand across my chest bone, and noticed the pink X-marked scar on my forearm was glowing with a faint blue. "Something's wrong with Kabayo. Not dire, but he's real worked up. I can feel it."

"What happened with Finn while I was gone?" He crossed his arms over his chest when I looked up at him, caught. "You think I didn't notice part of your cleaning frenzy had something to do with him?"

I chose my words carefully, not ready to spend our only night we could actually sleep lost in a fight. "Finn's not going to be an issue anymore. I think I made things clear enough."

Von studied my face and nodded. "You know, that's just evasive enough to work tonight. Well done. If you ever want me distracted so I can't interrogate you, wear exactly that."

"What, this?" I asked of the nightgown. It was white, with thin, silk straps. The gown was loose, but still showed a hint of my curves. It fell mid-thigh with a lacy ruffle on the hem and a small slit up the side. Mariang had bought it for me, knowing I'd never have the guts to go into a store and walk out with something like this.

"Like you don't know you're toying with me."

"Hello, you picked it out from my drawer."

"Yes, well, apparently, I love torturing myself." Von finished his Scotch and set our glasses in the sink, sighing when I stood at his side and started washing them. I knew he wanted to go straight to bed, but I wouldn't be able to rest if there were dirty dishes in the sink, growing whole planets of bacteria. "I think it's time we get some sleep, darling."

We went to the bedroom hand-in-hand, slipping into the covers and pulling them tight around us. Von slid my nightgown up to my waist in the dark, toying with the band on my underwear lazily. He kissed my lips just enough to make me swoon, but not nearly enough to sweep us both away. The blue and gold started to fall like pitter-patters of rain around us, and the bells tinkled a lovely tease of a song that muted out all other sounds. My legs fell open as Von moved atop me, deepening the kiss as he sucked on my tongue, his body undulating like a slow-motion wave over me. I could see our park, but just when my feet were about to step down, the magical world faded.

Von rolled off of me and lay staring up at the ceiling, his hand on his chest. "I want to set a date for the wedding," he said, catching me off-guard.

"Um, okay. I'm a little too tired to get out my schedule, but we can talk about it at least."

"We should start thinking about what *we* want. I know there's a fair amount of duty on our shoulders, but it can't always be everyone else pulling our strings. We have to choose a few things and stick to it."

I mulled this over, liking the logic that put the drama of Terraway on the back burner. "We haven't actually talked about what kind of wedding we want. What are you thinking?"

Von laced his fingers through mine under the covers,

and then dipped his toe under my calf to coax my leg to drape over his. His thumb lifted the edge of my nightgown and traced the inside of my thigh. He drew ticklish circles into my sensitive skin, scrambling my brains to where I would've said yes to whatever ridiculous kind of wedding he wanted. "I was thinking Fiji or someplace tropical for the honeymoon. I'm bored of Georgia. I want something new, something beautiful."

"Works for me. Anywhere that'll put a stamp on my passport, I'm cool with. What about the wedding itself? What kind of big day did you want?"

"Ah, now that's your department. I'm all about the honeymoon. I'm seriously rethinking this whole virgin until you're married thing. Were we set on that?"

"I think so." I debated a few seconds, but decided our lives were too harrowing on a daily basis for me to enjoy something that was meant to be amazing and special. "I don't have any wedding plans swimming around up in here." I orbited my hand around my head like it was a globe. "I was kind of thinking about eloping." I held up my hands to stave off any protests that might spill out. "Hear me out. Any kind of big deal thing means the council will have to be involved. You saw what happened when Sama knew they were assembling in Terraway. I don't want Ezra to get shot in the back with an arrow on my wedding day."

"Blood on a white dress would be agony to scrub out, sure."

"When I think about marrying you, my imagination

goes straight to our Brady Bunch life. I don't think much about the actual 'I do's."

Von spread my legs wider and tickled further up the inside of my thigh with the tips of his fingers as he mulled over my suggestion. "Can I wear a tuxedo? I look like a British spy in a tux."

I grinned. "Sure. I'll wear a white dress, if you want. Justice of the Peace on a Tuesday, and that's that. Then we're Mr. and Mrs. Vandershot." My eyes widened as soon as the words escaped my lips. "Whoa. That was way serious."

"First time it dawned on you we're actually doing this?"

"I didn't realize I was changing my name until I said it just now. October Grace Vandershot." I shivered. "That's freaky."

"So you don't want a big circus, and we can get married just us and our families?"

"Unless you hate the idea, yeah."

"If I wasn't about to pass out from exhaustion, I'd tear your clothes off and make love to you right now. Perfect woman, you are. Deal. Let me break it to Mum, though. She had her heart set on a grand affair."

Von had teased the inside of my thigh too much for his own good. I had chills and desires and all kinds of too much swirling through my body. My hips started to move of their own accord as I bit down on my lower lip. "Let's get married sooner rather than later. I want to be your wife already."

10

KINGS AND GRAVE ROBBERS

"Oh, thank goodness. They waited to start the meeting until you arrived. Let me take your sweater, dear," Lynna offered, ushering us inside the mansion. I stepped off the welcome mat and found myself scooped in her arms. It was then that I realized Lynna had been crying.

My heart sank. I knew the bliss of our little four-day hiatus had been too much. Ms. Vandershot had taken Anastasia, and Danny had moved back into the mansion, finally able to sleep without Von and me. It had been magical, just the two of us in my home together. Von and me being happy upset the equilibrium, so something terrible had to go down. "What is it? What happened?"

She squeezed me tighter as she shook her head. The desire to bolt from the affection tapped me on the shoulder, but my feet remained in place. "Run along to the conference room, kids." She leaned up and kissed Von's cheek before sending us on our way.

"Nothing ominous about that," Von lied. He leaned in as we walked through the foyer, passing the topiary that never changed, though everyone else in the massive house had. "I don't want to stay here long. Let's listen to whatever the council has to say about the battle and go back home. Anastasia was being a handful for Mum when we left, and she hasn't had to deal with a newborn in a couple decades. I don't want to desert them."

"Of course. And you know, in a month or two, we'll be able to bring Ana here for meetings, no big deal."

Von frowned, his hand on the small of my back as we neared the conference room. "Perhaps three or four months, just to be safe. I don't fancy tempting fate by putting her in a room with two Matruculans. We don't have the best of luck with these things."

"The best of luck with shapeshifting monsters? Yeah, I guess you're right." I greeted Alton, who stood outside the door to the conference room as a sentry. "You coming inside?" I asked, catching the door with my foot and holding it open for him to follow us in.

Alton pushed his gold wire-rimmed glasses up on his nose and worked up a wan smile. "I'm Duwende. We don't have representation on the council. I'm out here in case Ezra needs pulling. He's... It's been rough. I've taken it upon myself to be his constant shadow when I'm not helping Danny."

My shoulders drooped at the reality of just how much brokenness still surrounded us. "Okay. Thanks for helping out so much. I'll see if Boston or Graham can come over and give you a hand with them."

Alton offered me a smile and closed us in the room, shutting himself out of the cool kids' club. I was wearing nice jeans that hugged my hips and a green and purple t-shirt/tank top combo. Most of my other shirts had spit-up on them. "Gentlemen," I greeted the room, nodding my head at the men, who stood at my entry. "Good to see you all." My eyes fell on a couple new bodies seated at the heavy polished wood oval table. Carter stood next to his brother, who motioned for Von and me to sit with him.

Finn wasn't there. I looked around, but he was nowhere in the room. In his place was the seventy-plus man I knew to be the interim King of Dagat, having just met him briefly at the funeral. Mathias of the Green Lakes, or something like that. He scratched at the gills framing his throat and then ran his hand through his thick gray hair that had a sizeable coif to it.

The leader of Lumipad had been Sylvia when I'd first come into this room. Then Serena had overthrown her and abducted me. When Sama killed Serena to avenge me, I didn't know what would come of Lumipad. I expected another woman, but a fair-haired man with a bird-like shape to his face shook my hand. I'd met him for a millisecond at the funeral, but hadn't put it together that an Ekek could rule Lumipad. I'd just assumed only a

Manas could. My shoulders sank as I realized I was now the only woman in the room. Mariang had taken herself off the council a long time ago because she'd been so sick, and didn't feel like putting up with their constant bickering. Then Sylvia bit it. Now it was just me, and that weighed heavy on my shoulders.

Finn wasn't there. I didn't know what to make of that, but pushed it out of my mind when Von's arm slung around the back of my chair. Mason's hand found mine, and he brought it over to rest on his thigh so he could pull a little and take some of the burden off of Von.

Ezra was in black slacks, a white dress shirt and a subdued navy tie. There was a soulless sleeplessness to his eyes, which had bags beneath them. His hair was combed in front, but was sticking up in the back. For some reason, that little detail made my heart break for him all over again. He would never have permitted his hair to misbehave before his daughter was taken from him.

Ezra remained standing after everyone found their seats, garnering the attention of the powerful rulers. "As most of you know, Sama is the force behind the attack that took place at my daughter's funeral. We believe he was targeting the members of the council, so when you're in Terraway, I would urge all of you to increase your security and exercise caution. We can't be sure who's for us, and who's in Sama's pocket. King Aranya revealed himself to be against us when he raised his knife to King Kabayo."

I gasped, along with Mathias, Von, Mason and Carter.

My head whipped to Kabayo, who sat with his arms crossed over his chest and a smug expression on his horse face. "He's been dealt with in the same way all traitors to Terraway are handled. I ran him through with my sword, and now he's not a problem. Prince Langgam will be taking over his brother's throne within the week. Apparently, there was an uproar from the people of Sakuna when Luna tried to take the crown." He dipped his head to Lang, who returned the gesture respectfully.

My jaw was on the floor at all the changes that had taken place in a mere four days. I wanted to make sure Kabayo hadn't been wounded in his fight, to confirm that all of them were okay. I wanted to throw my arms around Lang and have a giant party to celebrate that his kingdom finally had a chance. I kept my words stuffed in my mouth though, since it seemed like Ezra was barely hanging on, and still had more to get through. "King Langgam, let me be the first to welcome you, and acknowledge your new title."

Lang offered up a polite smile, though I knew he had to be beaming inside. "Thank you, King Ezra. I'm sure I'll be coming to the council for advice and wisdom, once I'm instated at the formal crowning in Sakuna." He cast me a furtive glance that didn't match the congratulations I assumed he would be glowing from. He looked worried for me or something. My eyes shot to Kabayo again, and I saw his smugness melt into the same look of concern, like I might implode at any second.

I wondered how much crap I looked like. Perhaps I was getting to the point where a few nights of sleep wouldn't right all the wrongs.

Ezra pressed his hands on the table, his head hanging so his eyes stared only at the wood. It was like he couldn't bring himself to face anyone in the room. "King Kabayo and King Langgam stayed after Sama's army retreated after so short an attack. Upon examining Mariang's coffin, they found the little finger on her right hand missing." This garnered a few exclamations of surprise, but Ezra pushed through. "I was convinced Sama had come for more than my daughter's finger. He's shown no interest in her before. I joined them in Silo as soon as I could make the journey. We went through everything, every possibility, but it wasn't until we checked behind the castle toward the back of the royal property that we found what Sama was looking for." Everyone was sitting at attention now, no one daring to breathe too loudly. "Kabayo's crypt at the back of his property was robbed. The bones of his ancestors are safe, so we needn't worry about King Dakila or the great kings of the past being used in Sama's games."

Kabayo kept his eyes on the table, as did Lang and Ezra – all three afraid to look at me. A thrumming started in my ears like a slowly crashing wave. It pushed out the connections my brain was trying to make before Ezra led me there. Ezra's voice quivered when he finally brought himself to speak. "The only body that went missing was September Serendipity Reese – the daughter of Lady

October and her Reaper, Von. We can only assume that Sama sent his army to steal her body from us, which explains why the battle was so short-lived." Ezra finally looked up into my eyes across the table, and I saw timeless torment that would never relent for him. "I'm so sorry, darling."

I heard nothing after that for several minutes. No one spoke, and no one dared to move out of respect for our searing pain. My heartbreak felt like it must be painted all over the walls in spurts of red and streaks of the darkest black, as my insides were shattered and splattered for everyone to see. I was utterly and completely lost in my own personal abyss.

Mason was the first to stand, moving behind Von and me and placing a hand on both our shoulders. His body framed us in his strength as he started up a slow pull that was a drop in the bucket of what we actually needed. Von hung his head to give the tears that dripped down his cheeks a little privacy to invite all their friends to the awful party. No one spoke; they merely watched our pain respectfully. Kabayo studied my furrowed eyebrows and firmly closed mouth. The design that branded the two of us on our forearm lit up on him, glowing blue to alert him that I was either in danger, pain or severely internally compromised. I felt compromised, but I couldn't move. I couldn't speak. Nothing but white noise filled me from the inside, letting me know that whatever mess consumed me, I wasn't capable of processing it yet.

Von's fist pounded the table, making me jump. "Why?!" he yelled, demanding an answer from his surrogate father. "Why was her tomb not sealed? Why was there not a guard posted to keep watch?"

Kabayo took Von's accusations in stride, answering for Ezra. "Her tomb was sealed. Lady September was given the same honor a queen would have been given. I did have a guard posted there, but he was killed in Sama's quest to get into the crypt. Your anger's understandable though, and I won't rob you of it."

Von stood, shrugging Mason's hand off of his shoulder. "You understand my anger? You understand everything we've given up for Terraway? How many children have you lost? How many times has Sama tried to rape your wife in her mind when there's nothing you can do to stop it? You've lost a brother you helped raise? I packed Bishop's lunch every morning before school. *I* made sure he did his homework. *I* took care of every foul git he came across. I did everything I could to give my brothers a good life, but I can't work hard enough to keep them alive, much less happy. But you in your infinite wisdom understand my anger?"

Mason was ready for Von's clenched fists, which we both knew was a precursor to him launching one of them into someone's face. He wrapped Von in a hug from behind mere seconds before he lunged, and all but dragged him from the room, whispering words of solidarity in his ear all the while.

I wanted to go to him, to help Von in some way that would be a permanent balm to his torn soul. I wanted to, but I sat frozen in the chair, unable to move or speak. I heard Alton shouting for Von to calm down, and I closed my eyes when it dawned on me that Mason and Alton were no doubt using excessive pulling to subdue him.

I wanted to rescue Von.

I wanted to rescue myself, but I was sinking. I guess that's how you know you're not at rock bottom. There's that ability to fall even lower. I truly hoped I'd hit the dregs of the sludge of life by now. I shuddered to think at what could possibly bring me lower than this.

People were talking to me, but I didn't have the brain for conversation. It seemed my brain, like the rest of me, preferred a hiatus.

11

DANNY'S KISS

I awoke in my pea green bedroom at the mansion, not completely remembering laying down in the first place. As I sat up and rubbed my eyes, bits of the end of the council meeting came back to me. Lang had carried me to bed, which I now had the sense to feel humiliated by. I didn't want to fall apart, but some things couldn't always be helped.

Low mumbling caught my attention, and I realized that was what had woken me up. I swung my feet off the bed and tapped them on the carpet, softening when I saw that Lang had taken the time to remove my shoes. It was the little things that felt like sweetness, reminding me that though I felt very much afraid, I had family here who cared about the big things without forgetting the little things.

I tiptoed out of my bedroom and followed the

mumbling through the empty, unlit hallway to Danny's room. My fist lightly rapped on the door, and I heard a "Go! Go!" whispered before he opened it. I was glad he was talking to someone. His eyes were focused and his face sane when he poked his head out. "Hey, kid."

When he stood back to let me in, I was surprised to find there was no one in the room. I guessed he'd been talking on his cell, and had hung up for me. I don't know why that made me feel guilty – my emotions were all over the place. I stood in the middle of Danny's usually military-perfect room that was always in order and free of dust or clutter. Only now it, like Danny, was broken. There was crap everywhere, clothes on the floor, and Mariang's things thrown clear off her desk and scattered about the room. It looked like moshers had come through and trashed the place.

I knew he was expecting me to say something, but I still didn't have the words, so I just stood there like a shellshocked dummy, staring up at him so my eyes could do the talking. My daughter's bones had been stolen. I knew Danny couldn't have heard about Mariang's finger going missing, because he looked like he'd showered recently. He was dressed, clean and looked more balanced than I'd seen him in a month. Mariang's bedroom, on the other hand, was an utter disaster. I mean, her lamp was broken and in shattered pieces on the ground. Her dresser had been rifled through. The closet had piles of her never-been-worn clothes spilling out of it.

I'd never seen Danny disorganized, and wasn't sure what to make of it. He was grieving, so I guess cleaning his room hadn't been at the top of his priority list.

His caterpillar-like eyebrows pushed together as he frowned down at me. "You need something? I think Von's downstairs with Ezra and Mason. He stopped yelling not too long ago, so I'm guessing they've finally knocked a bit of logic into him."

I blinked up at Danny, not sure why I was here or what I expected him to say to me that might help. I opened my mouth, but no sound came out. I shook my head and lowered my chin, banding my arms around my stomach to hold myself together.

"I heard they told you about September. You still checked out?"

I guess me looking up at him without speaking for so long answered that question.

Danny's shoulders drooped, and dang if he didn't soften as he watched me not know what to do with myself. I hated that he was more together than I was. He moved his dirty clothes and dusty books with that same vellum paper Finn's books had off the bed, and onto the chair at his desk. Danny was flustered, not sure what to do with himself at having a guest in the room he'd shared for so many years with Mariang.

"Hold on, hold on. I wasn't expecting anyone." Danny quickly made the bed while I stood in the center of the chaotic room, unsure what to do with my hands. I scraped at the flesh once just out of habit, but the pain didn't center me like it used to. I couldn't feel anything. I dug my nails deeper, but still registered nothing.

When Danny deemed his disaster of a room passable, he gently took my arm. With his other hand wrapped around my back, he slowly lowered me to sit on the side of his bed. The sheets smelled like man feet, which is to say, totally gross. "You should rest for a bit, yeah? It's been a long time you've had too much happening. The council's mostly gone, so you don't have to worry about running into them. Lang's still here, and I think Mason and Carter, but that's all."

I said nothing to this, so Danny continued, swallowing hard as I blinked up at him. He ran his hand through his messy hair, just as befuddled as I was that he was the one I came to, mute as I was. He finally sat down next to me on the bed, hesitating, but then raising his hand to rub a circle into my back. He gave me a small pull I wasn't expecting. I could tell by his exhale that he needed the job just as much as Mariang had needed him. "Oh, that's better," he murmured, as if I was the one pulling for him. He was like me – lost without a purpose to drive him forward. He cleared his throat. "Kabayo's upset that he let something foul happen to your family. Left you a leather cuff to wear on your wrist."

My eyes conveyed that I couldn't guess why Kabayo would leave me that, or what I was supposed to do with it.

"I think it was supposed to cheer you up, to let you

know that he understands he mucked up. Kabayo doesn't know much about human women, so pretend the leather cuff is a vase of flowers or something." When my hand mindlessly raked at my arm again just to see if now I could feel something, Danny stole my hand and linked his fingers through mine atop his knee. "Stop that. You know it drives me mad." Danny played with my fingers, examining each one carefully. When he spoke again, his voice was gentler. "I never got to thank you for standing in front of me at the funeral. I mean, I knew what was coming, so I was prepared for it, but to have you throw yourself in front of me to save me from public humiliation? I don't know how to thank you for that. I was barely hanging on that day. You saved me."

I'd saved him, but I couldn't save my daughter, who'd been just a short walk away. Tears welled in my eyes, and I couldn't stop the flow. It was like losing her all over again.

"Hey now, that wasn't meant to make you cry. It's alright. You stopped them. No one's going to spit on me anymore." Danny mistakenly thought I was distraught about his public shaming. He shifted on the mattress beside me, bringing up the edge of the pink comforter to drape over our shoulders. He covered us and made what felt like a small fort where we could confess our worries. His arm wound around my hips, drawing me to his side so my cheek rested on his shoulder. When he planted a kiss to the top of my hair, that's when the floodgates really opened. I clutched his shirt and wept into the material, hating myself for leaning on someone who was probably having his first day of normalcy in a month.

I couldn't help it. Life was crumbling to pieces around me, and I was barely able to assemble enough sanity to stand on my own.

"Shh. It's alright. Man, I hadn't pegged you as a crier. I'm not all that great at this part of the job. Um, there-there?" He guessed at the right thing to do, awkwardly patting my back as I sobbed all the more. He kissed my forehead, making me feel five years old. I was so far from young anymore. I hadn't been a child in ages.

When Danny stiffened, my tears cleared just enough to look around to see what had startled him. I made out a glowing white blur floating before us, but Danny's hand went over my eyes, obscuring my vision. "Danny, what is that?"

"Nothing. You look tired. Are you falling asleep?" He sounded scared, forcing the idea of sleepiness on me.

But then I suddenly did feel drowsy, my eyelids drooping. "That's right," Danny cooed as he pulled too hard. "Go to sleep."

I shrugged out of his embrace. "What? I'm not tired. I'm in the middle of a breakdown. You're pulling way too hard, Danny." I heard a crash, and whipped my head to see the source of the sound. Danny tried to keep his hand up to block my eyes, but clear as day I saw her.

Floating two inches above the floor like a translucent apparition near the closet was a woman dressed in a long, flowing white gown. It was tattered at the edges, but still so pure a white that the dress itself appeared to be glowing.

Her sleek black hair was pulled into a bun on the top of her head like a ballerina. Her arms were thin and translucent, and I could see blue veins through the skin.

My racing heart seemed to stop at the face of Mariang staring out at me. Her cheeks were blushed with pink, making her arms appear that much paler. She was streaked in blood from her hairline to her chin, marring her beauty with gore.

It was then I realized Mariang wasn't staring at me – she was glaring with malice and purpose. My mouth fell open as a haunted house-worthy scream belted out from my diaphragm, filling the mansion with my horror.

"You're seeing things! You're so tired," Danny insisted, wrestling me down onto their bed as he shot waves of bliss through me. I thrashed and fought as best I could, but Danny's Duwende abilities, coupled with his brute strength, were no match for even the strongest will to escape.

It wasn't until Mariang appeared floating a foot above me, her dress hanging down on Danny's back, that I stopped struggling. She was pissed, but all I could see was my sweet sister dripping with the blood she seemed to have no end of. It dribbled down on me, making me shriek with fear and a renewed desire to get the crap out of there. "What's happening? You're not supposed to be here!" My scream reached new heights when her docile hand struck out at me, her sharp nails raking the skin on my cheek until I tasted blood. Her ghost-like body could touch things hard enough to damage them, though she herself appeared translucent.

I wasn't sure what hurt worse – the torn skin or that Mariang had raised her hand to me.

Danny was frightened as he turned to bark quietly at Mariang. "No! You can't do that! I told you that you could stay if you could control yourself. You can't hurt her!"

"You kissed her!" Mariang's voice was furious, but behind the sound there was a metallic edge that was grating and inhuman. Her delicate voice was now braced with steel, making her sound like herself, but not.

"I kissed her head! October's like a sister to me. You know I've only ever loved you."

"Help!" I yelled over and over, hoping anyone was near enough in the massive house to hear us.

Danny clamped his hand over my mouth in fear. "No! They can't take her! I need her, and she needs me!"

My terror was washed away in ripples until Danny panicked and shot a tsunami of peace through me. I wilted on the mattress, swaddled in feet-smelling sheets as the world and all of its problems left me in a blustery wave. In that surreal moment, my eyes closed as I felt myself leave me, too.

12

MY UPPER HAND

I opened my eyes to a bright light that couldn't be blinked away. I held up my hand to shield my eyes, but only found relief when a body stepped in front of the blinding glow. "That's better. I was beginning to think you were avoiding me."

A chill ran up my spine at the voice I'd hoped I would never hear again. I wanted to run far from the sound I'd once drawn comfort from. I remained on my back until I found enough of myself to sit up.

Mariang was a ghost now.

Danny had blissed me out, which meant I was dreaming. Sama had found me in my forced sleep, and there would be no escaping. I couldn't bang myself in the head to wake up this time. Who knows how long someone as practiced as Danny could knock a person out. I took a deep breath and decided to play the game. If Sama wanted me here, then I would be here. I wouldn't spend my life hiding, clinging to Von like a blankie I needed to fall sleep. "Help a girl up, will ya?"

Sama seemed surprised I didn't come at him swinging. Honestly, I was so turned around, I didn't think I could fight him with a clear head. Sama was a mind games master, so I knew I needed my wits about me if I was going to play his game. "Um, sure. Okay." He gripped my forearms and pulled me to my feet, surprised as I was that he hadn't been clocked across his chiseled jaw yet.

"Where are we? I can barely see anything; it's too bright."

"Terraway. This is the land of three suns, where the Goblins inhabited before you wiped them all out. Most people can't stand the brightness here."

"Hello, then why'd you choose this place for a reunion?"

Sama sounded confused, which meant I was winning. Even though my eyes were only opened to slits, I was winning. "I wanted the advantage, in case you were opposed to a reunion at all."

"Fat lot of good that's doing you now. I can't even have a conversation with you. It's too bright."

"There's a home we can use just over there." Philip motioned with his hand, but I couldn't see much.

"Are you expecting me to know where you're pointing? Dude, I don't know Terraway. Just lead me where I'm supposed to go."

His voice darkened. "You're tricking me. You want me to take you somewhere you can see, so you can overpower me again."

I placed my hand on my hip and huffed. "Fine, then let's stay right here. I'll just cover my eyes like an idiot and we'll have a good old catch-up just like this." I covered my eyes with both hands and moved my shoulders animatedly. "So, how's it going? Shoot my dad in the back with an arrow lately? Boy, do you know the way to a girl's heart."

"Ezra's not your father. I knew your father, and Ezra's not him."

I hadn't expected him to give me information that was so precious on a whim. "You knew my father? What's his name? What was he like? 'Knew'? Does that mean he's... Is he dead?" So many more questions came to me, but I couldn't work them all out of my mouth in a recognizable order. I didn't realize how much I craved knowledge about the man who'd given life to me and never came back to see how it all turned out.

"He's not dead." Philip let out an irritated huff that I'd turned his planned rapefest into a Q & A. "You truly don't know who he is?"

"Hello, does this look like the face of a girl who's got a clue?" I'm sure I looked pretty silly, giving him attitude while my hands were shrouding my face. "Seriously, Philip. Tell me who my dad is. If you know, you should tell me."

"You have all the clues; you're just refusing to put them

together." He pried a hand from my face to wrap it in the crook of his elbow. Then shielding my face from the sun, he led me forward through sand that was so hot, I was starting to feel it through my socks. I hadn't thought to give myself a wardrobe change in my transportation to my bliss world, so I was in the same jeans, green t-shirt and purple tank top I'd been in when Lang had laid me down in my bed.

"Don't make me feel like I'm a dummy. Not when you can actually help me." I wasn't sure it was wise to scold the powerful warlock, but I had nothing else to keep him in line, so I grasped at the few straws available to me. "Who's my father? And why didn't he ever come back for us?"

"Such importance you place on the idea of parents. Mine are long deceased, and I haven't given them a thought in decades. You're wasting your life, pining like this."

"Please, Philip."

He softened as he led me forward toward who knows what. "You called me Philip. I rather like your name for me. Sama means evil. I've been using it for so long, I can't remember my original name. Maybe it was Philip. I like to pretend you see past the evil that the world sees, your gaze cutting straight to the heart of me."

"Well, you only started being evil toward the end, so old habits and all. You really don't remember your true name? I guess I thought Sama was it." I huffed and stopped in my tracks. "I can't do this. You have to take me somewhere I can actually see. The sun's hurting my eyes, Philip. Anywhere else, really. You can pick."

"Very well. I'll take you home, then." He covered my eyes with his hand, I felt a whoosh, and when he let go of my face, I could see again.

"Oh, that's way better. Thanks."

His voice was grand, dripping with trepidation. "Have a look at my kingdom, *hani.*"

I suppressed a shudder. "Um, I can't actually see anything, you know. I still have bright spots messing with my vision. Give me a minute." I blinked a few times and saw the island with the trees peppered throughout, each one stripped bare. There was an ocean behind us, and the smell of the pure water revitalized my senses. "Oh, I remember this place. I guess I didn't realize this was your home. In all your time here, you never thought to decorate? Make it a little homey?"

Philip laughed, and the sound bubbled out of him, like he'd been holding onto the joy for too long. "Decorate? No, I've been a little busy with my army, and besting the kings of Terraway."

"Oh, right. You don't get bored here without anyone to pass the time with?"

Philip shook his head. "Terraway thought it was a curse I took on myself when I grabbed hold of the elixir to eternal life, but no curse in the world feels as good as this. Being young and powerful forever? I've perfected my magic. It's only a matter of time before the other kings bow before me, touting my curse as the biggest blessing in all of Terraway."

I cast him a dubious look. "How about we talk less about what a megalomaniac you are and more about this curse you took on yourself. It made you forget your own name? That's like, the saddest thing I've heard in a while." Second to Danny resurrecting his fiancée so he didn't have to live without her. That was sadder.

Philip pfft'd, as if the sordid details of how he'd gotten so powerful were beneath remorse. "It was so long ago; I don't know what my master's original plan for me was. I only know that nothing I did lived up to it, so he died as he lived – dissatisfied. I had one of my Amalanhigs tear his heart from his chest, and I put him behind me."

I swallowed, unsure how to handle a conversation where violent homicide was thrown around so haphazardly. "That sounds hard. Do you think it was worth it? Living without your Kapre master so you could be alone forever?"

Philip stiffened, and I wondered if I was about to catch myself a beating. "I'm not alone. I have an army full of subjects I can command at will. Not just the undead, either. I've found a way to create loyalty, to forge a family of my own. When they die in battle, I simply raise up more."

I didn't know what to say to that, so I stuck to nodding.

"And I'm not alone right now. I have you."

"Oh, hun. Most days *I* barely have me. That you're chasing me now? Kinda pointless. I'm bottom of the barrel these days. Not the prize you're thinking I am. Shows how thin your options are. Even with all your undead lovelies, you're chasing some other dude's washed-up woman?" I nodded once. "Desperate. Get a real girlfriend. I'm not even really here. This is all our dream."

Philip scoffed with a hint of a laugh to his attitude. "I can't believe you're still not afraid of me. After everything that happened the last time, you still talk to me like a girl who needs a strap taken to her pert little backside. I may be desperate, but you're the foolish one."

"You'd rather I cower? Something tells me you've got enough of that in your life – people bowing down whether you deserve it or not." I bumped him with my hip, trying not to be afraid. Most people stick to the "don't let him smell your fear" mantra. I've found it's more effective to just stop feeling fear altogether. "Tell me about my father. You're getting us off-track."

"Well, let's start from what you know of him. Surely your mother told you his name or showed you a picture."

"That shows how little you know about me or my life. Bev said his first name was Goodfer, and his last name was Nothing. Never saw a picture of him. Never knew his name. Doubt he knew mine."

"He knows your name, of that much I'm certain." There was a smirk to Philip's voice. "I could tell you, but I think I'll let you find out for yourself one day. The surprise would be the main event of our time together, and that's not what I had in mind for us."

I blanched, but was pretty sure I did a good enough job at hiding my distaste. "Don't be gross. I'm here willingly. Don't push it."

Philip chuckled darkly. "I think we both know I'll do as I please. You have so much spirit in you. Breaking you will be a satisfying victory. I haven't had one of those in ages. The other Omens gave in so easily to their fate. You're the only one who's risen to be my equal."

I jerked my hand from his arm. "I'm nothing like you. I didn't murder my teachers, and I don't command armies of darkness." Bruce Campbell can take care of those, no problem. I tried to summon my inner Bruce that could take out his boomstick and light up the night right good. My chin rose and my shoulders rolled back when my favorite horror movie superhero swelled in my spirit, giving me peace I couldn't have located on my own.

Philip was unperturbed. His hand rested on my back to lead me forward. "How many of your loyalists have died to protect you? And I saw you at the funeral of Lady Mariang through the eyes of my army. You commanded whole nations when they tried to spit on Danny. Admirable, but not so different than what I do. I force the undead to follow me, you force live subjects to serve your whim."

I guffawed, shocked at the things he was accusing me of. "I can't believe you just said that to me. You're a rotten jackhole, and I'm nothing like you."

Philip laughed loudly. "Oh, you're exactly like me. That's why you despise me so now."

"I despise you because my sister's a friggin' vegetable. I despise you because you tried to force yourself on me. You tried to mind-warp my fiancé. You shot Ezra in the back! Curse or not, if you value your life, you'll not push me today. It's been a long one."

Then it hit me. The hair on the back of my neck stood up, giving me chills that invigorated me. The way to take Philip down was literally at the tip of my tongue. I saw it all clearly, a master plan of epic proportions falling into place. No one had seen the solution, but there it was. I knew how to put an end to my eternal tormentor. I knew how to kill Sama.

13

PHILIP, THE GENTLEMAN

My intake of breath was the only indicator that I knew what had to happen next. Philip thought he had me, but as it turns out, I had him exactly where I wanted him.

Almost.

Philip had been talking, but I didn't care. I cut into his words with a curt, "I think we should meet."

Philip stopped abruptly, and I nearly pitched forward on the hot sand. He righted me, bringing my face up in his hand so he could search me for lies. Unfortunately for him, I was still blinking the errant stars from my vision, so I couldn't focus perfectly yet. It didn't do much for him as he tried to examine me for tells. "Why would you want that?"

"Because this is bullshiz. You want to scare me into being with you, but you won't see what it's actually like for me to be with you. It's cowardly. Let's try it for one week. A whole week of us being together, living under the same roof that's not in our dreams and see if we're even good together."

"You're up to something. You don't want that. You screamed when I touched you last."

I tilted my head to the side with an arched eyebrow. "I think that's a pretty typical response from any woman you force yourself on. I'm talking voluntarily this time, the two of us just seeing if we gel. Then if it works out, great. If not, we can move on."

Philip's voice came out insecure, which was my favorite shade when worn on a power-hungry megalomaniac. "We?"

I tried to soften my voice, to soften myself without letting him smell a manipulation. "You know I wanted to be with you before I found out it was all a lie. So if we're going to do this, you can't be lying to me. And you can't be Sama the Almighty Jackweed. You have to be Philip. I liked that guy." With every word that came from my mouth, I hated myself. I was seducing a rapist. I was hooking the man who'd hurt my sister.

I had a plan.

Philip's reply came back cautious. "You'll really come to live with me?"

"For one week if you promise to be Philip. If you promise not to lie."

He gripped my arm and all but dragged me the rest of

the way to his place in the middle of the sandy abyss. I tripped over the threshold, but righted myself when he stopped. He didn't release me, but shook my arm, his fingers digging into my bicep. "What's your game?"

"I'm calling you on your bluff! You're a chicken. You're just like every other man in my life. You say you want to be with me, but it's all a lie. You wouldn't know the first thing to do with me if I was really yours." I held up my hand and snarled. "And spare me the filthy innuendos. If we lived together, you wouldn't want me. You only want a conquest. You only want the fight. Once that's over, you'd move on." I sniffed, trying to work up a decent hurt expression. "You're just like the others. I want something real, but all you're willing to give me is a stupid dream."

Philip released me, stepping back so I could put my hand down and see the hut he'd taken me to. It was a simple four-wall wood room that had just enough space for the two of us. There was a bed in the corner, a tin bucket against the wall, and a basket that consisted of a few odds and ends atop the counter. There were jars of various heights on the counter, as well. "I thought witches had cauldrons. Where's your cauldron?"

He was staring at me as if *I* was the danger in the room. "You'd really come willingly?"

"That's what I just said. But I want some straight answers from you first, and a few promises." I tried to zero in on the conversation and make sure I said my piece. "If we ever get it on again, it'll be my choice, not yours. You don't know how to control yourself, so it's my call now."

Philip scoffed, but I could smell feigned bravado. "It's my call whenever I feel the desire for you."

"Then no deal. Don't you remember how good it was when we were both willing?"

Philip gulped and nodded. "Okay. I can grant you that one. What else?"

"I need to take a guide. I'm not from Terraway, so I'd never make it to your place alive. And I want your word that my guide lives. He goes free when this is all said and done."

"I can tell you how to find my island."

"Not good enough. I still don't know the area."

Philip mulled this over. "I'll give you a map so you don't need a guide."

"Oh, you'll give me a map either way, but I'm still taking a guide."

"What if I sent one of my men to bring you here?"

"How would that even work? I thought no one could get to you."

"No one alive, sure. But I've brought the undead to my island on occasion. The undead can survive the long trek that a live person couldn't."

"Huh. I guess that makes sense. But still no. I've been abducted too many times. You want to trust me? I need this to be able to trust you. I'm risking a lot here. You've got home court advantage." I cast him a dubious look, my arms akimbo. "You're really fussed about one guard? See, this is exactly what I'm talking about. Do you even want to be together for real?"

"Fine, but you can't take either of your Reapers. I won't be able to keep my promise to not harm your guide if you bring Von here. And Mason's got too hot a temper to be able to leave us alone. His love for you is too permanent."

I nodded, trying not to feel the sweetness of the smile in my soul that I had such devoted and amazing men in my life. "I'll have to do some thinking about who, but that's fine. They'd never let me come here anyway." I exhaled, bringing myself to speak the questions I wasn't sure I wanted the answers to. "I need to know you're not going to double-cross me or my guide, so I want the absolute truth, here."

Philip crossed his arms over his broad chest and leaned on the wall across from me. "I've got nothing to hide."

"Why did you do that to my sister?"

Philip watched me carefully. "Because she was weak. I thought Omens were prizes, but she was a normal girl. Captivated, then scared, then useless to me. You're my equal. After being with you, I could see the others I tried to mate with were a pale comparison."

My teeth ground together, but I swallowed the venom that would only blow my formulating plan. "Allie wasn't weak; she gave up everything to make sure I had a future. She's the strongest woman I know, and you took her from me. Do you care that you hurt me?"

Philip looked up at the ceiling. "I'm not allowed to lie to you, so no. I don't care that you're hurt. I care only as much as it affects you coming to stay with me."

I nodded, breathing in his toxicity and exhaling to purge it from my system. I leaned my hand on the light brown wooden table I could tell he'd cut and assembled by hand from the trees outside. "Good to know. There's just one other question I have for now."

"Ask me anything." His shirtless form didn't even draw my eyes, a fact that was not lost on either of us.

My voice came out a whisper. "Why did you steal my daughter's body from her grave?"

Of all things, Philip smiled at me. "Ah, that's something I'll have to show you, not tell you. Come stay with me, and I'll answer that question to the fullest extent. I can tell you this much: I did it for us." He moved his pointer finger between us. "And she's *our* daughter, not just yours. My immortality came at a high price. Having an heir wasn't a possibility until I found you. It's why I was searching for Omens. Your kind tends to be able to hold up under much more than the average resident of Terraway. I think it's the Matruculan blood that's stabilized by the human blood in your genetics. Makes you able to withstand true brutality and come out of it gracefully."

I exhaled my attitude. "Lucky me."

"Mariang was pitied for being so weak, but I don't know many who would be able to carry the weight of a world the way she did. No one was more delighted that you turned out to be an Omen than I was. That you think I'll let you go without a fight shows how little you know the monster you let into your sheets."

I shuddered, and he laughed. My eyes narrowed in time with my scowl that bloomed on my lips. "Don't pull that crap with me. You're trying to be gross to intimidate me."

"You're stalling. Kiss me."

"What?" I took a step back without thinking.

Philip advanced on me, pinning me to the wall of his hut with anger behind his smile. "Exactly what I thought. You have no intention of staying with me. You're just trying to stall for time so I don't remember you're wearing too many layers of clothing for my taste."

"Knock it off," I said, keeping my voice annoyed and light so he didn't sense the fear that gripped me from the inside out. "It was my idea to come stay with you, you jack-wagon. You want to kiss me? I've got nothing against that. Maybe wait for a second when we're not talking about my comatose sister, my dead sister, or my dead daughter to set the mood a little. I mean, honestly! Have you even met any women before? This is why I wanted a week together. If you think you can force a connection, you're wrong. You'll end up with another Allie on your hands. If you want me because I'm strong, stop trying to make me cower. It's childish."

"Don't lecture me!" he shouted, his anger building, trying to make his fury bigger than mine.

Just goes to show how little he knows the monster *he* let into *his* sheets.

I reached up and smoothed a few errant white-blond hairs from his forehead, softening him so that I had the upper hand. "If you want to be the man I come home to, then be a man. Don't try to scare a kiss out of me, you tool. Earn it, like a gentleman."

My insults, for some reason, seemed to knock a little sense into Philip, and he released me in the next breath. "I haven't been near you in so long. To see you command nations at the funeral and not be able to take you right then and there? It was the height of my self-control not to use the body my spirit possessed and plow his seed into you right then for all of Terraway to see."

I rolled my eyes. "Try harder. Something *I'll* think is gentlemanly. Care a little bit about what seduces *me*, not about the songs you want to sing in honor of your almighty psychic penis."

Philip barked out a loud laugh at my sass. "My 'almighty psychic penis?' That's the best thing I've heard in ages."

"You're supposed to be telling me the best thing *I've* heard in ages. Reel it in, Philip."

Philip's laughter died to a light smile on his lips, gazing down at me like... well, like he used to. His thumb reached up and grazed my cheekbone, tracing the lines of my face as if I was delicate – as if I hadn't been through too many battles. Part of me wished I could be delicate. His eyes lasered in on mine, observing more than I usually let people see. "I watch from afar, but it's not the same as going through it all. The wars you've fought, the things your young eyes have seen – it's a wonder you still look so innocent, like you have lifetimes of beauty yet to give the world."

I tried not to get too swept away by the words that hit me right in my tender spots. "Thank you. That was actually kind of amazing. Sometimes I don't think people get how hard it's been."

"*Sinta*, I've possessed thousands in your name, trying to free you from Geon's prison, to avenge the injustice done to you by Serena, to keep our baby healthy – all of it just to make sure life doesn't stamp out that light in your eyes." He rested his forehead to mine, and for a second, my master plan was a distant memory. "Some nights, your light is the only thing that keeps me warm."

"Dang. That... You really feel that way?"

"I do. You're really coming to stay with me?"

"For one week. But Philip, you've got to stop scaring me. No more trying to force yourself on me. No more fighting dirty. No more hurting me. You want a good woman? Then be a good man."

"You scold me like..." He trailed off, frustrated with me, but impressed that, as he'd claimed, I'd played his game like an equal.

"I think you're smart enough to want the real thing."

His voice came out like a growl. "I want you."

"Then let me come to you."

He nodded once. "Very well. Let's get started, then." Philip's hand wrapped around me, inching up the bottom of my shirt to press his palm on the small of my back. I tried to squirm away, but he held me in place. "Be still, *sinta*. I'm putting a map on your back. Only show it to your guide. I'll know if you've shown it to Von or Mason or anyone else. Only your guide can see it, and only using Terraway's light. Promise me."

"Only my guide. That's fine. It might take me some time to find someone willing to go with me, so be patient."

"Careful, now. This might sting a little." His hand started to heat up to a slow burn. My back and abdomen muscles clenched and spasmed while I bit my lower lip, trying not to cry out. "There you are," he cooed as the burn faded. He rubbed my lower back to soothe the ache. "You handled that like a champ. I can't wait to get you here, so do your best to hurry home to me."

"Can I ask you something?"

"You can ask me anything." His forehead touched to mine again, his lips so very close.

"What does '*sinta*' mean?"

The corner of Philip's mouth tugged upwards. "It means my true love. My soul's mate. It's the perfect word for you."

My heart ached in my breast when I recalled how early on Finn had called me that – how sure he was about us, about me.

"Kiss me, *sinta*," Philip said in a soothing coo.

I began to doubt my master plan when the bile rose in my throat. Philip's lips descended on mine, while the ocean in the distance warned me that I would soon make this nightmare a reality.

14

FAR GONE AND FAINTING

My head hurt like a hangover when too many bright lights woke me from the deep sleep I hadn't agreed to sink into. My mouth lolled open in lieu of asking the world what it wanted of me this time.

"October? Can you hear me?"

"Huh?"

Ollie's voice was warmth, and I was so very cold. "We've been trying to wake you for hours! What happened?"

My weak limbs couldn't move on their own, but if they could, they would've wrapped themselves around Ollie and squeezed for all they were worth. As it was, I couldn't even lift my head; I was too far gone.

Ollie was adamant. "What happened? You screamed,

and when we came up, you were out cold, Danny's room was trashed, and he was gone."

I wanted to answer, but I couldn't locate the muscles that might move my jaw to form words. Danny had somehow resurrected Mariang. He'd taken her as his ghost bride or something. It was all very Heathcliff and Catherine, which was great for fiction in the Moors of Wuthering Heights, but not so great for the reality of demon Cathy thinking I was jonesing for her boyfriend.

"Danny!" I worked out, though I'm thinking it sounded more like "Nanny!" I feared that if I tried to warn them about Sama, it would come out "Mama".

"Danny? What about him? Somebody phone Danny again!" Ezra demanded from my left. "Lynna, has he picked up at all?"

"No! What's happened to his room? He hasn't let me in since Lady Mariang... But I would've insisted if I'd known this is the state of the space he's been living in. What happened here?" She picked up a broken shard from the gold and glass lamp that had fallen to pieces on the carpet, examining it curiously. "Oh, heavens!"

I didn't want to know what "oh, heavens" equated to in Lynna's mind. It could be anything from a dust bunny to a hole in the wall. Either way, I couldn't turn my head.

Mason peered in my eyes using Von's gold lighter. "Pupils are dilated. She's been blissed out. I'm guessing Danny did this before he ran away?"

I worked out a barely intelligible "yes!" grateful that

Mason understood enough of my predicament to make himself useful.

Mason slammed his fist on the nightstand, making Lynna jump. "Two Reapers, plus extra Duwendes in the house! Both Von and I are here, and you're attacked under this roof while we were right downstairs? I hate this job! We can never stay on top of you. It's like you go looking for trouble."

Ollie was in no mood to relinquish the biggest temper to Mason, so he lifted his volume to match my protector's. "Calm yourself down or get out of here. Go check on Von. You're not helping anything with that kinda talk."

Carter's beefy and hairy hand weighed atop his older brother's shoulder. "Easy, Mase. Look around the room. See if there aren't clues here while she's coming out of her haze."

No one was more impatient with my haze than me. It took a full twenty minutes before I could move my mouth enough to talk again. My limbs were still totally useless. I explained as much of the situation to them as I could, but I understood so little of what had happened. "I know I slound crazy, but I not! I saw it right here," I slurred. I tried to lift my arm to point to the spot where Mariang had appeared near the closet, but my arm didn't move at all.

Ezra clutched his chest, and for a second I worried that I was about to give him a heart attack. "You're certain it was Mariang? You're absolutely sure?"

"I sure."

At my confirmation, Ollie dropped me from my leaning back position in his arms, leaving my body to flop on the bed as he darted to Ezra, who collapsed to unconsciousness under the weight of it all. I hated, absolutely hated being helpless, even more so when someone I loved was in agony. I was feet away from my poor broken father, but I couldn't get there.

When strong, hairy arms slid under my knees and behind my back to tilt me up to sitting, I expected them to be Mason's. The smell of patchouli was mixed with rocks, instead of the waft of woods that my favorite wolf always smelled like. My vision locked in on Carter's slate eyes that were worried, but still took the time to be kind. "Thought you might prefer being able to see the room. Are you alright, Lady October?"

"Where's Von?" I asked, making sure my lower lip didn't tremble, though to be certain, it wanted to. Ezra had fainted, and was just coming to as Ollie and Mason propped him up on the filthy floor, slapping his cheeks and calling his name. Lynna ran to get him a glass of orange juice, all while I sat there, doing friggin' nothing.

Carter's voice was gentle, trying to instill calm through the chaos. "Your other Reaper's in his cell in the basement. You cut yourself rather deep. Or Lady Mariang cut you. He's sweating out his grief and his desires in the cage with a blood bag until he comes back to his senses." Carter didn't know about my phobias, or I'm guessing normal behavior, because he offered me a drink from the dusty glass on Danny's nightstand.

"No, thanks." My mind raced as I thought about Sama and the promise I'd made to come to him without my Duwendes. It had seemed harrowing at the time, but now it seemed downright impossible. I could barely move, and I knew my two constant shadows wouldn't let me out of their sight, now that I'd been attacked by an actual ghost. On top of that, I needed to find a guide who knew the ins and outs of Terraway.

I waited quietly amidst the chaos for my body to come back to me, hoping when it did, the world would have righted itself.

15

THREE IN ONE

I packed a bag when Mason was in the shower that evening and Von was still in his cell. Von had since been declared safe, so when night fell, I still wasn't any closer to escaping or finding myself a decent guide. I'd managed to stuff my backpack behind the couch in the living room, but that's about as far along as I was on the master plan – which is to say, not far at all.

As I'd suspected, Mason and Von scarcely let me out of their sight. I finally gave up when night fell, vowing to try to escape tomorrow. My cheeks turned rosy when I changed into a nightgown that fell to the middle of my thighs. The flowy, silky material was held up by thin straps, and the whole peach-colored thing was lined with cream lace. It was beautiful, and if this would be my last night with Von, I wanted to feel beautiful.

I knew very well that marching headfirst into the lion's

den meant I might not come out alive. In fact, if I was being honest with myself, I was gambling on the rules of a world I didn't always understand. No one else had a plan, though, and I knew I couldn't live in fear anymore.

Fear didn't suit me; it never had.

Von swore when he came out of the shower in pajama pants, his eyes getting a good glimpse of me in all my virginal glory. In reality, other than the fact that the nightgown had spaghetti straps, it wasn't all that racy. It was a tribute to how modestly I usually dressed that Von gave me the glad eye over what was basically a lacy mid-thigh sundress. But you know, call it a nightgown, and things get PG-13 real quick. Von rubbed his hand over his bare stomach. "You look... You look like you wouldn't be wearing that little scrap for long if it was just the two of us in this mansion. Pack it for the honeymoon?"

"Sure."

He pulled a cinnamon stick from the case on the nightstand and chewed on it, so I knew he was itching for more blood. My cheek had been disinfected and cleaned up from Mariang's assault, but the skin was still broken in two striped diagonal lines down my left cheek. Von took in a ragged breath. "You look amazing and smell delicious. It's quite the effect you have going there."

I frowned. "Oh, you want me to sleep downstairs?"

"Not dressed like that. I want you in my bed posthaste."

I quirked my eyebrow at the man I adored. "Post-haste,

eh? You've got to stop using those sexy words around me. But seriously, I don't want you to lose it. I'll sleep on the couch."

"No, no. I'm fine. Glutted myself on blood earlier." His smile was forced, and I could tell he was tipping on the edge of self-loathing. He'd wanted so very much to not have to drink blood at all anymore. "How's that for sexy talk?"

"The very sexiest. Mason already asleep in one of the other rooms?"

"No, he's downstairs talking to Ezra. He'll be up soon, probably in one of the guest bedrooms down the hall." Von made his way to me and kissed my lips, making me swoon for him in ways that made me sure I was doing the right thing. I couldn't live in fear of Philip. He had to go down. I wouldn't be able to have a life with Von if Philip was still trying to get at me. And I had a kind of far out there idea for how to wake Allie, but was afraid Philip would only try and torment her if I did. No, Philip had to die if Allie and I were to live.

Von and I wasted no more time with words. After a few kisses that kept building into our usual hurricane of passion, we were tumbling around on the floor of the bedroom as we shed our clothes in our minds in the imagined park that was precious to us both. The gold and blue swirled and sparkled around us, knocking purple and green leaves off the trees as nature danced to cheer us on. "When we get married, I'll take you away from here,"

Von promised, though we both knew it was wishful thinking.

"Where? Where will you take me?"

"Anywhere and everywhere," he murmured between breathless kisses. "I love you."

I slowed our kiss so I could have a quiet moment with him on the colorful grass. "You know I'd do anything for you, right? I'd give anything to keep you safe."

"I know, baby. Me too." Von tasted my lips with a low moan that made my whole body fall in love with him.

"I don't like that Philip got to you, taking your hair and controlling you like that. I don't like that he found a way to tear us apart."

Von stopped the kiss, our magical world fading around us and bringing us back to the light beige carpet of our bedroom in the mansion. "His name is Sama, not Philip. Philip is fake. Sama is very much real. Call him by his proper name."

It was rare Von bossed me. Instead of responding verbally, I tilted my head to the side, my legs still wrapped around him.

Von deflated in my arms. "Sorry. That was harsher than I meant it to come out, yeah? I just don't want you to confuse him with the monster he truly is."

"Trust me, I know he's a monster."

Mason knocked on the door, giving us a courtesy heads-up so we could untangle ourselves before he opened it. "I'm sorry, guys. Ezra's requested I stay in here with you both tonight. Eventful day, plus she's got an open cut still." He held onto the doorjamb in his brown plaid pajama pants and white undershirt, almost as if he was nervous to let himself inside.

"That's more than fine. We were just about to turn in." I smiled up at Mason, though I knew Von was cringing that our time alone was being infiltrated.

"Come on, mate. All wolves are welcome in here." Von pulled back the covers and flopped onto his side of the king-sized bed.

I crawled into the middle, not realizing until Mason slid in on my other side that he hadn't planned on turning into a wolf that night. I was nervous, and very aware that I was engaged and sleeping in a bed with two men the same day I'd kissed another in my dreams. I was pretty sure Mrs. Brady never had these problems. I was aware of every movement, and immediately wished I was wearing sweat-pants and a frumpy shirt.

Von took the lead, feeling my nerves. "Night, darling." He kissed my lips just once, and then rolled me on my side so he could spoon me. He palmed my stomach, his thumb moving up and down over my navel in a slow tease that made it hard for me to relax. "Did you want a snog as well, Mase old boy? My lips are puckered and ready for you."

"Pass." Being spooned by Von put me face to face with Mason, who brought the covers up over all three of us. He reached out and held my hand, bringing my other arm to loop under his neck so I couldn't scratch myself in my sleep without hugging him awake. Then he snuck his knee between mine, so I could use his leg like a body pillow. "Goodnight, *hani*." Then Mason nuzzled his nose to mine and pecked my lips three times before closing his eyes, content now that we were together.

They loved me, which made it impossible for me to escape.

16

DRUNK GUYS ARE FUNNY
LIKE THAT

The house was still during the night, until around two in the morning, when I heard a mumble of voices coming up from the main floor. I tried to extract myself from Von's lax grip without waking him, but clumsily managed to rouse both of them in the process. "Where are you off to, love?" Von's eyes were still closed, his lips puffy. He was pretty much the cutest vampire I'd ever seen.

"Can't sleep. I'm going to go get a snack. Be back in a few."

My whisper woke Mason, who sat up. "I'll go with you."

I placed my hand on Mason's chest, gently pushing him back down onto the mattress. For good measure, I stroked the hair that peppered his toned belly under his t-shirt, smiling when he made precious noises of utter contentment. "No, no. Go back to sleep. You want me to bring you anything?"

Mason was only half awake, so he didn't catch my dubious glare when he mumbled, "Always offer to bring me food dressed only in a nightgown. Fantasy come to life."

I paused to kiss Von's lips, and then Mason's, stealing just a moment where we were together, and life gave us a few breaths that weren't so harrowing. I loved them with a fierce protectiveness, and knew I couldn't allow the rest of our lives to be spent always looking over our shoulders for Sama's next attack. I leaned down to touch my cheek to Von's, unable to make myself leave without one more simple touch. "I adore you," I admitted.

"I don't blame you," he replied, his charm still in full swing, even mid-sleep. It was the perfect thing to say, and Von was the perfect guy for me.

Within seconds, Von was already asleep again, so I climbed over Mason, whose hand grazed the back of my naked thigh, giving me goosebumps as I righted myself. I quietly opened the dresser drawer and pulled on my jeans, and then zipped up one of Von's hoodies over my night-gown, shoving a pair of socks in the pocket.

Mason was sitting up now, rubbing the sleep out of his eyes. "Where are you really going?"

"To the kitchen. I heard Ezra moving around down there, and don't want to walk around in my nightgown in front of my dad."

Mason paused, craning his neck to confirm with his keen hearing that Ezra was in fact downstairs. "Okay. You'll be safe. It's only Ezra and Carter."

"Like I said. Lie back down, sweetie." I waited until Mason complied, and then tugged the comforter up over his chest, kissing his forehead. When his eyes finally shut, I made my way down the stairs, hoping for a brilliant diversion to come to me so I could get on with my master plan.

Ezra and Carter both ceased their conversation and stood from their stools at the counter when I came into the kitchen. Only the light over the sink was on, and I could tell they had been trying to drown their sorrows in the bottle of rum that was sitting between their crystal tumblers. "Good evening, October Grace. What are you doing up at this hour? Trouble sleeping?"

"Yeah. I would ask what you two are up to, but I'm guessing nothing good, judging by your breath. What's bothering you?"

Ezra sank back down onto his stool. "Only the things you already know. Danny's simply gone. He's resurrected a portion of my daughter's spirit, and he's taken it with him. Sama's set on getting into your head. Sakuna's on the brink of a major hierarchy change yet again. I'm actually surprised it's taken me this long to open a bottle."

I gawked at the half empty bottle, and then narrowed my eyes at Carter. "You let him drink that much? You know he doesn't have the stomach for it. Dad!" I put the cap on the bottle and glared at Carter's glazed, impish grin. I pulled a slice of bread from the box on the counter and slapped some peanut butter on it. "Take this to bed. We'll talk about Mariang and what to do about it all in the morning. You're not going to solve anything at this hour, young man." I was worried about Ezra, but it came out as pissed. "Go on to bed. I was hoping to have a word with Carter anyway."

"I'm sorry!" Ezra moaned, his mouth sticky with peanut butter. "I let her down, and now I'm letting you down. I'm utterly worthless!"

My shoulders drooped, and I knew Ezra wasn't with it enough to make rational decisions. "It's alright, Dad. But it's time to go to bed now."

"'Young man,'" he echoed as he stood from the stool, leaning heavily on the granite counter. "I haven't been young in so long."

Despite the time-sensitive nature of my master plan, I wrapped my arms around Ezra's waist and buried my face in his chest. "It's okay. We'll find Danny and reason with him. What he brought back? It's not the Mariang he loved. He'll realize it soon enough, if he hasn't already." I glared at Carter. "Help me get him to bed."

"Me? You seem to be mothering him well enough on your own." Even though he argued with me, Carter stood and took Ezra's arm around his shoulder. He wore a black tunic and the same kind of I'm-ready-for-anything military black pants that Finn and Mason often wore.

"Yeah? Well, you break it, you bought it." We carefully

maneuvered Ezra to his room, laying him on his grand bed that had so clearly been designed for two, but only held his lonely form. I smoothed his blond hair back from his brow and kissed his forehead, tucking him in with his heavy teal and brown comforter that had gold trim on the edges. There wasn't much I didn't love about Ezra. He'd taken me in when I'd had no one, and claimed me when neither of my parents would or could. I loved him, and because of that, I knew I couldn't let Sama cause him another night of restless sleep. I scribbled a note on a pad of paper on his nightstand and folded it, tucking it into his breast pocket for him to find when he was sober. I swallowed thickly and placed my engagement ring in his pocket, and then fastened the button so it didn't slide out. The note explained things well enough, so hopefully Von didn't think I was leaving him. I couldn't very well go off with Philip for a week wearing Von's engagement ring.

I leaned over Ezra's body and kissed his prickly cheek, knowing that of all the people I loved, Ezra was near the top of the list. "Goodnight, Dad."

Ezra mumbled a farewell, but he was already snoring when I tiptoed out with Carter.

Carter chuckled next to me as we made our way back to the kitchen. "I haven't had a drink with Ezra in ages. Probably not since my coronation."

I whirled on Carter, my finger in his face. Even though he was much bigger and taller than me, my anger was nothing to be trifled with. "Next time the two of you go thinking you're pirates and can drink as much rum as you want, remember that you're old men, and cut yourselves off after two drinks."

"I'm not an old man!" Carter frowned at me, affronted. "I'm twenty-nine years old."

"Oh, so not sixteen? Then you should know better, old man. Get my dad drunk again, and you'll see a side of me you don't want to."

Carter had the nerve to let his eyes travel down to my backside appreciatively. "I can't imagine there's a side of you I wouldn't want to see all rolled up in my sheets."

I popped his chest bone with the flat of my hand to move him back a step. "You're drunk. Stop being a flipped-up jackwagon. You know I'm engaged, and you know I used to date your brother."

His gaze drifted where it most certainly wasn't welcome. "Oh, Mason always does the noble thing. I'll bet that even with all the sleeping together you three do, he's still never seen your softer sides."

I glowered up at him. "Stop talking to my breasts. Keep this up, and I'll knock you clean out and leave you right here for Lynna to step over in the morning when she starts up breakfast. I don't think anyone'd have trouble believing you got your face kicked in just because someone didn't like the look of it."

"You've got quite the mouth on you." He reached for the bottle of rum, but I grabbed it from his hand. "I was needing that. Terraway spirits don't have the same sweet flavor. Topsider drinks are far more enjoyable than ours."

I sized up his rosy cheeks, his easy smile and the slate eyes that kept losing focus. "You're the perfect amount of drunk for what I need right now." I gripped the neck of the bottle tight in my fist. "How about we take the rest of this to Terraway? Finish it up just the two of us."

Carter eyed me curiously, leaning away with his hands on the back of his hips. "You're trying to get me liquored up."

"I'm trying to get you to take me to Dagat." I decided this was the best opportunity I was going to get. "I need to talk to Captain Finn, but I can't get there without someone to port me down."

"What about Mason? I'm thinking your keeper wouldn't want you running off with me." He leaned in and stage-whispered, "I'm the bad one. He's the responsible son." Carter stank like he'd bathed in rum.

"Take me to Dagat, and I'll hand over the rest of the bottle. Just a quick trip. Oh, thank you!" I pretended like Carter had already agreed to it and scampered off to the living room, snatching up my backpack and slinging it over my shoulder. I slid on my socks and shoes, ready to go.

"Wait, why are we doing this?" Carter's eyebrows pushed together as he frowned, following me into the living room.

I whirled on him, my hand on my hip as I huffed dramatically. "We already discussed this. Ezra asked you to take me down to Dagat. He needs me to deliver this back-pack to Finn. Kinda time-sensitive, so if you don't mind…"

Carter scratched his head in true caveman fashion. "Ezra didn't… I don't remember that."

I forced out a light chuckle, looking up at him with affection. "Dude, how drunk are you right now? Better trust the memory retrieval to me." I chucked his shoulder like he'd never hit on me, like we were old friends, and like I pretty much knew he'd do whatever I asked of him.

Drunk guys are funny like that.

He harrumphed as he tried once again to sort out the events of the evening, but put up no further protest. "Okay, little Omen. Hold tight to your big, strong king. I haven't ported drunk in years. Might not be the most graceful landing you've ever been dealt."

"Make it quick, then." I moved into Carter's body space and clung tight to him, holding my breath until his arm wrapped around my back to keep me in place.

He was counting down from five, which made me more than a little nervous. None of the others who'd ported me needed to psych themselves up before the plunge.

I closed my eyes and knew as Carter reached "one" that there was no turning back.

17

FROM FIERCE AND GLORIOUS TO SLAVE

When I opened my eyes again, I made an instant vow never to ask a guy I didn't really know who'd had too much to drink to port me anywhere. We landed in a pile of limbs in the dead of night. After a solid "oof!" Carter passed out on top of me, his mouth lolling open in a loud snore.

It took more than a little effort, but I eventually managed to slide out from under him, dusting myself off. Carter was a king, so I knew he'd be okay at the porting spot until he woke. My brain quickly snapped to filter out a list of priorities, starting with job one: locating some *baga* root so I could breathe.

Broken-off memories of Finn bringing me here when I was on the brink of death with my back skin peeling off flooded me. My chin turned to the right and left, trying to locate something familiar so I dug for life in the right spot.

The marsh stood out in my memory, so I bolted to it, dropping to my knees when I found a three-pronged stick jutting out from the squishy grass. A blue vine hung in my face, tapping the top of my head over and over while I moved as quickly as I could. I nearly cried out with relief when I unearthed the gnarly root, choking it down in plenty of time (or with two seconds to spare. You never know with Terraway). I searched around in the moonlight for another root, just in case, and shoved it in my backpack.

I didn't remember much of the journey to the Dagat palace. The last time I was here, Finn had run with me in his arms the entire way, and I'd been barely alive. I heard a steady trickling of a stream I couldn't see, and the plink-plonk of a twig or a nut dropping from a tree on my right. I could smell the greenery that surrounded me, breathing it in deep to acclimate myself to the world I knew I didn't belong in. For the time being, there seemed to be only one clear path forward, so I started down it at a light jog, keeping my head down in hopes that only the stars would take notice of me.

About two renditions of *All the Men in My Life Keep Getting Killed by Candarian Demons* from *Evil Dead the Musical* passed in my head before I heard a faint chittering that made my pace pick up to a run. In my periphery, I saw the same three-tailed monkeys swinging from branches that I'd noticed during my first trip to Dagat. They hadn't bothered us then, but it seemed that now I was here without Finn, I was persona non-grata. They began to throw nuts from the trees at me, some of them hitting my arms and whacking my head as I made quick work of the journey. They chittered and pelted me unrelentingly, punishing me for leaving my Reapers at home.

The run turned into a sprint when I heard footsteps pounding a stone's throw behind me, picking up speed to overtake mine. I made the mistake of looking over my shoulder, like a dummy. I let out a bitten-off scream when I saw a gilled Kataw chasing me, his triton clutched in his hand and a non-negotiable look of rip-tear-kill on his face.

"Stop!" he called to me.

He looked so big and ferocious, I nearly obeyed him, but turned back to the path and kept running instead. Relief spread over me when the spires of the palace came into view in the distance above the trees. If only I could outrun him a little more, I could get to Finn.

I made it about a third of the way into my next rendition of my favorite *Evil Dead the Musical* song before my foot slipped on something under a smattering of foliage. The next thing I knew, I was being hoisted up into the air by a large net. "Ah!" I cried out, clinging to the sides to try and fight my way out like a fool.

"Are you tired of running from me yet, little sandwalker?" the soldier teased me with a bite to his tone.

"Get me down! I need to talk to Captain Finn. I'm the Omen, and I need to see Finn." I hated throwing around my royalty card, but I didn't see any other way out of this.

The man frowned and clicked on his finger lights, shining them so he could get a good look at my face. He squinted up at me with too much skepticism for my liking. "You're not the Omen. Lady October is regal and travels with her two Reapers. Do you really expect me to believe an Omen would travel to Dagat without her protectors?"

"I don't care what you believe! Cut me down from here, or I'll do it myself. I need to see Finn, so you can either take me in like a gentleman, or you can arrest me and bring me to him. I don't much care. Either way, I need to see Finn, and I don't have much time."

"If it's all the same to you, I'll take you in as a feisty little prisoner, then. The captain can decide what to do with your legs once he gets a good look at you." He reached up with his triton and sawed only half of the rope netting loose, letting me tumble out and fall with a painful crack on the ground. "Up you get. Try anything smart, and I'll run you through just to be rid of the hassle. I was hoping for a quiet night tonight on my patrol."

I kept my mouth shut as he jerked me to my feet and yanked my arms forward, tying them together so deftly, I knew there'd be no chance of wriggling out. The wisps of the rope cut into my wrists, making them burn and itch as he led me forward like a slave.

I wanted to pummel him, but didn't trust that I'd make it to Finn alive if I took a chance on besting the muscular military man. He started out at a march, but looked up at the sky a few minutes in. "Can you run on those puny legs, little girl?"

"I outran you well enough before you got lucky and that stupid net caught me. Let's go. If we can get to the palace faster, so much the better."

"Oh, how I'm going to enjoy throwing you in the dungeon. Let the more eager soldiers have their fun with you. Or perhaps you'd be better suited for what's left of the harem?"

"Just run." I rolled my eyes and tried to keep up when the soldier picked up his pace so much that I had to really concentrate to keep up. It was counterintuitive to run without pumping my arms, and when the palace was finally in sight, I tripped over my own two stupid feet and did an ungraceful, totally painful face-plant in the dirt. The soldier dragged me a few feet just to be a jerk before stopping to right me.

I shrugged off his help and stumbled to my feet myself, sucking the blood off my busted lip and blinking a trickle of red out of my eyes.

The man looked down at me, examining my face with a grimace. "Now you're probably more suited for the dungeon than the harem, but don't think that'll get you out of going wherever Captain Finn sees fit to throw you." He shook his head at me in exasperation. "Impersonating the Omen. Like I wouldn't see right through that." He tugged my rope, and despite my scraped knees, I managed to follow him at a slow trot. "I was at the funeral of the late

Lady Mariang, you know. I saw Lady October stand for the shamed Reaper. She was fierce and glorious. You're nothing but a child."

I didn't bother arguing, but trampled along in silence. I was grateful the three-tailed monkeys had stopped throwing things at me, and more grateful still when we reached the edge of the woods.

Lit by only the moons was the golden castle that shimmered even in the dead of night. The tall columns seemed to stretch to the heavens, small as I was next to them. The third floor was outlined in rubies, the fifth in opals. I hadn't taken the time to appreciate the magnificence before, but now all I wanted to do was gape at the beauty.

Of course, the jag with the rope was jerking me along, so I didn't have the time to gawk like I wanted to. He took the golden stairs three at a time, which I didn't have the capacity for. My scraped-up knee was shaking, and I worried about it going out on me if I slipped on the smooth surface.

The soldier saluted two guards who'd been posted at the entrance. The one on the right managed a shadow of a smirk at my captor. "Evening, Lieutenant Emil. Looks like you found a prize for the dungeon. She give you any trouble?"

"She tried. I'm taking her to Captain Finn. Is he ashore tonight, or did he go home?"

The taller of the two scoffed. "You know the captain never goes to his home anymore. He's in the study. You can take her on back." The tall guy with a death wish pinched my butt as I walked over the threshold. "I guess I'll be visiting the dungeon on my break today."

I made him jump when I barked at him like a rabid dog. If they wanted to treat me like an animal, then that's what they'd get from me.

18

MY NEW DOGGY

We went through two more checkpoints before reaching a long, narrow room that held only a globe in the center, sitting atop a gilded stand. The sphere seemed to be lit from the inside. The only other lights were rows of flickering candles lining either side of the room. Finn appeared to be deep in thought as he stared at the globe, startling when the bang of the door announced our entry. "What the... What are you doing here?" Then he stood straighter, barking out a command that made me jump. "Unbind her hands! Are you mad? That's your Omen you're leading around like a criminal!"

Emil's head snapped toward me, his mouth falling open in stunned horror. "The Omen? You weren't lying?" With nervous fingers, he took a balisong knife from his belt, flicked it open and cut the ropes off my wrists. Then he dropped to his knees, head bowed before me in a complete 180 of his previous swaggering personality. "Forgive me, your grace. A thousand apologies will never be enough."

"You're right it won't! Prepare yourself for the gallows, Lieutenant. Since you've clearly lost your head, I see no reason for it to stay attached to your shoulders."

The worst part was that Emil didn't protest more than a sharp intake of breath, prostrate before us.

I moved forward, placing my hand on Finn's arm. "There's no need for that. He was just doing his job. He didn't know it was me. I didn't tell him who I was," I lied. "He was just keeping your woods safe."

Finn put his boot on Emil's shoulder and used the leverage to shove him flush to the ground, where the lieutenant remained without a fight. It was frightening to watch Finn's brutal nature combine with his unquestionable authority. "Be that as it may, you're bleeding and limping. I'll match your injuries blow for blow on his body if it's not your wish he's executed."

I moved to stand between the defeated man and the irrational one, splaying my arms out to guard the poor dude. "I need to talk to you, Finn. Let Emil go. This is more important than that. It's just a little blood."

Finn glared at Emil and finally nodded. "Very well. You may keep your life, Lieutenant, though you shouldn't thank me for it. Thank your Omen for your food and your life."

Emil crawled to me on his hands and knees, not

looking up as he pressed his lips to the top of my black sneaker. "Oh, jeez. You don't have to do that. Honestly. It's all fine. I get it. You were doing your job. It's why I didn't put up too much of a fight." When he remained on all fours at my side, I lowered my hand to his head, hoping it would communicate some sort of kindness to him. I didn't need someone kissing my feet, and I leveled my hard gaze at Finn to tell him as much. "Emil didn't lay a hand on me the entire time. I got caught in one of your rope traps, and then I fell while I was running a few times. He's a good soldier. Did everything by the book."

Finn closed the gap between us. Anger painted his features that were only dimly lit by the flickering candles. He jerked my chin upward so he could better see my face. "You're lying. You've got marks all over you."

"Then put a muzzle on your stinkin' monkeys. They pelted me the whole way until Emil found me."

"What are these slashes on your cheek from?" He thumbed the injury Mariang had marked into me.

"I cut myself shaving."

Finn shot me a withering look. "I've been going insane down here, hoping you're okay, and you come to me like this?"

"Well, if you'd shown up to the council meeting, then you'd know exactly how okay I am. Then maybe you wouldn't bark like a lunatic at your lieutenant."

Finn looked deep into my eyes, saying too much without opening his mouth. He had lines of sleeplessness etched on the corners of his eyes, making him look far older. There was a hardness to his green pools that seemed to pierce straight through me in punishment. Though he tried to push anger to the forefront of his emotions, I could see plainly that Finn was miserable. "Fine. Emil belongs to you until you leave our land, then. Do with your new pet as you see fit." He leaned down and punched Emil across the face, making me yelp.

I fell to my bloody knees and wrapped my arms around Emil's thick neck. "Do you have to be so mean? This isn't you. What's going on? I didn't give you your will back just so you could do *this* with it."

Finn jabbed his finger to his chest as if he was trying to punish his sternum. "This is exactly who I am. It's what you didn't have to see because I kept you safe from it all. You came here for what purpose, I can't even begin to guess. I don't owe you holding back anymore. This is who I am, *Lady* October."

I clung to Emil, pressing my cheek to his as I ran my fingers through his hair to calm us both. He was panting through his fear of being nearly executed. "Well, it's ugly. So ugly, I can barely stand to look at you."

"Then what did you come here for, if not to look at me in all my glory? Did Mason bring you?"

I stood, but Emil remained at my feet. Finn moved his boot to rest on the back of Emil's neck, anchoring his lieutenant's head to the marble floor. Emil bowed without hesitation, his butt sticking up behind him, not resisting the degradation. I scraped at the backs of my hands with building anxiety. "It's kind of private, so could I talk to you alone for a minute?"

Finn removed his boot from Emil's neck and snapped his fingers, as if the lieutenant was a dog. "Leave us, but don't go further than the door. And don't you dare rise up off your knees until Lady October leaves our land. Then I'll deal with you as I please."

"Oh my gosh! Do you hear yourself? We all get it; you're big and mean, and we're all just shaking in our boots." I hated myself when Emil kissed my shoe again and crawled quickly out of the room, shutting the door behind him. "That was unnecessary. I can't believe you treat your loyal men like that."

"I treat anyone who crosses you like that, whether they're my men or not." He held my arm too tight, jerking me to his chest with too much force. "I don't know what you're hoping to prove by coming here. Ezra wouldn't dare send you to Dagat without the whole team at your side. And just where is your dreamy fiancé?"

"Probably still sleeping with Mason in our bed. No one knows I'm here except Carter." This bit of news relaxed his grip due to surprise, but Finn still held my arm in a way that felt controlling. I didn't much like being controlled. "I tricked Carter into taking me down here. He's passed out drunk at the porting spot, so you might want to send one of your men for him in the morning."

"I'll send Emil now."

"No, not now. Not before I tell you why I'm here. I need your help, Finn."

"My help? I thought you made it clear you didn't need me or my help anymore. You've got Von. Where's he right now in your hour of need? What need was so desperate that you came here without an escort?"

I waited until it seemed he was done with his indignant ranting. My voice was quiet when the words tumbled out of my mouth like a confession. "I need your help because I know how to kill Sama."

19

ONE WHOLE MINUTE OF CANDY

"You're crazy! Your plan isn't a plan at all! It's a guess, October. A guess. You want me to gamble your life on a guess? We don't even know all the ins and outs of that particular kind of magic." Finn shook his head. "I'm not taking you there. Not in a million years. Not if your life depended on it, which it doesn't."

I finally jerked myself free, staring up at him defiantly. "You think my life doesn't depend on this? He put my sister in a coma! You have no idea how close I am to being totally wiped out by this guy every single time I close my eyes. I mean it, Finn. I can't live like this, because he'll kill me. It has to stop, and I think I'm the only one who can put an end to it all."

"It's suicide! I can't protect you from Sama." He stepped back and pointed at me as if publicly calling me out, though we were the only two in the room. "You're marching to your death, and I won't lead you there. You really thought I'd take you? Of everyone, you thought your hooks in me were so strong that you could get me to say yes to this? Do you really think I'm that weak?" He held my biceps and jerked me back and forth again so hard, my teeth rattled. "I came here to escape you! I dreamed that you would come and find me, offer yourself to me as the bride I wish you could be, but this is how you come? This is why you're here? Because you think I'll help you die? Don't you know me at all?" He jerked me around again, his grip too tight for my struggle to reason with.

I knew Finn was strong, but I didn't grasp just how immovable his muscles were until I was desperately trying to get the crap off his bad side. "Get ahold of yourself! You're scaring me, Finn," I admitted, loathing the truth of that statement.

"I'm scaring you? Good! I didn't think it possible to knock a healthy fear of the world into your brain. I should've done this ages ago." He breathed into my face through his clenched jaw. There was too much tension – always too much with us.

I didn't want my voice to break, but I wasn't used to Finn being this rough with me. "Sama wouldn't let me bring one of my Reapers. I came here because I know you'd stop at nothing to save me. Even if it was hard, you'd try until the end. I need someone who'll try with me."

"Make no mistake, this would be the end. It would be

the very end. I want no part of your death. I wanted to share a life with you, not end us both so stupidly."

I swallowed and cast around for a second option. "Then just give me a guide. Let me take one of the soldiers you don't need so much. I don't know how to get around Terraway, and Sama wrote the map to his house on my back using some spell, so I can't see it. All I need is a guide, Finn. Can I take Emil? Anyone, I don't care! Just someone who won't rape me."

Finn glared at me, and for once, I truly felt how much bigger than me he was. "Straight back to Ezra's is the only place you'll be going."

I finally managed to shove him back so I could have two inches of space between us. "Don't you get it? I'm dead either way. And it's only a matter of time before Von and Mason are targeted. And the attack at the funeral? It was meant as a diversion so Sama could steal September's bones. The council was attacked because of me! Ezra was shot in the back with an arrow because of me! Sama has to go down, and I'm the only one with a map and a plan. We can't just keep dodging him, always on the defensive. You're a fighter, same as me. You know what we're doing to avoid him isn't sustainable. He has to go down."

Finn's nostrils flared with his waxing and waning temper, his full lips wanting to shout at me, I'm sure. "Let me see this map."

My eyes widened that I'd actually made a little progress. "Sure. He said you can only see it with Terraway's light. I'm guessing that's either your suns, or it's the finger lights. Not sure."

I was about to turn around and lift up the hem of my nightgown that draped over my jeans and stuck out under my hoodie, but Finn beat me to it. He marched me to the nearest wall and practically shoved my front to the cold surface, ripping my nightgown and hoodie up my back. Luckily the material hitched under my breasts that were pressed to the wall, but my heart raced at Finn's temper. I don't think I'd ever seen him so unforgiving. He gasped and dropped to his knees, so I'm guessing the map had revealed itself to him. His fingers flitted along my spine, landing at my hips where he held onto me, thumbing the small of my back. "We never knew where he was sequestered by the last Kapre. Every few years, some of his followers try again to reach him, but it's no wonder they can't. Even the Mer can't swim out this far."

He blew on my skin, sending a simultaneous warmth and chill through me. I knew he could see the goose-bumps. I knew he could see my fluttering shut eyelashes since my cheek was pressed to the cold stone. "Knock it off," I warned. "I didn't come here for that."

There was a crazy amount of sexual tension I didn't want to be part of, but there it was, dripping over our bodies like honey, making him look sweet enough to taste. Finn leaned in and lowered my jeans an inch down my hips. I should've elbowed him in the jaw. I should've walked away.

But I didn't. I stood there, my front pressed to the cold, while Finn warmed my backside. His full lips kissed a line along the lowered edge of my jeans, pausing at my tailbone, where he sucked on the ridge until I moaned, my back arched. My brain wanted me to run, but my body was controlled by my traitor tailbone in that moment. My body lingered, indulging in what it wanted – something lovely. Something delicious. Something succulent. My life had been so dark and harrowing. I wanted a whole minute of candy. Luscious candy with no thought of the ramifications of indulgence.

So I let my body go down the candy aisle of certain doom for one whole minute.

2 0

TOO MUCH WANT

t wasn't until Finn unbuttoned my jeans that my brain took over, running the car off the road to avoid a head-on collision. "No! I'm engaged, and that's not changing. I told you I didn't come here for that. I came here because I knew you'd help me live."

"You planned this, didn't you? To show me the map first. You knew it'd link me to the map, settle in my brain, and then you *couldn't* take anyone else."

"What are you talking about? Linked you to the map? What does that mean? Sama told me I could only show my guide. Did the map do something to you?"

Finn stood, lowering my nightgown and hoodie, and standing too close for the redness in my cheeks to fade. I was too embarrassed to turn around and face him. I couldn't even face myself. His hand gripped my hip as he spoke, with his other hand on the wall above me, bracing himself and caging me in at the same time. His voice was quieter now, more controlled. "Sama uses magic that takes time to develop. He's had decades to study, and the magic he attempts demands too much concentration for a person with a single lifetime to invest in the learning curve. He's testing you. I'm guessing he didn't want you to go running to Daddy or your keepers about this?"

"He didn't want Von or Mason, no. Made me promise."

"This was his way of testing you. The first person you show the map to is the only one who can see it. Then it imbeds in their brain, so they see it every time they go to sleep until they reach the place the map calls them. I can see it just fine using my finger lights, but if Emil came in, he wouldn't be able to see any trace of it."

I palmed my forehead. "Of course Sama would make it so that he would know if I turned on him."

"Sama's got many faults, but being careless isn't one of them." Slowly, Finn reached both arms around me and refastened the top button of my jeans, just to show us both that he owned my button. He stroked the band of my underwear, and my stomach reacted by sucking inward without checking in first with my brain. His hands remained under my nightgown but overtop of my jeans, encircling me in his protection I knew all too well could sour on a hot dime. His thumb traced my navel as if he knew exactly how to play my body so I would dance for him.

He was not wrong.

Finn's voice was low in my ear. "Well done, trapping me to go with you. Now I won't be able to dream of anything else until I personally take you to Sama."

"I didn't mean to trap you. I mean, clearly I didn't know that would happen."

"Hmm." He sounded dubious, but I didn't care. I had my guide. The sooner we could get there, the sooner this might all be over – for better or worse. "I need a few things from my house before we go." His fingers slid from my stomach to my hand, holding on tight so we didn't lose each other.

Sudden lightness at his compliance lifted my pitch up half an octave. "Really?"

"Really. I want some kind of reward for saying no to you for this long, though. Personal best."

This would be our last journey together, I was certain. After this, I would be able to let go of the hand that held me closer than I could stay. Part of me wanted to stay, but the rest of me knew it wasn't enough to get me through.

Finn led me to the exit and opened the door, clicking his fingers at Emil like he was a dog. Emil hadn't risen while he was alone in the hallway, and kept his head bowed as he scurried along on his hands and knees behind us. I squeezed Finn's hand. "Finn, I don't like this. It's totally demeaning, and it makes me look like I condone this sort of thing, which I don't. Let him go back to his normal job. He was good at it. Honestly, he didn't lay a finger on me."

Finn was less grouchy when we were holding hands, so I let us remain together for the time being. "No. You can rule your kingdom as you like. You can make Mason and Von jump for you all day long. This is *my* land. I was trained the same way my men were. Emil's grateful to have his head still. That's all the mercy I'm willing to part with tonight."

We passed through another set of doors, revealing us to too many soldiers who stood at attention at Finn's entry. "This is the Omen, not some random jungle rat Emil brought in. Take a good look so the crime doesn't happen again."

Several sets of eyes registered the shock of letting me be led in bound, passing several checkpoints where no one had noticed who I was. I didn't blame them. I'd been Vogued for the funeral. Here I had two violent slashes across my cheek from Mariang (the not-so-friendly ghost), and I had dirt on my clothes. I sported several bangs and scrapes from the monkeys, Emil and the stupid fall from the net. I was a mess, but I didn't care. I cared that Emil was on his hands and knees behind me. I cared that I was some cruel off-with-their-heads queen who would encourage such jackassery. I stopped walking when we reached a vast hallway that was encrusted with sapphires in the gold crown molding, with six guards lining the walls on either side. Keeping my voice low, I leaned on my toes to speak privately to Finn. "I'm not playing around with you. Let Emil up off his knees, or I'll walk out of your castle on mine."

Finn's green eyes glinted with anger that I would deign to cross him in front of his men. That wasn't what I wanted to do, but I couldn't go through with the wicked queen act. I just couldn't. He snarled at me with a low rumble. "You wouldn't dare."

In response, I slowly lowered myself, my bloody knees almost reaching the gold floor before Finn gasped and jerked me back up next to him. He clicked his fingers at Emil. "You're dismissed. Go see to King Carter of Hayop. He's sleeping off some merriment and mistakes at the porting place. See that he gets back safely to his people. Say nothing of the Omen being here." He raised his chin and looked around the room to his men. "No one saw the Omen here. Is that understood?"

A resounding "yes, sir!" echoed off the walls, making me jump. Emil kissed both my feet before rising to his, keeping his head down as he bowed to his captain. Finn all but dragged me to the exit, squeezing my hand as I stumbled out of the castle and bathed myself in the moonlight.

Finn didn't speak; he was too mad. He simply looped his arms through my backpack and stomped through the sandy beach, not stopping as his feet hit the water.

Anxiety climbed up in me. I wanted anything but the very same water I'd been molested in and watched Garrick die in. "Finn, wait! I'll just stay here. There's no need for me to go into the water. Get what you need, and I'll wait for you here."

Finn stomped forward with my hand painfully winched in his, not caring that I was starting to freak out as the water quickly rose up my legs.

"Finn, stop! I don't want to do this!"

"You don't get to choose. This is the way. You wanted a guide? This is where we're going. You questioned me in front of my men. Soldiers have died for less. You push me to the edge, and now that Sama's tricked me into going with you, you're unhappy about the route we're taking?"

"Wait, we have to go through the water to get there?"

"It's the quickest way. Anything else is a complete waste of time. Trust me to be the guide for once."

"I do trust you, it's just that I..." I glanced around at the water that lapped at my ribs, making me want to recoil from the fingers that felt like they were everywhere on me. "I told you I don't know how to swim! I don't like the water, so be cool while I wrap my mind around this whole thing."

Finn kept forward, and in the next two steps, hoisted me up. My legs instinctively wrapped around his hips and I clung tight to his neck, pressing my cheek into his soft gills as I held on for dear life. Finn finally came down from his fury and held the back of my head, pressing my body tight to his chest. "You break my heart when you say things like that. *I am* the water. You say you don't like it? You're saying you don't like *me*, and I know that you *love* me."

I didn't respond to this. Of course I had too many feelings for Finn. I wanted to run from them – to run from him – but I was too busy clinging to him to get away from either of us. "Let's take the long way. Please, Finn. I can't do the water. I can't do this!"

His hand stroked from the crown of my head down my back and cupped my butt. "Listen to me; this is happening, so I wouldn't spend all your breath fighting it. Put your lips on mine, and I'll get us there safely, just like last time."

I was holding on too tight, the ocean at my back threatening to pull me away from my lifejacket and spin me out into an unmarked grave. "Don't you dare kiss me," I warned.

Finn chuckled, though I couldn't tell you why. "I think I'll wait for you to beg me. Much more satisfying that way."

"That'll never happen." My cheek was too afraid to leave him, lest I get swept away, so the side of my face slid from his gills up his throat where my cheek rested against his.

I shivered when Finn whispered, his lips dragging on the shell of my ear. "My mouth is right here. Why are you avoiding my lips? How do you expect to breathe underwater?"

I knew he was teasing me, but it was working. There was too much want in the air surrounding us. I had a great many strengths to my name, but when it came to Finn, I was weak. Finally, I turned my head just enough and parted my lips, sliding them onto his and fighting the instinctual urge that rose in me to kiss him. Finn pinched my nose, leaving me wanting as he ducked us under the water and pitched us forward.

MAUDLIN CONFESSIONS AND
MAUGRIN'S ATTENTIONS

I'm not sure how long I screamed, but Finn stopped his missile-like speed about halfway to his house to bring me to the surface. My head broke through to fresh air, and embarrassing as it was, I couldn't control the quivering my lower lip did. He kept his voice even, so I didn't permanently go over the freak-out edge. "Hey, I need you to calm down. Our underwater hearing's pretty clear. You're alerting the Mermen for miles that you're here. If you want stealth, maybe screaming isn't the best way."

I felt like I'd endured some sort of medieval water torture, forcing unnecessary truths out of me at random. "When I was in kindergarten, I would steal things out of people's lunches in the morning when we had free play time. I was so hungry, and I only took the things I knew they wouldn't like! When I was seven years old, I accidentally spilled water on one of Ollie's schoolbooks. I got scared and told him Bev did it, and they yelled at each other all night long! I should've told him the truth, but I was afraid he'd hate me and leave me with Bev." Confessions throughout the ages bubbled up in me as more fresh air crawled its way into my lungs. "When I found out Gideon touched Allie, I drove his Cadillac to the nearest church, spray painted 'child molester' on the side and put sugar in the tank. It was stuck there for a week!"

"Easy, *sinta*. You're not dying. I've got you right here, and I'm not letting go."

I tried to let Finn's words breathe calm into me, but I was stuck on verbal vomit. "I stole Bev's necklace! It was in her hoard and she never wore it, so I didn't think she'd notice. I just wanted to look pretty for the eighth grade dance! I swear I was going to put it right back in the tuna can where I'd found it when I got home. She noticed it was gone while I was at the dance and thought Allie took it. I came home and she'd blacked Allie's eye! I didn't mean for her to take the blame! I told Allie what I did, and she wouldn't let me confess to Bev. Said one black eye was enough for the both of us. My sister got hurt because of me! I'm a terrible person!" My chest heaved, and I started to hyperventilate. "I used to... And this one time Judge was... and I tried to help him, but I broke the... My fault!"

Finn kept one hand on my butt and palmed my chin with the other. "*Hani*, you have to stop. You're going to attract too much attention. You can tell me anything you like when we get to my house. *Our* house." He watched me nod pitifully and then pressed his mouth to mine again, taking us under. He glanced around, and I could tell by his heart that pounded against mine that he was nervous. He shot forward faster, holding me tight.

I thought somewhere along the journey I'd hit the peak of my nerves, but apparently, there was a whole new level of anxiety my body could feel in any given moment. Cold panic shot up my spine when Finn pulled his mouth from mine and turned his head to the side to yell at someone, who I'm guessing had fins. "Back up, Maugrin! You know what happened to the last man who attacked me. You really want to try your luck when it's one on one?"

I felt a hand that was certainly not Finn's push up the leg of my jeans to examine my calf. My fingers dug into Finn so deep, I was certain I'd leave marks.

Finn reached in his belt and pulled out what looked like a flashlight. With a simple click of the button on the handle, a legit retractable full-sized triton popped from the hilt. He slashed it out in warning before Maugrin had a chance to answer.

"One on one? I was thinking two on one with this little beauty you've got wrapped around you. Where'd you find her?"

"That's none of your concern."

I turned my head and opened my eyes in the ocean that was lit only by the stars and Finn's fingers. I made out a thick Merman fin that was green, scaly and looked like it had some sort of fungus growing on the ridges all the way up to his waist. His chest wasn't nearly as broad as Finn's, and had dime-sized nipples. He was balding on top, but only enough to star in a Rogaine commercial, not start auditioning toupees. His trout-like mouth drooped at the corners when he spoke, jerking back from Finn's weapon. "I just wanted to see if you'd share your legs. I meant no harm to you, Captain."

I gripped Finn's waist with my thighs tighter than was probably comfortable. Finn's voice lost its edge, but he didn't retract his triton, keeping it aloft between us and Maugrin. "There'll be no sharing, and you'll keep your mouth shut that you saw a pair of legs in this ocean if you want to live to see tomorrow."

"Keeping the prize for yourself? Looks like Banak wasn't the only greedy bastard in the ocean." Maugrin's eyes darkened with intent. "You should share the bounty before it's taken from you, Captain. You never know how fast word might travel about your lady's legs if I'm denied."

So quick, I didn't have time to protest, Finn shot me out in the water behind him and lunged for Maugrin. My arms flailed around in the abyss, trying to hold onto something that couldn't be grasped in your fist. My legs kicked without direction, somehow slowing my progression downward as panic choked me around the throat. I didn't understand. Finn promised he'd keep me safe in the water. He knew I couldn't swim.

I watched the fight unfold as I slowly began to sink.

Finn flicked his wrist, and the edges of the triton slid out further, making it easy to slash through Maugrin's bottom half, all the way down from waist to flipper. With another slice, he divided the fishy tail in two, shouting with fury that scared me almost as much as drowning. "Now you've got a pair of legs to die for. To the bottom of the ocean with you." Then to shut up Maugrin's cries of pain and horror, Finn socked his temple hard enough to knock the older guy out. For a few seconds, Maugrin remained suspended in the water, and then started sinking toward me.

Finn retracted his weapon and shot downward, scooping my floundering body up in his arms just when I thought my lungs might burst. His mouth found mine and he breathed life into me, steadily bringing me to a higher level. I'd hoped he would bring us to the surface, but he shot forward under the water, aiming himself like a relentless arrow that had only one target.

FINN'S FIDDLE

I shivered and tried to pass off my hysterical tears as ocean water that steadily streamed down my cheeks when Finn unlocked the door to the main floor of his house. My limbs were useless; the adrenaline coursing through my body left me breathless in more ways than the obvious.

Finn was shaken, I could tell, but it was only evidenced by the rapid thrumming of his heart. Other than that, he was Captain Finn – always in charge and never hesitating from a fight. He didn't set me down, but carried me toward his round bed I'd promised myself I'd never lie in again. His hands dried parts of me as he walked into his bedroom and laid me down. His fingers swept carefully over my convulsing body as too much of the *way* too much crashed down on me. I was freezing, terrified and knew I'd made the wrong choice in seeking out Finn to take me to Philip.

My teeth chattered, and I wasn't sure if the trembling was from nerves, or the cold that felt deep set in my bones.

When I was dry but still shivering, Finn took off my shoes and socks, kicked his own off and climbed into the bed with me. He pulled the comforter up over us and kissed my eyelids, "You're safe now. No one can get into my house but me. I told you I'd keep you alive."

"You d-dropped me in the ocean, you j-jag!"

I couldn't believe he chuckled at that, but he did. An affectionate smile swept over his features. "I kept you from getting mixed up in the brawl. Maugrin's an elder in the village. You don't get to live that long without knowing a thing or two about fighting."

"Your s-soldiers are so a-afraid of you. How come Maugrin wasn't? Why'd he try and t-take me?"

Finn held my body and rolled onto his back, taking me with the motion so I was lying on top of him, my muscles still locked as fear continued to wash over me. His hands drifted to the backs of my thighs, and he massaged me over my jeans. "Because of these things right here. Legs are a fascination in Dagat. And he wasn't respectful as he should've been because he's an elder. Makes a man foolhardy to've lived that long, and escaped death who knows how many times. Makes you feel invincible." He brought his hand to tap under my chin, tilting it up so he could look into my eyes. "But he went down just as easily as anyone who comes up against me. No one's invincible, October. Not even you."

I swallowed hard as we looked into each other's eyes. I was unable to ignore his words or our solid connection anymore. "I don't want to die," I admitted, "but I know it's a possibility. I know how dangerous it is, what I'm doing. But I also know I can't live like this. Ollie and Allie didn't sacrifice everything so I could have a life where I was afraid to go to sleep."

"And what would they say now if they could see you going off on your own to fight the man who put your sister in a coma?"

I examined the curves of his face, his hard cheekbones that made him look forbidding. I didn't mean to fixate on his full lips. I touched his short brownish-blond hair that never dared to obscure his handsome face. His green eyes seemed to glow with intensity as he watched me study him. My shivering finally calmed down in his warm embrace under the covers of our own little haven in the middle of the ocean. "Ollie will be mad, but he'd expect nothing less. No one messes with Allie and gets away with it. She's a good person, and the world doesn't have enough of those. He'd do the same thing in my position."

Finn's adoring expression made me debate between looking away and leaning closer. "It's your fire that made me fall for you the first time. That very first council meeting where you put us all in our place."

I glanced around the room I'd spent many nights in, swallowing hard. "I swore I wouldn't come back here."

"But you keep coming back to my bed. I admit, I

haven't had much reason to come home. I sleep mostly on the mainland. It's hard to sleep in my bed without you in it. I don't like the feel of my house without you to come home to."

I knew when my mouth opened, I'd choose the wrong words. "I didn't want to miss you. I try to never think about us at all." I cleared my throat, my tone sharpening. "But that's not why I'm here."

"Whatever the reason, I'm glad you came back." I wrestled with my two selves until he whispered, "The suns will be up in a couple hours. How about we get a little sleep before we start our journey?"

I shook my head, bracing myself on my hands and knees over his body so I wasn't laying on him anymore. "No. Pack what you need, and let's get out of here. If I sleep now, I'll dreamwalk with either Von or Sama. Sama's probably pissed I'm taking so long to get to him, and I don't think I can keep this a secret from Von in our dream space."

Finn met my eyes, saying too many things that I knew would only be more complicated if he actually opened his mouth. My cheeks felt hot, and I was very aware of how close our bodies were. When he finally spoke, he lifted his head so the sultry words were delivered right into the crook of my neck, his lips toying with my body. "You're not wearing your engagement ring."

I shouldn't have shivered, but my neck was my sweet spot, and Finn was playing me like a fiddle. "I didn't think

Sama would be too thrilled about me spending a week with him while still clinging to Von. I took it off so Sama didn't suspect I wasn't giving our little trial run a fair shot."

"Very clever. Let me see the map again." His fingers were stretching under my nightgown, lifting slowly as I swallowed hard.

Clarity came to me just in time. "No. You already saw it. You don't need a map to pack a bag, which is what you're supposed to be doing." I climbed off of him and stood in the center of his room. "I'm engaged to Von. Ring or not, that's not going to change. Von's never done a thing to you. He doesn't deserve this."

Finn took his time rising from the bed, puffing out his chest as he towered over me with an unreadable expression. "We both know he's not enough for you. You're a conqueror, like me. It's in our bones. He's a joker. Utterly useless."

I narrowed my eyes at Finn and kept my voice deadly quiet. "Do not insult Von in front of me ever again. I'm here for work. Your opinions on my personal life are of no use to me right now. Let me make myself perfectly clear; I don't care about our past. I don't care about my engagement. I don't care about global warming, puppies, kitties, or anything except for killing Philip. All I can think about is putting my knife through his chest. Anything else is white noise."

Finn stood and returned my glare for a solid five seconds before he backed down, throwing clothes, *buhay,* and food for me into his pack so we could get going. "I've got a small boat out back. I could swim myself maybe halfway there, but towing you and our packs, I might not make it even that far. It'll be slower, but it's safer this way."

"Fine. Whatever. Let's just end him."

BAKUNAWA AND BEGGING FOR IT

The world was quiet out in the middle of the ocean. Finn alternated between paddling and propelling us forward by swimming behind the boat and kicking his legs like a motor. When he exhausted himself, I took over the paddling, letting him sleep curled up in a ball in the small rowboat like a puppy. In slumber, he snuggled my ankle to his chest, like it was his teddy bear. The nighttime lights in the sky glittered off his windswept hair, illuminating him only in parts, and making him look positively precious.

I paddled us toward a small mound I could see in the far distance. I'd only just saw it after Finn drifted off, and I guessed that was where Sama's lair was hiding.

There was too much quiet, too much time to think about my life and all the mistakes I'd made. I wondered if Von and Mason had woken yet, and if they'd found my note with Ezra. I wondered if Von had finally reached his statute of limitations with me, and if he was finally tired of it all enough to leave me for good.

I know *I* was tired of me.

At this hour, I was just plain tired. I knew the suns would be rising soon, and I had nothing but adrenaline and a healthy fear of being mind-raped keeping me awake. My heart broke for Allie, who'd had to go through all of this alone. Sama never taught her anything about reaping; she hadn't even been awakened. He had a second Omen locked and loaded, and he let Terraway suffer anyway, so they would have to rely on his rations. Then he'd made Allie suffer. I wonder how long she resisted him, or if she'd been gullible like I was, believing the dream to be just that, until he turned on her.

I needed my sister. I needed one of my sisters to be alive, but they were both stuck in some horrible in between. Allie was unconscious, and Mariang was a flicker of who she once was, off with Danny, who was reaping the disaster he'd sown.

I looked over my shoulder to make sure I was still aiming for the small mound in the distance. I frowned, course-correcting when the mound was much farther to my right than I realized. I paddled in long strokes, wondering if it was such a good idea to exhaust myself so early on in the trip.

I put the paddles up for a minute to give my arms a rest and stretch out my back. I couldn't even see Finn's village anymore. In fact, there hadn't been anything around for hours, except for the small mound. I turned to examine it for signs of life, but it wasn't in the right place again. This time it was yards to the left of where I'd been aiming the boat. My eyebrows drew together as I watched the island in confusion. My mouth fell open as the perimeter slowly began to widen, making the mound appear to be the beginnings of a larger island. I'd heard of optical illusions, but this was too much a shift to be shoved in that bag of logic. I studied the island, gasping when it went completely under the water.

"Finn?" I squeaked out, not wanting to disrupt his sleep, but too confused to let the weirdness go unaddressed.

When he didn't stir, I carefully got down on my knees, swallowing the scream in my throat as my small movement rocked the boat slightly. "Finn? Something's weird out there. I need you." I placed my hand on his leg, squeezing his calf to wake him.

"Huh?" He'd been drooling, and his eyes were barely open when he gripped the side of the boat to sit up. "What's wrong?"

"The island keeps moving, and now it's disappeared!" I whispered, afraid that somehow if the ocean heard me tattle, it might retaliate with brute force. "Come look."

Finn ran his fingers over his face, wiping his mouth on the back of his hand as he moved to his seat across from me. "Okay, what now?"

I pointed to the nothingness in accusation. "There was just an island there. It was small, then it got bigger, and now it's gone! What is it? Is it some sort of magical Terraway thing?"

"I don't see anything, and we're nowhere near the island. Whatever you thought you saw, you didn't. Trick of the light maybe."

I frowned, but didn't bother arguing. I knew what I saw. Or at least, was pretty sure I knew what I saw. As if in vindication, the mound rose again, only this time, it was a fair bit closer than I remembered it being. "There! You see that? It was bigger last time, but that thing there. What is it?"

Finn squinted, tilted his head and then stood. "I'm not sure. Hold on a second." I don't understand how he dismounted from the boat with barely a splash into the water, but my favorite surfer dove down to get a look at the island or whatever from under the surface.

I didn't expect him to reappear in the next second, climb into the boat with terror on his face and grab the oars. "It's the Bakunawa! We're headed straight for the Bakunawa! I'm turning us around. We'll head the rest of the way on foot. I don't care if it takes longer."

"Wait, what's the Bakalama?"

He rowed like a man possessed, his muscles rippling and straining without tiring as he moved us eastward instead of westward. He was too into rowing to explain, so

I respected the struggle he had with the oars moving through the sea, as if it were as dense as pea soup.

I kept my eyes on the mound that kept going down beneath the choppy surface and reappearing yards closer each time. "Finn? I think it's following us. What is it?"

Finn swore and put his whole body into the effort of rowing with renewed vigor. "It's a sea monster. You remember the sigbins from Sakuna?"

I nodded, recalling my favorite sweet little monster, Edward Scissorteeth. He'd been a terror to the civilians of Sakuna, but he was my puppy. Well, he was a mini dragon of sorts, with small back legs, a scaly goat head and sharp teeth a weapon like him needed. "You're saying a sigbin swam all the way out here?"

"Sigbins are tiny, like dogs. Bakunawa is bigger than anything you can imagine. Big as some of your tall Topsider buildings. He's a water serpent with a head like a sigbin. That island? It's part of Bakunawa's tail."

"Get out," I remarked, incredulous.

"I don't know what he's doing in our waters. We have charms in place that've kept him out for decades. That he's breached our walls? It's bad, *sinta*. It's real bad."

"Like, we're about to die because of a sea monster, bad?"

"Like, all the Mer people need to get out of here now, bad."

"Where are we going?" I had zero sense of direction

anymore with no landmarks, but I had a sneaking suspicion we were going back the way we came.

"I'll call Kabayo through the council link. He can take you to Sama after I draw out the map for him. I'll deal with the dreams of the map my whole life, if I have to. I need to get back to my people and warn them."

I wanted to whine that killing Sama wasn't really something that should be put on hold, but I held my tongue, knowing a whole race of people deserved to live. "Okay. I don't need Kabayo, though. Just draw out the map for me, and I can go by myself. Is there a point of land you can drop me at along the way?"

"No, we're going straight back to my people. We don't have any time for side stops. You have no idea how enormous Bakunawa is."

"Ah, man! You know Ezra's going to find me if I don't get a move on."

"I'm not arguing with you on this! Kabayo's going with you, and that's the best you'll get. Otherwise I'll take you right back to Ezra myself and let him deal with your terrible plan. Honestly, sometimes I don't get you, and other times I'm afraid I completely understand you."

"What's that supposed to mean?"

He grunted through a long stroke, gritting his teeth as he spoke. "It means that you're just like Sama! You have a goal, and you'll sacrifice anything to get there, even yourself. I used to think it was one of the things I loved about you – your eternal focus. Now I see that you're just insane.

I fell in love with your insanity, thinking it was honorable."

"Are you joking right now? I'm trying to end *your* bad guy! I'm about to hand myself over to someone who makes my skin crawl so *your* world can survive. What's not honorable about that?"

"You're ready to throw a whole race of people to the bottom of the ocean so you don't have to be patient. It's impractical, this manic plotting you do. Even now, I know you're furious that I'm taking you back to my house instead of bringing you to the lion's den. Hundreds of thousands of people, October! It's more important than your plan being put off a day or two."

"Two? Are you serious? You think I have two days I can kill just waiting around sipping tea? Every time I go to sleep without Von, I'm afraid I might not wake up, that I'll end up like Allie. Then your whole world dies. Philip's mind games are exhausting to stay on top of! I'm afraid I'll say one wrong thing, and he'll turn on me, like he did Allie. Suck on that, you jag. I'm set on my timeline because it's also a countdown clock for Terraway. And that's millions of people, not hundreds of thousands."

"I'm not discussing this with you. I'm trying to get us there." He gave a few more vigorous strokes with the paddles and then lifted them into the vessel. "It's not worth the effort of keeping the boat. Come on, I'll swim us there." Sweat was pouring down his body as he shook his arms out. They looked heavy and not sturdy enough for rowing.

"I'll row us for a bit while you catch your breath. Take a second. If you pass out halfway there, Dagat dies too, you know. Rushing this is dangerous. Take a breath."

"I'm fine."

"Shut up and breathe."

Finn did a deliberate spluttery breath of exasperation in my face. "I'm all better now. You cured me. Let's go."

"Would you stop being so stubborn? You're barely upright! I'm not going to die in the middle of the ocean so you can be a big man!"

Finn stood like a surfer, perfectly balanced and ready for action, though his hands were twitching from overuse. He hitched my pack and his over his shoulder and lifted me up, gripping the front of my hoodie and yanking me to him. His arm wrapped around the small of my back, pressing my body to his like I was friggin' Scarlet O'Hara, my hair blowing out behind me in the breeze. "Don't you know by now?" He thumbed my lip just to toy with me. "I am a big man."

He leaned in, closing his eyes for the kiss he'd said I'd have to beg for first. I don't know why I leaned in. I can't explain why I rose up on my toes as the small boat rocked on the waves that were starting to grow choppier. When my mouth met Finn's, my lips moved on instinct, nipping at his lower one that always seemed to tease me like a forbidden treat.

Finn's body melted around me, but he didn't kiss me back. His jaw went slack as he let me suck on his bottom lip, inviting but not participating. It took me five whole seconds of making love to his lip before I realized there was no music or colors dancing for us. My cheeks flushed pink, and my breathing grew uneven. I pulled back, horrified at the thrill of triumph that flooded his face. He held up one hand in innocence. "I was going to breathe for you, nothing more. I told you the next time we kissed, it would be because you wanted it." He leaned in and whispered low in my ear, "And boy, do you want it."

"I... I... It was an accident. I thought you were... so I..." I buried my face in my hands. "Oh, just let the sea monster eat me already! I'm so embarrassed. I'm sorry, Finn."

"I'm sorry you can't admit what everyone knows. You love me, and if there wasn't a world to save, I'd take you right here and make love to you until you forgot every other man's name. But for now, we have to go." He held me tight in his arms, preparing with too much smugness to jump us overboard.

We were about to take the leap that would terrify any non-swimmer to her very soul when the boat was bumped by something underneath the wood. I shrieked and clung to Finn as the small boat lifted off the surface of the water. My stomach leapt into my throat, strangling the scream that surely saw no end when we kept rising. A rubbery, gray tentacle the thickness of the length of a car brought us higher, suspending us twenty, thirty, and then forty feet in the air.

24

NO PLACE I'D RATHER BE

The rowboat cocooned us as best it could, but it wobbled slightly on the arm of the sea monster, the size of which I'd vastly underestimated. Finn knelt us down in the boat, his shaking arms giving me zero hope that we'd actually survive this. "We have to jump and take our chances swimming."

"Won't it see us? Won't it catch us? Won't it eat us?"

"Yes to all of it, but what choice do we have? Wouldn't you rather to go out swinging?"

I didn't have time to sort through my regrets, knowing each second we were still alive was a luxury. "Leave the backpacks here, then. They'll only slow us down."

It was the best plan we could come up with, but it didn't matter. The sea monster started moving west, carrying us on our precarious perch. The tentacle lowered a little when the boat moved unsteadily from side to side, so that now we were only twenty feet above the ocean's surface. Finn and I were on our knees at the base of the boat, clinging to each other like children who'd once thought themselves warriors.

"Are you ready to jump?" Finn asked, peering over the edge. His expression hardened as he leaned back to place his chin atop my head. The wind I hadn't felt much of before whipped at us, due to the increased speed at which we were now moving through the ocean. "Scratch that plan. I can't jump wide enough to clear his tentacles."

I glimpsed over the side, swallowing the bile that rose as the stars showed me just enough of the nightmare to keep me in the boat. Underneath us were tentacles thick as roads, winding like blacktop through the water, and stretching out too far around us for us to jump free and land in the ocean. "So this is it? This is how we die?" It wasn't despair; it was stating a grim fact.

Finn sat down carefully in the boat as the monster moved us far faster through the water than we could ever hope to go on our own. He pulled me into his arms, bracing us against the wind that made me shiver against him. "If it is, then we die together."

A tear rolled down my cheek, but that was the most I allowed myself to carry on. The moisture was immediately whipped away by the wind, for which I was grateful. "I never got to finish the Mer books I was translating. How does it end? Does Lissima end up with Ricardo?"

Finn cupped my face with one hand to shield me from

my wildly flying hair. He stared into my eyes, looking at me like I was something special, like it was worth getting swallowed whole by a sea monster if it meant we were together. He slowly shook his head. "I'm not spoiling the ending for you. We're going to get out of this somehow. There'll be no giving up, no saying goodbye. It's a bump in the road." He motioned to the space below us. "Bakunawa's not tearing us apart. He's saving us, taking us somewhere."

"Is that supposed to make me feel better?"

"It's supposed to make you not give up. He's a sea serpent, which means he's got a lair. No one knows where, but I assume he's taking us there to add us to his collection of bodies."

Finn was right, but it hadn't occurred to me that the fact that we were still alive meant that the sea snake had a purpose for us still. Something dinged in my mind. "You said snake, but it looks like he's got lots of tentacles, like an octopus. Are you sure it's the right sea monster? Not that it matters. I mean, if you're being abducted by a sea monster, does it matter which one it is?"

Finn had the wherewithal to chuckle, which either meant he'd gone insane, or the situation wasn't as dire as I was making it out to be. "He's got a head like a sigbin, a body like a snake, but his tail's split into sixteen tentacles."

"Precious."

"I'll get us out of this," Finn promised, though both of us knew he had no idea how. His eyes searched the ocean for possibilities, but there was nothing in any direction – just the void of the dark swallowed by the ocean.

"I'm sorry, Finn. This was all my bright idea. I just wanted it to be over! I wanted Sama gone, and I didn't stop to ask if there were any heinous sea monsters before I dragged you into the ocean." I buried my face in his chest. "I'm so sorry."

"You came to me. You could've gone to Kabayo. You know he loves breaking the rules and pissing off the council. He might've taken you."

"I know! And you're the person I want to save, not the one I want drowning in the middle of the ocean!"

"You wanted to be with me. Maybe not in all the ways I need, but some part of you knew I'd be good for you. You left your fiancé in the dead of night to come to me. You crossed worlds to get to me, but you still can't admit that you're in love with me? That it's me you should be with?"

I kept my face fixed firmly to the side, my cheek buried in his chest so he couldn't see my guilty expression. "We're about to die, Finn. This is hardly the time for all that."

His arm around my back tightened. "This is the only time left for it! This might be all we have, and you're still lying to yourself? Admit when we're inches from death that it was worth it! Admit that you needed to see me."

"Shut up, Finn! This isn't helping anything."

His anger rose to a shout. "You might want to marry him, but you want me, too. Admit that I'm about to die because you couldn't live without me!"

"Stop it! Stop saying it!" I wriggled free of his grip, venturing a few inches further toward the helm, regretting the distance between us the second it made itself known.

"October!" he shouted, his voice booming above the wind that whipped at my hair as I turned to look at him over my shoulder.

My heart pounded for too many reasons, and I knew that whatever I did or didn't do, I would regret it. The boat shifted, and I lost my footing, tipping toward the helm and smacking my chin on the seat. Tears sprang to my eyes, and I knew I was on the edge of losing my mind into the depths below. My hand was shaking as I gripped the side of the boat, needing something sturdy to hold onto so I didn't fall apart into a million emotional pieces I'd never be able to stuff back inside.

Before I shattered, Finn was on all fours behind me. With steadier hands than mine, he slid me onto the floor of the rowboat, shielding me from the wind as he rolled me onto my back. His body caged mine in, his eyes holding my fearful gaze as he leaned down to lay atop me and let the boat shield us both from the elements. "Easy now," he warned, brushing the tangles back from my face. "I'm here."

I didn't say "We're not going to make it out of this alive." That much was obvious. There wasn't time for a rescue, or to plan a way of escape. There was only this last moment, and I didn't want to spend it crying. I swallowed hard, and pushed out Terraway, Sama, the sea monster, and even the people I would be leaving behind that I loved. In our last moments, there was only Finn, and only me. I hadn't been "only me" in so very long.

I don't know how Finn found the strength to be tender, but when his knuckle dragged down my cheek, a layer of calm brushed over me, taking my panic down a notch. It wasn't pulling; it was simply Finn, calming me with the reminder of everything we were to each other. His voice was tremulous but gentle, as he tried to say the perfect parting words to our lives lived on the shore. "No regrets. There's no place I'd rather be."

I reached up and held his face in my hands, tracing the prominent features. They could look deadly in a breath, but always melted into softness for me. "Take me someplace other than this," I pleaded, tilting my throbbing chin so my lips brushed against his. I wanted to be anywhere that wasn't here, even if that meant admitting things I wasn't ready to examine.

"Beg me."

"What?"

"Beg me to kiss you."

My lower lip quivered uncertainly, but finally, after all my fighting, my weakness for him won out. "Please, Finn. Kiss me. Take me away from here."

Finn palmed the back of my hand that rested on his cheek and exhaled a brief smile. "I know just the place."

With that, my mouth crashed onto Finn's. During what was most certainly our last moments, I chose to leave reality and escape into beauty – however imperfect that paradise might turn out to be.

25

A HOME FOR THE BIRD AND THE FISH

We tumbled onto a tropical-looking beach, surrounded by green and silver that danced around us, painting our bodies and sparkling on the pure white sand. I felt Finn all around me, pressing on top of me and beckoning me to mold around him as only my body knew how to do. His shirt came off – I'm not even sure which one of us tore it and threw it at the hollowed log that sat at the peaceful ocean's shore.

"Tell me you see it," Finn begged between kisses. His movements were a mixture of fluid and frantic, tugging on my lower lip and even biting it when his passion grew to be too much for a normal makeout to contain.

I slowed the kiss enough to look around, taking in the sparkling beach, the palm trees that had been brushed with a hue of purple on the trunks, the blue ocean that looked so clear, it had to be fake, and the green – oh the glittering green of the palms and the swirls of the luscious color dancing through the sky. What drew my eyes and drew out a gasp was the cottage sitting on the edge of the ocean. The siding was a cheery yellow with white shutters framing the windows, which were open to the gentle breeze. "Whose house is that?"

Finn stopped kissing me abruptly, hovering above my body with a look that suggested I'd said something shocking. "You see it? You're not going to disappear now that we're not kissing?"

My eyes grew to saucers when the implications of my choices and the things that felt out of my control slammed into me, punishing me with the scarlet letter "A" I knew I'd well deserved. "No! But I can't be in love with you! I love Von! I love Von!" I said the words that cut him over and over, willing them to take me away from the tropical paradise I had no right to be part of.

Finn palmed my chin in that controlling way he had, his mouth set in a tight line just inches from mine. His thumb and forefinger gripped my jaw, turning my head to the side as he leaned down to whisper through clenched teeth. "I knew you loved me. So you love Von, too. I already knew that. But I want to hear you say it. Admit that you loved me this whole time." His fingers dug so hard into my face; I was certain he'd leave marks. His passion mixed with anger as he started slowly dragging his lips down the side of my neck. My spine twitched and my body reacted in ways I hadn't meant it to. My legs parted and Finn settled between them as if he belonged there – as if *we* belonged *here*. "Say it," he growled. "After everything, I deserve to hear it."

I didn't want to say it out loud, though the evidence surrounding us was incontrovertible. I swallowed, and then let a whisper birth from somewhere inside of me that I'd tried so very hard to gag and stuff in a trunk. "I love you, Finn."

A tear escaped the corner of my eye, trailing down the side of my face and landing on Finn's hand. He swiped at the tear, and then stuck the finger into my mouth, moaning as I sucked on the tip. It tasted like sorrow, shame and too much admiration for a man who I knew couldn't stay mine. When I released his finger with a pop, he slid the hoodie over my head, gasping at the nightgown I hadn't worn for him. His lips touched down on my sternum, slowly teasing me and drawing out the pang of need that never seemed to go away.

"Not here," I insisted, holding my nightgown firmly to my chest. "Not here, and not now."

"How about in our house?" Finn offered, his chin jerking toward the cottage.

"Huh?"

Finn rolled off of me and gave me his hand to help me up. Our fingers linked together as he led me to the cottage, not bothering to knock as he walked over the threshold. "This is our house. In our dreams, this is where we stay. Our kiss takes us here." He paused, looking over his shoulder to find me frozen on the wooden porch that fed into the ocean off a long dock. "You said there wasn't a place for us to live. I'm a fish, and you can't swim. But here? We can be together in our secret place. We can have a whole life in a world designed just for us."

I stood there, fist clutching my peach lacy nightgown as my eyes poured over the details of the life I hadn't expected to manifest before my eyes. It was a modern looking cottage, but not too flashy. The inside was done up with enough Topsider conveniences that I could see through the open door – a fridge, stove and a couch. There was a touch of Finn's world too – a lantern hanging on a hook on the wall, a hammock off to the side of the living room in front of the picture window.

The backs of my hands started to itch, and I couldn't figure out why or how I got here, staring down the barrel of a life I'd convinced myself wasn't possible.

Finn moved to stand before me, his feet firmly planted inside the cottage, claiming the territory in the name of our future. "Welcome home, *sinta*."

I couldn't hide the fear in my expression, nor the overwhelming feeling that I didn't belong here. My gaze fell on a picture frame that rested atop the end table next to the beige couch. "Is that me?" My feet finally moved inside, shuffling over the smooth wood and tracking sand onto the brown and lavender rug in the center of the living room. I fingered the frame, holding it up to make sure I hadn't gone insane. With this many lives, it was getting harder and harder to be sure.

"It's us," Finn explained, standing beside me and smiling down at the picture. There we were, barefoot and grinning at each other like two lucky SOBs who weren't about to get eaten by a giant sea monster. We were holding hands and walking on the beach, not a care in the world.

I couldn't remember the last time I'd smiled like that. I couldn't remember the last time I'd smiled. I conjured up a good representation to try and match the photo, but I knew my staged one fell flat. I knew my fake smiles, and the one in the photo was no fraud. I was genuinely happy there. There was an inscription on the bottom of the frame that read, "If you live, then I breathe."

"This... This isn't real," I explained, placing the frame back on the end table.

"It's real enough." Finn linked his fingers through mine and led me into the kitchen, pulling a coconut from the fruit basket on the counter. He took his knife from his boot and gave the side a good whack that made me jump. "Try it. You'll like it. Came from the trees right outside."

The water dribbled down the furry sides of the fruit's shell. "I've never had coconut water before. At least, not straight from the source." I took the half a shell he handed to me and tipped it to my lips, swallowing the bland, yet somewhat sweetened liquid that was both thicker and thinner than I anticipated. A few sips dribbled down my chin. My wince announced that no matter what world I was in, I wouldn't be too fond of spills. "Oh, that tastes good, but I'm a mess now."

Finn's gaze locked in on mine, not blinking as he slid the shell from my hands and placed it in the sink. *Our* sink. He didn't say a word, though I knew he could've said any number of cheesy things about helping me take my clothes off. Instead, he cleared the space between us, lifting me up in his arms and pressing my back to the wooden wall. His lips crashed into mine, tasting the coconut and savoring the flavor of me.

He didn't ask me to come to the bedroom with him, he simply took me there. Green and silver twinkled around us like spots of overexposed light popping in our vision. I scarcely took in the details of the bed that was all ours – not mine, and not his, but ours. We tumbled onto the red sheets, tangling our legs and twisting our fingers in each other's hair to get a better hold on the life that felt too real to be so. I didn't want to think. I didn't want to analyze. I didn't want anything but more of this. It muted the pain that came with having a defective conscience. I tried to rationalize the tryst away by telling myself that this wasn't real. I wasn't actually in a bed with Finn; we were still in the boat.

But part of me knew. I was only kissing him here because we'd been kissing in the boat. This bliss was tainted with the stink of betrayal. As Finn's hands lifted my nightgown and his lips kissed a hot line up my midsection, I was betraying Von, who thought I was cuddled up next to him in our bed. He was willing to share our bed with Mason as often as reaping demanded it of us. He was happy to stand by my side and wait like a gentleman until we were married to bed me in real life.

He was happy, and I would make us both miserable for reasons that were only selfish. I wanted, so I took. I was no better than Philip. My body betrayed me, twisting and writhing for Finn. I heard guttural noises birth from my lips as Finn made himself at home in my curves. He was a mixture of kissing, sucking and biting, and I was a blaze of firing neurons and oversensitive nerve endings that did exactly as he commanded.

I loved Finn.

I loved him, and I hated myself for the crime.

I hated myself, but some days I was all I had, despite the beautiful beach, the cottage and the man who'd brought me here. I couldn't come here again, and I knew I had to get out now, if I didn't want another spontaneous psychic pregnancy on my hands.

My fingers fumbled on the buckle of Finn's pants, holding the button closed. "We can't. This isn't real, and I'm not yours."

Finn opened his mouth, his face contorted with pure hurt I'd inflicted upon him, but before he could tell me exactly what he thought about that, the green and the silver were ripped away from us. The wind found us again as the sea monster's tentacle dumped our boat unceremoniously out into the ocean.

26

HONEY, I'M HOME

'd never been skydiving before, and something tells me that even with the comfort of a parachute, I wouldn't enjoy the weightless out of control feeling that rushed through my body. I could scarcely put together my surroundings in the proper order before I realized I was heading straight for the shore that hadn't been there when we'd started our kiss. My body went one way, and the hoodie Finn had removed from me went somewhere else.

My scream scared me, as I had no knowledge of when I'd started making the awful sound. My body sliced through the air like a well-aimed missile, cresting and coming down with a hard splash into the water.

I was so close to the shore, but the water was too deep for my feet to find purchase in the murky sand beneath the green-tinged water. To almost make it, and then drown in the last ten yards felt like the punch in the gut I deserved. I should die in obscurity, drown in the cold ocean that had somehow turned muddy and sickly, and then have my remains be eaten by the sea monster so Von couldn't find me.

If he didn't find the note I left in Ezra's pocket, would he think I'd ditched him? When Finn turned up missing too, would he assume we'd run away together?

My arms punched through the water, fighting for breath so I could explain things to Von. I had to go back to the real home I had with him, instead of living in a fantasy – if he'd still have me.

My lungs burned and my disoriented body flailed until a strong hand closed over mine, yanking me up the few feet I needed to break the surface. I could barely see, even though the dawn was doing its best to alert me to my surroundings. My body was hefted out of the water when my lifeguard finally reached shallow enough ground. I was *Baywatch*ed out of the depths, my legs dangling as I clung to my hero.

"I feared you were lost, so I sent my servant to find you."

My body froze when my vision cleared. I coughed into the shirt of the man who was certainly not Finn. I was smack in the arms of Philip, stunned as I watched the slight breeze gently brush his white-blond hair. It was so shocking to see him in real life that I merely gawked up at him while he carried me toward the shore.

"I admit I forgot about your inability to swim. Apologies for the way Bakunawa brought you to safety. His body's too large to get too close to the shore."

My heart pounded in my chest, and the blood flowing through me felt like ice. I didn't have my knife on me, and struggled to put the pieces of the plan together in my mind. I wanted to get it all over with, but I was so cold and inundated with holy-crap-I-almost-drowned that I couldn't bring my muscles to reason. "My guide!" I protested, wriggling to get down and find Finn. My small effort of struggle was ignored, and Philip carried me toward the very same hut he'd taken me to in my last dream.

"Your guide can swim, as you should've learned to do long ago. He'll be able to rest along the shore, but he won't be able to go past that tree there," he motioned with a jerk of his head to a tall, branchless trunk to his left. It was barren, the bark stripped, leaving it sad and naked for all to see. The tree itself looked cursed, as the rest in the naked forest were. "There's a heavy charm that marks my territory. You're only here because I'm carrying you in myself. You wouldn't be able to find it on your own if I weren't here to help you. I would've explained it all to you earlier, but you haven't been to sleep since we last parted."

Philip glanced down at my wet and petrified face as Finn's voice reached our ears from a few yards down the coastline. He was calling out my name, scared that I was lost in the ocean. I opened my mouth to reassure him that I was alright, but Philip shot me a deadly look that made me shrink in his arms. "She's not your concern anymore," he called to Finn, clutching me tighter. He didn't pause for Finn's anguished cries and war-laden threats. Philip's grip on me tightened as he carried me deeper into the stripped and naked forest.

27

THE BLACKNESS OF OUR FOG

As soon as I had enough of my bearings together, I struggled for Philip to let me down. Now that we were alone, he complied, touching my feet to the hard soil and sand mixture that didn't seem fertile enough to grow anything. The urge to vomit rose up in me when I tried to work up the gumption to kiss him in a welcoming "I'm so glad to see you, honey" kind of way. He wore a beige shirt and black pants, his white-blond hair standing out against the natural colors that surrounded us.

Distraction came at me in the form of a dog barking. The howl was calling out a warning for… something as it tore a path through the branchless and barkless trees that were way too close together. Had they branches, they would've been all intertwined to the point of not being able to see a single thing. As it was, the morning suns shone on the last thing I expected to see running toward us.

It wasn't any old dog. Sandy, my neighbor's pit bull came bounding toward me, tongue out and cautioning me to stay back with a warning growl. "What the... Is that my dog?" I quirked my head up at Philip in confusion.

Philip smiled that I was talking to him, asking him normal questions, like how a regular couple might converse. "I had one of my Ekeks sneak to the surface and bring him to Terraway, and then an Amalanhig brought him here for you. I thought you might enjoy someone familiar on my island to make you feel more at home."

My knees buckled and I dropped to the ground, opening up my arms and welcoming Sandy with the hug we both needed. "Hey, boy. I sure missed you. What are you doing here, huh?" I snuggled his bowling ball head to my chest and scratched under his chin while he licked my face in earnest.

"He's groveling, as he should be."

"Groveling? Sandy's my buddy. He's never done a thing to need groveling for." I kissed the top of Sandy's head. "Poor baby. You're probably terrified being here. I'm with you now. Nothing to worry about."

Philip wore a superior smile that told me he knew something I didn't. Judging by the touch of evil he had in everything he did, I wasn't sure I wanted to know the source of his smirk. "Let's get you dried off. Then we can talk about your mutt."

I frowned up at Philip as I released Sandy, who stayed close to my heels. "His name is Sandy, not mutt. Be nice."

Philip chuckled, looking not as evil, though I held tight to my healthy fear of him even as he tried to relax me with conversation. "Oh, sweet girl. I miss you ordering me around. The only thing I get is blind obedience. I rather enjoy the sound of you thinking you have any control over me."

I shot him a baleful look, which he smiled at. I touched my forehead, grimacing as my brain started to catch up. "Oh, I need to go back to the shore. My backpack's there with all my things."

"I have plenty of things for you and your dog. What did you call him? Sandy? There's nothing you need back there. Your guide will locate it after he exhausts himself trying to find you, I'm sure." Sandy rubbed his side against my ankle affectionately. "I've got a treat for you both in the hut." Philip led Sandy and me to the clearing I'd seen in my dream. In the center of the perfect circle was a simple hut, framed by the stripped trees. It was the same no-frills hut he'd shown me before, but the realness of actually being here made me gasp.

"Our palace, milady," Philip offered. He opened the door and ushered me inside, introducing me to the one-room abode that was exactly as I remembered it. My knife was in my backpack on the shore, so I searched with careful eyes for anything I could use as a makeshift weapon when the time came.

There was the same tin bucket in the corner, a hand-made wooden table, and a basket on the counter, along with jars of various sizes. I was shivering in the center of the hut, dripping all over the planks of the wooden floor. "Do you have a towel or something?"

"I do." He didn't move, but stared at me, as if seeing me in his house was the most fascinating thing that had happened in months. Since he was sequestered here by himself, I guess it probably was.

My fists climbed to rest up on my hips. "Well, are you just bragging, or can I actually use it to dry off here? I'm kind of dripping all over the place."

He narrowed his eyes skeptically. "Why did you come here?"

I blinked at him. "Are you serious? I just crossed an ocean by way of a sea monster, and you want to know why I'm here? I told you, I wanted to give us a shot where I didn't have to be afraid of you invading my mind, and you could see if we'd actually be good together for real. This way we can figure out if we should be together, or if we should move on."

"See, that's the reason I've been running over in my mind, but now that you're here, it doesn't add up. Why would you give yourself over to me, unguarded? Knowing what you do about what I did to your sister, why would you come here?"

Sandy looked curiously between myself and Philip, head tilted to the side and ears flopping.

I huffed, arms akimbo. "Because I'm a masochist, apparently. I've got a thing for lost causes, and you're about as lost as they come."

Philip's head turned to the side, his dimpled chin tightening as he sized me up. "A little impertinence is charming every now and then, but you'll do well to remember that I'm the master here. I'm not a lost puppy in search of redemption. If you're hoping to change me, you've come on a fool's errand."

I cast him a look of deep displeasure. "You're pushing your luck, dude. I don't need a monologue on how it's impossible to change a man. That's a tune I'm well familiar with. I just need a towel."

He watched my attitude a few more seconds before moving to a chest and pulling out a blanket. The cream fabric was fuzzy, and as he wrapped it around me, he pulled me closer to him, his hand on my hip. I wished Finn hadn't removed my hoodie. My peach nightgown was sticking to me, drawing attention to areas I didn't want Philip thinking he was welcome to explore.

It was now or never, and I knew the "never" option was too tempting to seriously consider. I took a chance and rested my head on his chest, ignoring Sandy's irate bark at my bold move.

Philip's hand drifted up, combing his fingers through my dripping tangles. I could hear the erratic beats of his heart and knew he was just as nervous as I was. It was a big deal, him letting an actual person onto his island of isolation. I was a risk, just as much as he was a risk to me.

"I have to tell you something, and I need you to not freak out."

His hand stilled in my hair. "What is it?"

I swallowed, driving the knife into my heart for the greater good. "When we kissed in my dream, it's not the same as kissing an awakened Omen in real life. There's hallucinations and colors, and it's, well, it's pretty trippy." Sandy went nuts, barking and growling until I snapped my fingers. "Hush up now, boy."

"Why are you telling me this?"

My hand climbed up to rest on his beige shirt. "Because I want to kiss you. I want to see what kinds of colors we make together."

Philip moved his hand under my chin, and I reminded myself not to flinch. He tipped my face up, and beneath the unrepentant warmonger I knew him to be, I could tell that he was also a man who wanted to be desired. Of all the things he could command, he couldn't make a woman *want* to be with him.

Philip's eyes zeroed in on my lips, and though we'd had sex before, this definitely felt like virgin territory. "Philip?" I whispered, leaning up so our mouths weren't more than a few inches apart. I didn't want to know what he smelled like, so I tried not to notice the sharp oaky scent that wafted into my nose unbidden. "When was the last time you kissed a woman?"

His eyes hardened in time with his grip on me, tightening me to his chest so I could barely breathe. "The last time I kissed a woman was the last time we kissed, so do the math from then."

My tone remained soft. "I mean in real life, not in an Omen's mind."

A flicker of utter loss sliced through the anger in his eyes with all the delicate grace of a butterfly's wing, making him look lost in a storm of his own making. "I can't remember. If it happened, it must've been lifetimes ago. I've been here for ages, locked in my island."

I didn't have to fake sympathy for him; my heart did a very real tug in my chest, unable to fathom what kind of monster I'd be after enduring that kind of isolation. My hand rose to touch his cheek, stroking the barely prickly skin as I gazed up at him with true compassion for his plight. "Oh, honey. You don't have to be alone anymore." I leaned up on my toes, brushing my lips to his too briefly to be considered a kiss. Philip was motionless, savoring the first kiss he'd had... maybe ever. At least in this lifetime, I was his first, so I took great care to move slowly.

The kiss unraveled, going deeper in layers I wasn't sure I understood the depths of. Sandy was angry now, but his growling and barking were drowned out by the banging that started introducing itself to our kiss. The drums echoed all around me, bashing inside my head and making me lose all sense of who and where I was. There were flutes with Mason, trumpets with Finn, and beautiful bells with Von. I should've guessed Philip's kiss would come with the ominous heaviness of pulse-pounding kettle drums.

When my skin was reverberating with the steady thrum that warned me of just how stupid I was being, colors started trickling into my mind. The red and yellow from Mason, the green and silver Finn had given me, and the blue and gold I'd bathed in with Von were replaced by a black fog that had tinges of royal purple to it. The fog moved like a thick snake around us, spiraling and climbing upward until we were wrapped tightly in the tension that only seemed to build. My tongue beckoned his to come out and play. The dance they did together was strange and seductive, yet somehow delicate.

I waited for the carbonation feeling to run through my body and over my skin, welcoming the strange sensation when it announced the breaking of Philip's curse I'd set out to undo.

Philip let out a moan of longing mingled with distress as his hands coiled around my back. His tongue touched mine, and the kiss deepened beyond what I'd needed it to be. I tried to let the kiss fade away, but Philip held me tighter, wanting more.

It didn't matter. His curse was broken, which meant that Philip was mortal again.

THE TRUTH ABOUT SANDY

It took too long to extract myself from Philip's lips. A graceful decrescendo was hard to execute without arousing suspicion that I wanted to murder him where he stood. Finally I was granted a whole foot of space when Sandy bit down on my leg. "Ouch! Sandy, no!" I stumbled to the only chair in the hut and flopped down on its wooden seat, shaking the imagined fog clear so I could see what was in front of me. A few drops of blood ran down my leg under my jeans and stained my sopping white sock.

Philip braced himself on the wood wall, his hand on his chest. "That was incredible. That's what I've been missing? That's what that cursed Kapre kept me from all these decades?"

I winced, realizing that I'd just kissed a super old man. Add rapist to that, and you got yourself the winner for the worst kiss of my life, courtesy of Terraway. I tried to appear enraptured, gazing up at him in wonder. "Was it everything you imagined? Because that was worth a trip across the ocean for me."

"Is it like that every time?" He motioned me to him. "Again."

Sandy stood between me and Philip, growling low at the man as he readied to attack. I checked the puncture marks from my dog's teeth and guessed that Philip didn't have any modern first aid supplies handy. "Sandy, you've never bitten me before. What's gotten into you?"

Philip's breathlessness was replaced by a smug smile. "Oh, he's not thrilled that you've taken up with his oldest friend."

"Is that supposed to make sense to me?"

"I guess there's no harm in it now. You gave me that gift, so I suppose I should give you yours." He reached for a wooden jar on the counter and dipped his knuckles in, pulling out a handful of crimson dirt. "You have no idea how hard this was to find, Levi. How long I searched through the eyes of thousands of muted souls. So many years of turning over every rock to find this for you. Though the search wasn't entirely without joy, I'll admit. I got to see the world through their eyes," he said wistfully.

My mouth dropped open. "That's what the rations were for? So you could live a life and see the world away from the island you're stuck on?"

"Wouldn't you want to see the world if you could? I

know your dreams. You see big and beautiful things you'll never venture to in real life. The rations dull their minds so I can float in and out, experience the world with my spirit while my body's stuck here."

I wanted to get into a heavy ethics debate, but that would be admitting that I thought him worthy of saving, which I did not.

He mumbled a few incoherent words and blew the red dusty dirt out at Sandy, coating his maw with the powder. An evil upward turn of Philip's lips came to his face when Sandy sneezed. "You didn't think I'd be able to find it, did you. You thought yourself cursed forever, banished to wander the Topside as a simple dog. I've been sneaking residents of Terraway up there for a year now. It wasn't so hard to use that same tunnel to get you down here, back where you belong. I was just waiting until I had something to make the trip worthwhile. But I found it, Levi." Philip's eyes danced with excitement, making him look much younger. "One of my soldiers found the old Kapre's missing ruby. I ground it up and used it to undo your punishment. You're free, brother. Actually free."

I stood, indignant. "What are you doing to him? Don't piss me off, Philip. Leave my dog alone."

Philip didn't listen to me, but addressed only Sandy. "It's time. Either you tell her, or I do."

My eyebrows creased in confusion. "Tell me what?" This was supposed to be the moment I stabbed him through, and now I was caught up in half a riddle.

A low growl started in Sandy's chest, rippling up as he bared down and braced himself for... something. Philip's eyes watched with delight as Sandy started whining at my feet, like he was apologizing for some crime I had yet to discover.

Then suddenly his body twitched unnaturally, his right shoulder elongating and stretching out, losing its caramel fur and looking more like... like a human's. I yelped and hopped backward, my hand over my mouth to stifle the incoherent shrieks that announced my freak-out. I'd seen this before when Mason transformed from wolf to man.

Sandy twitched and convulsed, growling and barking with pained fervor, until lying on the floor in the middle of the hut was a fully grown, naked man. He had auburn dreads, and too many muscles to be anything other than a bodybuilder, or like, a Viking or something.

I plastered my body to the wall, my breath coming in shallow pants when I realized the truth. "Matruculan?" I guessed, my hand moving to my chest to still the rapid jumps before my heart grew legs and leapt out of my chest to head for safer, less magical ground.

Philip nodded, his eyes on the man who had only seconds ago been my dog. "Of course."

Suddenly all the too-sentient-for-a-dog things became clear. Of course a dog wouldn't bring us takeout when we were starved. Of course a dog would've attacked us at some point when we trespassed onto his absent owner's property. Dread washed over me in waves. I'd told Sandy my deepest fears and confessed my secrets to him growing up. I didn't have a mask of "I'm fine" around him. I'd slept in the dirt with him on more than one occasion, and now here he was – a man who looked to be pushing thirty, lying at my feet, and in desperate need of some clothes.

Despite the fact that I was freezing and still wet, I cast my blanket to the floor as an offering, hoping someone would explain what the flip was going on.

"Give him a moment. He hasn't been upright in... how old are you? Well, add nine months to that." Philip drew a pair of shorts from his trunk and cast them down on the man, who was still assembling his bearings on the floor.

The only thing I felt was the blood draining from my face when the implications of what Philip was hinting at started to become clearer. "You mean... This is... But I don't have a..." I plastered my back to the wall, my arms sprawled out to brace myself as my knees began to debate whether or not they wanted to hold me upright.

Philip leaned down and clutched the man's hand, pulling Sandy to stand on unsteady feet after he slid on the pair of shorts. Sandy's auburn dreads had caramel streaks throughout. His nose was... I mean, it was my exact nose. His eyes were the same shape as mine. His expression – well, I'd never seen anything like it. He was awash of shame, fear and hope, though I scarcely understood my own jumbled emotional state.

Philip slapped Sandy on the back and all but shoved

him toward me. "Darling, this is Levi, my oldest and dearest friend. He was an apprentice with me many lifetimes ago, sent to work for a very difficult and short-sighted Kapre. One day, we stumbled upon a way to make what was thought to be an impossible curse, and used it to bless ourselves. The elixir of *Matalo* was our creation, but our master punished us for our ingenious discovery. Said we weren't worthy of such responsibility." Philip sniffed at the offensive memory. "I was sequestered to the island here, so I could live out my eternal days alone. Levi was banished Topside, confined to his Matruculan animal form." Philip watched me watch Sandy, petrified as I was. "I've been working to weaken the magic these last couple weeks after one of my soldiers found the Kapre's lost ruby. I was able to step out of the enclosure to take you into my island. I still can't venture far, mind you, but it's progress." His hand rested on Sandy's thick shoulder. "With the help of the dust from the ruby our master held a few of his curses in, now Levi's free of that part of his punishment."

"I can shift whenever I like?" Levi clarified, wary.

"Indeed, brother." Philip grinned at Levi, and then turned back to explain it all to me. "Through the years, Levi's found ways to weaken the punishment from time to time, as I've done with my own afflictions. It's how I'm able to send my spirit out, and how he was able to spend a handful of days as a human on your side before being forced to turn back into a dog."

I was well past the point of freaking out, but when Sandy turned to Philip and engulfed him in a warm hug, all language left me completely. "Thank you, brother," Sandy exhaled, gripping Philip with love I couldn't understand. "How I've missed you."

Philip kissed Levi on both his cheeks, and I could tell they'd both been starved for physical contact by how tightly their fingers dug into the other's skin.

When they finally released each other, Levi stepped back to admire his friend, clutching his shoulders with a look of admiration that was mingled with deep hurt. "You're different now. The isolation of this island's twisted you, brother. You want, so you take. You can't have my daughter, though. That must be clear to you."

My body was plastered to the wall, as if I hoped to make my bones part of the wood. My limbs were trembling when Levi turned to me, his hazel eyes painted with compassion that Philip just plain didn't possess. "October Grace?" His voice was deep, stirring something in my chest I hadn't known I needed to be able to suck in a full breath. I'd been suffocating for far too long without that sound that rang in my bones like truth. The vines and webs that had been tangled around my heart began to loosen, giving up their death grip on the organ that had never been allowed to beat in the same rhythm as the rest of the world. "Do you know who I am?"

He could've told me a hundred times, wore a sandwich

board and rented a plane to fly a message in the sky, and I still wouldn't have understood him. I opened my mouth, but the effort of trying to get sound to come out was one step too many. My knees finally gave up, buckling beneath me as the island faded to nothingness.

THE DESPERATION OF PHILIP
AND LEVI

Someone was slapping my face, but my arms were too weighted to reach out and punch the offender. I hadn't slept in I don't know how long, and my body was begging for a pillow and a nap.

My eyes fluttered open, and flooding my vision was Sandy— er, Levi. He had hazel eyes, and long auburn and light brown dreads tied back in a leather lace. He had Ollie's square jawline, Allie's smaller ears, three freckles on his left cheek, and my... my everything. I wanted to run, but I was too mesmerized. Too entranced. I hadn't let myself need a father growing up because one simply didn't exist. Now he was here, bracing me so I could sit up while I gawked at him.

I didn't have any words. I'm sure I should be pissed, reaming him for leaving us with Bev. But if he'd been a dog, what could he have really done? Would he have been a better parent than Bev in his dog form? Did he love us? He couldn't be totally negligent, since he'd taken up residence right next door to be near us. Did he love us? Had he wanted us, and not walked out rather than stick around? *Did he love us?*

"You fed us," I remarked, wishing the first words I was saying to my father were more meaningful and eloquent. "When we were starving, you brought us food."

A fierce emotion beamed through his whole being while he clutched me as he knelt on the floor. "You were so small. I was afraid you might die so many times. I don't know what happened. Beverly wasn't like that when we were together the first time. I watched her for months before I took my chance, used all my strength and turned human for the night. She was kind, meek and funny. Then over the years she grew... I was wrong about her."

My clumsy finger lifted up and poked at his face to make sure he was real, and that I wasn't hallucinating. I depressed my finger to his cheekbone, his jaw, his forehead. "It was the stone. She had the sagrado stone hidden in her hoard. It poisons humans, so it warped all of us in one way or another. She was a full human, so it bent her mind the worst."

Levi's arm behind me froze as his expression fell into horror. He took a moment to process the blow. He swallowed thickly, his eyes filled with palpable shame. "I gave her that stone. I thought someone was following me, so I told her to hold onto it, that I'd be back for it someday. I had no idea it would be bad for her." He hung his head. "I did that? I turned her into a monster? I'm the reason you were beaten and neglected?" I didn't expect tears to form in his eyes, but when his nose turned pink and his voice caught, I found I couldn't look away.

Ollie rarely cried. Allie broke down when the dark moods struck her, but Ollie was steadfast. I wasn't sure if that was a good thing or a bad one, but watching Levi's three tears roll down his cheeks blew my mind. Every detail about him added a new explosion to the vivid image that was my new dad. "You stayed. You couldn't be a person, but you still stayed? Why? Was it because you wanted to watch the stone?"

Levi shook his head, letting out a nervous scoff. "I couldn't care less about the stone. I couldn't have used it to save Terraway if I tried. I put a blessing on Bev and you kids so you could touch the stone without it turning you to rock. Same one I used on myself to steal it in the first place. I didn't realize it would mutate Bev's personality." He shook his head, his tone mournful and angry. "I stayed because of you kids. I so wanted to be there, to have you call me Papa, to take you away from that awful trailer and build you a house. I wanted to bring home firewood and take you three on trips. I wanted to do homework with you, and take you all hunting to kill a beast and bring it home for Beverly." He clutched me with just enough fire to make me believe that someone actually wanted to claim me, to put his last name on me and work hard so I could play.

I hadn't played in so very long.

"You wanted us?" I knew it wasn't wise to ask a question that could so easily go south on me, but there it was, the only thing I really wanted to know.

More tears slid down the thin scruff on his cheeks, making his voice catch, and tugging at parts of my heart I'd thought were long dead. His answer came out in a fierce whisper. "I would have treasured you, my girl."

Philip's voice interrupted the tender moment, which made me want to double kill him. "*You* had the sagrado stone? You stole it from the Kapre?"

Levi glanced over his shoulder to his friend. "He deserved it for what he did to us. He imprisoned you first, and I knew I was next, so I took the stone with me Topside. Terraway knew he had a spare sagrado stone; he deserved to be persecuted when he lost it. Did they make him suffer?"

"No, *I* did. I found my first subject to control, and knew exactly where to aim him. Our master didn't see it coming. I avenged our pain as much as I could, brother."

Levi seemed satisfied with this answer, though he never took his eyes off my gaping expression. "None of it matters anymore. Had I known it would warp Beverly, I would never have trifled with the stone at all." He closed his eyes and pressed his forehead to mine. "I'm so deeply sorry I did this to you all."

I didn't have words, so I stuck to gripping the back of his neck to make sure he didn't up and disappear on me.

Philip broke in with annoyance in his tone. "I needed that stone. I searched everywhere, raised whole armies to find it!"

Levi shrugged, still supporting my weight with his arm. "I would have given it to you, had I known you needed it. Our master banished us for being power-hungry and wanting too much control over life, and he goes and keeps one of the few sagrado stones to himself in his collection of precious gems? It was the worst kind of hypocrisy. So I stole his treasure. What did you need it for?"

Philip was incredulous. "It's not one of the few sagrado stones anymore, it's the only one left! Terraway gave up hope it even existed. They've been relying on the Omens to fuel the suns. Terraway's been withering for the last couple years. It's only because October found the stone and split it between the nations that they're alive at all."

My eyes narrowed as my fight came back. I sat up on my own and barked at Philip. "You don't give a crap about Terraway. You wanted to destroy the stone so everyone would have to rely on your rations."

Philip looked down his nose at me. "That's where you're wrong, darling. I only needed the rations so I could send out my spirit into dulled souls. If I had the stone, I could grind it up, bless it and use it to break my imprisonment. I could be free of this island if only you would've brought me that stone! So many times I tried to get you to tell me where it was."

"You'd grind it up? You'd let Terraway die off just so you could get off a tropical island?"

Philip's fists clenched at his sides as he shouted at me. "You have no idea how many decades I've been here! I would do anything to be free! I don't care if the whole of Terraway burned up under its suns. I would be free!"

Levi slowly helped me to stand, taking care with my unsteady form so I didn't collapse again. He moved his body to position his shoulder between Philip and me as a partial shield. "You'll not raise your voice at my daughter. And you don't know what you're saying. You wouldn't let Terraway die. You must know of another sagrado stone if you were set on grinding one of them up. I only took the Kapre's because I knew there were others to keep the suns regulated."

"You had your family. You had freedom to move around and explore a whole world! I've had nothing but this island for over a hundred years! Nothing!"

I didn't expect Levi to wrap his arms around Philip. Philip wasn't a super huggable guy to begin with, but Levi didn't seem to mind. He squeezed Philip and kept his voice steady with a tinge of sadness. "Brother, what happened to you? I loved your grand dreams once upon a time. Why are you chasing nightmares now?"

Philip's voice came out mournful, dripping with utter

loss. "I can't be alone here anymore. I need to conquer, to explore, to feel a woman's touch. I can't do this anymore!"

"We'll get you out," Levi promised. "You used the Kapre's ruby to break me of my curse. I'll find a way for you to be free, too. Now that I can help you? You'll be out in no time at all."

30

WHAT FATHERS ARE BUILT FOR

My brain started working again, but admittedly kept hiccupping whenever my vision slid over to my father. He looked like a Viking, like Mason. I thought back over my conversations with my favorite pit bull, but couldn't think of one where I'd confessed the awful things Philip did to Allie and me. Levi had been separated from Terraway for over a century. He had no idea the dire situation Philip had put everyone in.

I needed to kill Philip, but I now had the added obstacle of getting Levi to let me do it, without being able to clue him in.

"She's not here for you," Philip said in response to something I hadn't been paying attention to. I'd been too busy gawking at my father and plotting how to murder his bestie. "She came to be with me."

Levi was no longer hugging his friend, but stood

between us again, his voice firm, but not unkind. "And she can stay as long as I'm here. It's not proper for her to be here with you like this. This is the first time I can actually voice my opinion on her life, so you'll let me have this. You won't give me a voice only to take it away when it displeases you. Find another man's daughter. You can't have mine."

My heart swelled. Though I didn't much care for anyone making decisions for me, I was grateful for the extra anti-rape barrier.

Philip started pacing, hand to his forehead as he fished through the reasons he could say to my father without getting punched in the face. "It has to be her. I've searched through so many dulled minds, but hers didn't have to be muted for me to get inside. I could talk with her, enjoy the Topside through her imagination. She's shown me things that... It has to be her."

Levi was firm. "Well, it can't be her. Once we break you out of here, you'll see there's a whole world of women with sharp minds you can entertain yourself with."

"But I can't... You don't understand! She's the only one who's been able to carry my child! All the others have died or lapsed into comas."

My whole body forgot the master plan and started shaking with rage I couldn't put a cap on. "Allie's in a coma, and he's the reason! He drove her insane when he tried to knock her up by sleeping with her in her mind, and now she's in a hospital bed!"

Philip held up his hands when Levi rounded on him, wrapping his hands around Philip's neck without a second thought. "You did *what* to my daughter?"

"Allison invited me into her mind! It was weakened with drugs, so I slipped inside."

Screw the plan. I was done. I lunged at Philip, ready to tear his eyes out. "My sister would never do drugs! You pushed your way inside!"

Levi removed one hand from Philip's throat and caught me around the ribs, maintaining his place between us. "Is that true?"

Philip was livid. "She wanted me there, just like October! She was happy when I came to be with her. It was only when she found out who I was and who she was that she started to get confused."

Levi maintained his hold on me, but set his jaw against Philip, his other hand still clutched around Philip's throat. "Confused how?"

Philip struggled to swallow. "Confused like she didn't want me there anymore, but I know she did! She let me into her mind in the first place! I don't care what she said, I know she wanted it!"

I let out a shriek of indignation. "That's like, the international rapist motto! I'll kill you! I'll kill you!" My anger turned itself onto Levi when he was calming me down instead of dealing with his assjack buddy. "Don't you dare defend him! You have no idea what I've been through because of your friend."

"I'm not defending him; I'm telling you to control yourself. Sama's immortal, so if you do come to blows with him, you'll surely lose. I'm the only one who can deal with him. Trust me to do exactly that."

"Trust you? I don't even know you!" The moment the words belted out of my mouth, I wanted to stuff them back inside. Sure, Levi was new to me, but Sandy wasn't.

Suddenly I was engulfed in Levi's arms, his fierce love evident in how tightly he held me, shaking me at every fifth word that came out through clenched teeth. "All you need to know is that I'm your father. I've been waiting for an opportunity to show you who I am since you were born. I've loved you for your entire life. I fed you, brought you clothes, chased away predators, watched out for you and never once turned my back on you. You say you don't know who I am? I'm your father. I was built to make sure you never have to be in situations like this. Let me handle it."

A tear squeezed itself from my eye, surprising me that this was the first time I'd let loose such raw emotion during this whole debacle. "I can't sleep. He comes into my mind and tries to get me pregnant. I didn't know who he was at first. I thought he was just a dream!"

Levi cupped the back of my head and squeezed. "I'll take care of it."

Philip was fuming that I'd given him up, and I swear I saw a glimmer of hurt in his expression that I'd turned on him. "You come here to be with me, and this is how it turns out?"

Levi opened the door and ushered me outside. "Go back to your guide. I'll come get you when we've finished catching up."

I was so turned around; I didn't know how to stuff all my mixed-up emotions into one sentiment. I looked up at Levi, lost for words. Then I threw my trembling arms around his neck, pulling him down so I could whisper in his ear, "My kiss made him mortal, but he doesn't know." I pressed my cheek to his, my eyes closing in case when I came back, he was somehow vanished. "Please don't leave me," I begged, voicing the insecurity that had plagued me most of my life.

Levi paused, and then gripped me in a hug that was so loving, I could barely understand the depths of it. Unending devotion flooded through me, awakening the dead ions and pumping new life through my tired soul. "Never," he promised with a ferocity that made me actually believe him. "Go to your guide. I'll come for you in a few minutes."

Letting go of Levi was one of the hardest things I'd had to do, including all the impossible things I'd had to tackle as of late. I tried to memorize each detail of my father in case... Just in case.

31

PHILIP'S DAY OF RECKONING

I stumbled back the way I'd come with Philip, retracing our path through the nude trees until the dirt under my feet gave way to chalky sand. When my eyes fell on Finn, who was slashing violently at the air facing my direction, I halted my immediate instinct to run toward him.

"Finn?" I called, making my way closer to where he stood.

Finn faltered, his head whipping around to locate the source of my voice. "October? Where are you? Are you hurt?"

I was careful not to let my feet pass the protection of the island of solitude. I guessed that I'd never be able to get back inside once I stepped out. Leaning as far over as I could, I reached out and placed my hand on Finn's arm, making him jump. "It's me," I assured him, grateful he didn't up and chop my hand off. "Come on in. I think I need your help."

Finn stumbled forward, now that someone on the inside had granted him entry. "How did you do that? I've been calling you for ages, trying to find a way in." He was sweating from head to toe, visibly exhausted.

"I took a chance. You alright?"

Finn leaned over to steady himself, his elbows on his thighs as he exhaled loudly. "No! I'm not alright. I've been panicked that I marched you to your death! What's happened? Did you do it?"

Finn was the only person I'd confessed my master plan to. I shook my head, lowering my voice to a whisper. "I kissed him, so the curse is broken. He can die now. But he found my dad, Finn! My dad's his long lost best friend. My dad is Levi, the apprentice who got kicked out of the last Kapre's service with him. He's in there now, yelling at Philip for everything he did to Allie and me. I don't know how to kill him without getting Levi involved."

Finn straightened, looking down his nose at me. "First off, his name is Sama, not Philip. Second, no one knows what came of Levi. He lived over a century ago. Maybe Sama found a way to cheat death, but I think we'd all know it if Levi had done it too."

"If you know what he looks like, then come to the hut and take a look. Either way, make sure you don't hurt him." I squeezed his hand. "I have a dad, Finn!"

Finn's expression was dubious, and not excited, as I'd

hoped he'd be. "We'll see about that. But sure, I'll let the council have him instead of gutting him myself."

"That's the spirit. This way." I grabbed his wrist and pulled him in the direction of the hut, but he didn't budge. "Let's go."

"Not yet. I'm still getting over the shock of you being gone and then being here. Give me a second. You're really okay? He didn't..."

"Nothing happened. I kissed him, and then my dad turned from a dog into himself. It's been a little surreal. Not quite the Brady Bunch I'd pictured, but you know, what else is new?"

Finn pulled me closer, tilting my chin up with the butt of his knife. "Don't ever vanish like that again. I can't take you disappearing."

"What if I was a magician's assistant, and it was all part of our scammy act?"

"Not even then."

"You're no fun." I scratched a spot on my elbow. "Let's kill Philip and be done with it."

"Sama," Finn corrected me. "Don't go getting confused. It's a monster we're dealing with, not a man in love."

"I know, I know."

"*I'm* the man in love." The corner of his mouth tugged upward as he looked down at me, taking in the scope of my hopeful expression. "That was some kiss. Did you really see it? Our life together?"

I nodded, swallowing my guilt. "I saw it."

"I love you, you know." Then he palmed my chin and brought my face close to his, planting a kiss to my lips that made my heart race. When he released me, I had to blink away the traces of silver and green that impeded my vision. "I told you I'd find a place where we could be together."

"Philip first, then we can talk about all that." I didn't exactly know how that conversation was going to go, but I knew that everything short of a Brady Bunch reunion could wait until after Philip was dealt with. I started forward, but Finn stayed in place. I turned to face his expression that wreaked of displeasure. "What's wrong?"

"Sama. You keep calling him Philip. You're scaring me. Now I'm wondering if you don't really understand how bad he is, that you think he's redeemable, or that he can be reasoned with. Tell me you understand that he's got nothing for you but the worst of intentions."

I nodded, tucking a lock of hair behind my ear. "I know he's bad. The death penalty's around for a reason. And you can hold your breath about Santa Claus, because I know the truth about him, too."

"Who? Focus, October. *Sama*, not Santa. When we get in there, I need to know you won't hesitate on me."

I took my backpack from him and pulled out the over-large balisong blade he'd given me for protection so long ago, opening it to ready for the fight. Examining my face in the reflective surface of the blade, I noted the differences in my optimism that were plain on my features. Maybe at one point I might've thought Philip redeemable. I'd gambled on many a prisoner's rehabilitation into society, and lost more times than I'd won. I knew there were some crimes you could be absolved from, and that others went too deep to scrub away.

I could see in the steadfast coldness of my eyes that my sins couldn't be escaped – that eventually I'd have to pay for all of it. But today was Sama's day of reckoning. "Don't worry, Finn. I won't hesitate."

TAKE ME HOME

We heard shouting before we saw the hut. It was the incoherent rantings of a man enraged, and the excuses of a defendant with no solid defense. "How could you do that? You knew they were my daughters, and you seduced them anyway?"

"Your magic runs deep, Levi! I knew if I was ever going to be able to have a child, it would have to be from a lineage with more cunning and more magic than the usual selection. I knew you would've blessed your own children. I tried other women – you have no idea how hard I tried – but it was only your daughters. Allie couldn't carry the baby to term, no matter how many times I tried." The sounds of fists hitting flesh reached us, making the hairs on the back of my neck stand up.

Finn held his finger to his lips as we moved through the bare trees, pausing before the sand beneath us grew polluted with dirt and bramble. He was right; it would give us away if we continued forward. The crunching underfoot would be too loud.

I could only make out a few angry words from Levi that were peppered between the punches. When Philip finally begged for mercy, the punching stopped. "You deserved that, you know. You took my Allie away from me. You warped her mind to take her away from her brother and sister so you could get her pregnant? You wouldn't have been able to keep the baby even if she had carried it to term. You're stuck here! What was the plan? Let me tell you the nightmare it is to have a child you can't get to."

"I have spies. I have allies all over Terraway. I've been able to help Ekeks and Manas get Topside when the famine was too brutal. I would've had them snatch the baby and bring him to me. I had a plan! I would've cared for your grandson and trained him to be as great and powerful as we are. I would've been better than our old master, who was always limiting us."

Levi's shout rose to a roar. "You would've cared for my grandson? What of my daughters? Did you care for them? My Allie's in a hospital!"

Something about the possessive way Levi claimed her as "my Allie" rallied hope in my breast and stirred up faith in my soul I hadn't known was there. To hear him put his stamp of ownership on the sister I loved jerked emotion to my tear ducts. Would that Allie could witness our father's devotion.

I could hear the danger of Philip reclaiming his bearings, yelling with fury instead of apology. "You don't get to judge me! See what you wouldn't consider, stuck here for an eternity!"

"I would never ruin your family! Give me a thousand years in this prison, and I wouldn't take what was precious to you just to use it up and throw it away. My Allie deserved better than this!"

Philip scoffed. "Allie was weak. I chose her because I assumed she'd have your purity of strength, but she was barely able to fight through the first trimester."

I lunged forward, animalistic in my rage that he'd insult the girl who'd shown unswerving strength of spirit when it came to raising me. Finn caught me around the middle, cupping his hand over my mouth and holding me back. "Wait, October."

Levi's voice dropped to a deadly quiet that sent a chill up my spine. "Say it again. Tell me how you used my daughter, almost killed her and then have the nerve to call her weak. Tell me how she survived you, but she still measures out weak."

I closed my eyes, picturing with perfect clarity Philip's calm and cocky countenance as he uttered the unforgiveable. "Allie was fit for one thing, and she couldn't even be of use for that. She made for amusing sport before I tired of her." His over-enunciation of the last bit made me see red in my murderous haze. "Your daughter is weak."

I probably should've expected the body flying out the

open doorway to be Philip's, but I yelped all the same when he landed in a pile of limbs not five yards from where Finn and I stood. Levi stormed out of the hut with purpose in his eyes and murder in his fists.

He was fast, but I was closer, so Philip got a shoeful of my wrath first when I broke from Finn's grip. Errant cussing flew out of my mouth as I let loose on the man who'd haunted me – my own personal, tangible ghost. I punched him across the face, but my anger still wasn't satisfied. Allie wasn't with me, so until she was, Sama would pay. I slashed a line with my knife across Sama's thigh when he kicked out to get me off him.

"October, stop!" Levi yanked me off of Sama and tossed me backward with Mason-like strength. My body bounced three times before a tree stopped me, bringing me banging to a halt when my shoulder smacked into the hard bark. It was then I remembered that being Matruculan with uncut hair made you as strong as The Hulk, *duh*, and Levi had long dreads that swung out wildly as he turned his fury on Sama.

My dad was a friggin' superhero.

Levi pointed his finger to me in warning. "It's my duty to end him. You stay put."

My eyes found Philip's that shone with malice as he pierced me with his snarl. "I loved our daughter enough to try and bring her back! I took her bones and gave them flesh! Without me, she has no chance of coming back to us!"

It was the punch in the gut I wasn't expecting. Without thinking it through, my mouth opened just before Levi reached Philip, and I yelled, "Dad, stop!"

I think the only thing that could've stopped him was me calling him by his proper paternal title. Levi skidded to a halt and whirled on me, his face filled with wonder. "So long I've waited to hear you call me that." He shook his head at me, his hand over his heart. "But it doesn't matter what he says now. It's his final hour."

"But if he can give me back my daughter, let him live just long enough for that!" I hated the begging in my voice, but I realized that when it came to September, I would lower myself to any depths, even begging the man I hated to give me hope. I moved to stand on unsteady feet, my balance off after the rough landing. "Please, Philip! Where is she?"

Philip's snarl softened as he sat up, clutching the gash I'd given his thigh. "I can take you to her body. I've almost got her reanimated. I just need a few more things, and we can have her back."

Finn moved closer to Philip, his knife drawn and too much purpose in his eyes. "Finn, stop! Where's September? Where's my daughter? Give her back to me!" The horrible cracking in my shout scared me with my loss of control. I needed my daughter, and if there was a small chance she might be saved, I would fight to the death for that sliver of hope.

Levi's voice was steady, making mine seem all the more

unbalanced. "I know the magic he's speaking of. It's one of the original modifications the first Kapre made to civilians of Terraway to ensure we were all buried properly. It wouldn't bring her back, October. It doesn't bring any of them back. It gives us their shell. Trust me that you don't want your daughter's shell without her soul."

"I can give you more than a shell!" Philip's promise made my heart soar with confusion and anticipation I didn't know how to keep in check.

I turned my head to the left and the right one time, making up my mind on the spot. "I need to see her. I need to make sure it's not possible."

Levi's shoulders lowered, and an immovable look came into his eyes. "Trust me to know the rules of this world. Trust me that I wouldn't kill my granddaughter, that I would save her if there was a chance."

I was too caught up in my own dilemma. I was too focused on Levi and the loyalty he swore that would ask me to leave my daughter to the dust. I was too lasered into the hazel that was identical to mine, and all that it stirred up in me to have my father not just be near me, but also *want* to be near me.

I was lost in the swirling moment, so I didn't pay attention when Finn's knife swung out from behind Philip, piercing through the villain's back. Once, twice, three times he ran Philip through, all at different points along his back. I screamed as Philip made a sound like he'd merely been shoved from behind. His head bobbed back and flung forward as Finn retracted his knife and stumbled away from the bloody mess. Then Finn fell to the ground, as if caught up in a random fainting spell.

"No!" Levi shouted, surprising me by running to Finn, leaving his oldest friend to flop on the dirt as he struggled for life and breath. Levi knelt at Finn's side, gripping his upper half with frustration I didn't understand. Finn hadn't been stabbed. Finn had been the one stabbing Philip. "It was *my* responsibility! October's *my* daughter! *I* was meant to die for this, not you! I don't even know you! You don't belong in this fight!"

"Die? What? Finn, what's wrong?" I expected him to maybe have tripped over a stick or something, and for that to be the source of his fall. When Levi dragged Finn away from Philip so he was a safer distance apart, I saw with horror Levi's hand that supported Finn's back was coated in blood.

"Finn!" I ran to him, dropping to my knees on his other side. My hands flitted over his face as I checked his weakening pulse. "You're okay! You're fine!" I was frantic as I leaned him forward, gasping that there were identical stab wounds on his back that matched the ones he'd given Philip. I screamed like a lunatic, losing the parts of my mind that normally went into nurse mode.

Levi lowered Finn to the dirt, clutching his hand as Finn fought for breath, his eyes wide. "Sama and I put a protection on ourselves before we took the elixir of *Matalo*. If someone tried to kill us, they themselves would be killed in the same manner. It's why I threw you back. I didn't want you to kill him. *I* was supposed to kill him. This was to be my sacrifice!" He focused on Finn. "Soldier, tell me your name. Tell me what message you'd like passed on to your kin, and I'll deliver it myself. I'm so sorry. This battle wasn't meant for you."

Finn's eyes were wide as he choked on blood that spat out onto his lips. He looked scared, frantic to undo the wrong that had been done to him. He touched his chest over and over, but no relief came. I could tell he'd punctured both his lungs. He mouthed something when his shocked eyes were finally able to focus on my face.

I sobbed over his body, trying to think of something – anything that could make it all not be real. "What, Finn? Tell me anything. I'm here. I won't leave you."

"Take me," he choked out when I leaned closer. Our noses were almost touching, bathing me in what couldn't possibly be Finn's final breaths. A tear dripped from my cheek onto his.

"Anywhere. I'll go with you anywhere," I promised. "I'm sorry. This is my fault. I love you, Finn. Tell me how to undo it!"

He gasped again, each movement making his mouth open wider, as if he hoped to be able to fill his lungs that had never seen much in the way of limitations before. His Kataw enhancements allowed him to hold on much longer than Philip's now lifeless body had. A tear spilled from the corner of his eye. "Take me home, *sinta.*"

I didn't need any other words to know that he wanted *our* home. Our cottage on the beach. I nodded, gulping through a sob that this was how this great man in my life would come to an end. I gathered him to me, coating my hands in his blood as my lips brushed to his. I tasted his blood, inviting his insides into mine with our tongues, so I could carry him with me. As the kiss deepened, I tasted the ocean and coconuts. I tasted salty air and heard trumpets. I saw violent streaks and lightning bolts of green and silver as my lips trembled in time with his.

Then I saw our cottage. I grabbed Finn's hand as my feet touched the pure white sand and ran for the safety of our home. "Hurry!" I yelled, panicked that we wouldn't make it. The sky was gray, a storm rolling in to darken the sunshine I'd taken for granted.

Finn ran beside me, strong and young, filled with all the things I'd always loved about him. I tripped on the sand and he righted me, holding my hand tight so we didn't lose each other. Green, glittery lightning struck mere feet from us, driving our panic higher still. "We're almost there! Don't lose me, October!"

"Never! I'm right here, and I won't let go." I charged forward, running with everything in me to the safety of our special place. The sand was the worst kind of obstacle, slowing me down so it felt like my limbs were moving through thick molasses. The cottage seemed like it was an eternity away, but I was determined not to let his hand drop. I glanced down and saw that my palm was slick with his blood, making my grip slippery. "Hold on! I've got you!" I heard the horrible desperation in my voice that cracked with too many tears and too much stacked against us.

I don't know how we reached the porch, but when I flung the door open and stumbled inside, my foot caught the floorboard at just the right angle. I pitched forward into the cabin, crashing down and knocking over the end table in the process. The perfect picture of our future shattered as it hit the floor, but I didn't care about broken glass. The inscription of "If you live, then I breathe" on the frame mocked me with echoes of a life that could never be. I clutched the bent frame to my chest as I sat back on my heels, heaving with a gust of relief that we'd done it. "We made it! I can't believe we did it. Finn, are you…" I turned to get a glimpse of him in our home, but where he should've been, there he wasn't. "Finn?"

The ocean went silent, and the green and silver that lined my periphery began to fade with every blink. "Finn?" I stood, noticing for the first time that the trumpets were gone. My legs moved of their own accord to the doorway, finding Finn's footprints in the sand leading up to the cabin, and then vanishing. I clutched the frame in one hand and braced myself on the doorjamb with the other. A guttural, anguished cry erupted from my innards, spilling out onto the ocean that felt unbearably empty. I screamed his name out at the world that was supposed to be ours. "Finn!"

The sky began to darken from gray to black, like

someone turning down a dimmer switch. I dropped to my knees and tore at the back of the picture frame, snatching the photo from the shards. I gazed on the life I would never have and pressed it to my broken heart. My last cry came out a desperate whisper. "Finn!"

And then the perfect world we could've shared faded to black.

33

PHOTO OF FINN

 I didn't dream for the longest time. Whole blankets of dark nothingness stretched out before me, separating me from time and awareness. My arm started to burn, and the only thing I saw was the mark of loyalty Kabayo had given me. The swirling Xs lit up in a brilliant blue that awakened me from my muted existence.

But that was all. I saw and felt nothing else. I was alone in my dark world, and though there was nothing to occupy myself with, the solitude felt like a warm blanket I couldn't bring myself to part from. I rolled over on the floor of my mind and ignored anything that resembled reality.

I'd been through too much, lived too many lives of war. My hands were coated in Finn's slick blood, so I clutched them to my chest, feeling the crinkle of the photo paper I couldn't let go of. I couldn't see our faces of adoration, gazing into each other's eyes, but I knew they were there. I knew a whole life had existed in some alternate plane, and I'd lost it all. I'd lost Finn forever, and when I awoke, I knew I would lose Von for all the reasons I should.

The blood between my fingers was precious to me, so I clenched my fists to make sure I kept as much of Finn with me as I could. For all the handwashing I'd done in my life, I would swear off the obsessive habit forever if it would give me just a little more time with Finn.

He'd loved me, and I'd let him die. The logical side of my brain argued that I couldn't have known that Philip had installed that failsafe in himself. But looking back at the many conversations Philip and I had shared, the hints were there. What megalomaniac wouldn't use a failsafe? My rational side was gentle with my ocean of pain, assuring me that there was no way I could've leaped to the reality of the situation from that logic.

But I wasn't logical, and holding onto Finn's picture as tight as I was, I knew I wasn't rational. I was in a world unto myself, drowning in guilt I knew I would never escape from. I shouldn't have come to Finn's country. I should've gone on my own, or taken a guide only so far. There was something in me I hadn't been able to squelch that chased after Finn. Then as soon we finally caught each other, we were separated forever.

I'm sure life was going on, and the world still spun, but I wanted no part of it. I'd killed the thing I loved. The world didn't need me muddying up the place.

So I stayed in my darkness, clutching the photo of Finn to my chest, and praying it was all a dream.

~

TIME PASSED – I'M NOT SURE HOW MUCH, AND THE ODDEST thing about it was that I didn't care. I felt my body being jostled at one point, nose flooded with the barn-ish smell of Kabayo intermingling with the ocean.

I clung to my photo, my fingers locking when someone or something tried to pry my hands open. I screamed and protested when the picture fell away from me as a wet rag swept over my hands, taking Finn away from me forever. I wondered if my protests were only in my mind. Perhaps my physical body was compliant with whatever fate had left to dole out in punishment for my many, many sins.

I searched for the picture, but as I suspected, the second I let go of Finn, he disappeared. I cursed myself for tripping over the entrance, pitching forward and dropping his hand. Maybe if I hadn't, he'd still be here with me.

I heard a jumble of voices – explaining and then shouting. I heard the ocean, and then cars. More shouting.

I wanted no part of it – any of it. I wanted to sleep without Philip, without Finn, without Mason and even without Von. For once in my life, I held tight to my solitude, not letting anyone infiltrate it.

The abyss was my very best friend, muting all that I couldn't face with my precious darkness that kept me warm. When I felt my body being shifted, I clung to the darkness, fighting with everything in me not to understand the voices that were aimed in my direction.

I didn't want to hear any of it. I wanted to be alone, so the darkness was where I stayed.

34

CHAINSAW AND CHIN

I sat in the darkness, hugging my knees as I replayed Finn's last moments, then Mariang's, then Garrick's, then Bishop's, and then September's. My love was toxic, so I knew it was best for the world that I stayed locked up. My mind was the perfect prison, and I accepted my punishment with grace, knowing I deserved every bit of it.

"I thought your mind would be more adventurous, that there'd be more to do here. This is it? This is all there is? We gotta get out of here, sweetheart."

Despite the fact that I wanted to be alone, my head jerked up in surprise at the voice I'd heard no less than a zillion times. A sudden beam of stage light shown down on the man sitting next to me, illuminating his cocky can-do attitude and the best chin of my life. "Bruce Campbell? What are you doing here?"

He was older than he'd been in *Evil Dead*, but no less glorious. Hints of salt and pepper brushed back from his temples, and the boyish playfulness in his eyes enraptured me, as it always had. At any age, Bruce Campbell was glorious. "What am I doing? I'm boring myself to death, I guess. Really? This is your imagination? Where's the tree fort? Where are the fast cars? Give me a blank canvas like this, and I'll do something crazy with it."

"I bet you would, but this is my world, and I've had enough crazy." Bruce Campbell was the shiz, and this was the best I could offer, as far as a shared adventure went. I was ashamed.

He waited a whole five seconds before letting out an exasperated sigh. "Come on, sweetheart. Let's go dig a tunnel and see how far down this thing goes." He stomped his boot to the black floor.

"You're not real, and I don't have a shovel."

Bruce's face soured, his chin dimpling in time with the space between his eyebrows. "Of course I'm real! I would never say something so mean to you."

I picked at a thread on the knee of my jeans. "You know, I used to think that you were my guardian angel. That if you could fight the evil dead, the army of darkness and all that, somehow I could make it through a normal day. Now I'm not so sure."

Bruce held up his hands and shook his head. "Oh, no. Don't blame this place on me."

I glared at him. "Well, if you don't like it, then you can leave."

"I don't believe this." Bruce stood in frustration, offered his hand to me and yanked me up. "This isn't how I raised you to be."

I looked around incredulously. "Um, you didn't raise me. I don't even know you in real life."

"How many of my movies have you seen? TV shows? Didn't you do a paper on my autobiography for your great American hero assignment? I raised you better than this."

I think it was when he slapped the back of his hand into his right palm that I started to smile. The upward turn of the corner of my mouth felt foreign to my features, but I couldn't help it. Bruce Campbell always made me smile. He had that way about him that charmed me every time. "Whatever. You couldn't pick me out of a lineup of two."

"So what? Do you think Ash would've rolled over and taken a nap when the Candarian demons started attacking?" He waited for my answer, his arms crossed over his chest. "That wasn't a rhetorical question. Would you have watched that movie if I wussed out in the second act?"

I hugged my middle and hung my head glumly. "No. I guess not. But this is different. This is reality. I've buried too many people. I need a break."

"Then go watch the friggin' *Brady Bunch*." He shook his head in disgust. Part of me felt the deep shame that Bruce Campbell had finally shown up in my dream, and I was blowing it all over the place. "You're losing your fight, and that's not you. Only one way to fix it."

I lifted my chin and raised my eyebrow, waiting for his miraculous cure. My body jumped back when he pulled a chainsaw out from the darkness. It was somehow already wet with blood. "What are you doing?"

"Giving you a head start because I'm a nice guy. You want to stay here? You're gonna have to fight me for the space. *You* may've given up on you, but *I* haven't."

I cast him a dubious look as I backed away slowly. "You're not going to chase me with that chainsaw."

"Well, first I'm going to chase you, then I'm going to catch you. Then you die. So either wave your white flag now, or start running."

"Put that thing down."

Bruce's eyes were wild, as I'd seen hundreds of times before when he got super passionate in a scene. He had the best crazy eyes. "You want a life worth going home to? Then you have to fight for it, sweetheart!" He pulled back the string on the chainsaw, starting up the rickety engine on the first try.

I'd expect nothing less from my own personal superhero.

Bruce took a bold step toward me, raising the chainsaw to shoulder height.

I knew that look in his eyes. He wasn't stopping for nothing. I'd seen him cut off his own hand with that very chainsaw. Dude wasn't messing around.

I shrieked and bolted through the darkness. More unnerving than the roar of the chainsaw was that while I was running with everything in me, Bruce was walking, his footsteps somehow echoing around me in time with my pounding heart.

I searched for something – anything to hide behind, but Bruce traveled with his own spotlight, so wherever I hid, I was revealed whenever he got close. "Stop it! Just let me be alone!"

"Oh, you'll be alone, but you'll also be in pieces."

I was furious as I ran, that this was the best my imagination could give me when Bruce Campbell showed up in my dream. "You're a jerk! I'm allowed to grieve, you know. I'm allowed to be sad." My muscles started to feel the exertion, but I didn't slow down.

"Nobody's stopping you from being sad. I'm telling you that the world's still moving out there, so staying here's not an option. Checking out's not an option. Donating your hands to science? That, I can help you with."

I screamed as I ran through the nothingness, not seeing anything, but feeling a breeze that started to grow colder. "Leave me alone!"

"You're already alone!"

His words hit me like a ton of obvious bricks. I was alone. I was fighting and running and hiding not just from the horrible things, but from the good things, as well. I was running from Ollie, who didn't deserve that. By giving up on myself, I was giving up on Allie, who needed me even if

I was broken. I was running from Ezra, from Mason, from my friends who, flawed as they were, loved me each in their own ways.

I was running from Von, who'd earned the chance to tell me off once and for all.

I was running from myself, but no matter how far Bruce Campbell chased me, I would always have me – for better or worse.

"Okay! Okay, I'll go back! Just put the chainsaw down!"

The cold breeze started to slow my muscles, growing arctic and painful. A needle-like chill infiltrated my skin and started to seep into my bones, rendering my body clumsy, and not fit for a chase. I stumbled, tripping over my own two feet. I held my arms out, bracing myself for the fall, but steady hands caught me before the floor did.

The noisy chaos of the chainsaw was gone, and I found myself righted by my superhero who had like, the best chin in the whole world. He looked down on me with something akin to pride and gave me half a smile – which as it turns out, was just enough. He released me, chucked my shoulder and said, "See? Told you I was real."

I let out a short laugh, but it was marred by the cold that swirled through me. With rapidly stiffening arms, I reached up and looped my hands around his neck, squeezing him tight to thank him for the tough love. I silently begged him not to leave me when I returned to my life, and it all fell apart. "Tell me it gets better."

"Candarian demons haven't killed me yet. I've got high

hopes for your ending, too." He wrapped his arms around me, and somehow that simple motion gave me just enough of my bearings to hold my head up, no matter how grim my ending turned out. He gave me another tight squeeze, flooding my icy limbs with optimism that I needed at least one of us to feel. "You did good, kid. Now go on home."

35

WASTING HIS LOVE ON ME

The ice in my veins wasn't unfamiliar, but it was painful. The first sound I heard when the world started coming back to me with all its lights and colors was my own scream – not a totally reassuring sound that I'd made the right choice.

"It's working! I knew it! I'm here, love. Don't worry. We had to do something drastic to wake you."

I winced at the leap from total darkness to too many lights and sounds. My eyes squinched shut as the ice tore at my insides, raking a path along my ribcage that froze me in my supine position.

"Take the corroded soul out slowly," I heard Ezra command Von. "Work in layers, otherwise you'll put her under all over again. We need her awake, even if she's in pain."

It was as if the cold was being peeled back like single

pages from a notebook, not giving me much relief as I shouted incoherently.

Von's hand was warm, spreading heated honey through my arm that slowly trickled into my torso, taking over the real estate the ice had claimed. Mason's grip on my other hand was reassuring, letting me know that no matter where I ran, they would come for me.

It was incredible, and I didn't deserve it. "No," I protested, trying to slide my hand out. The pain was my penance, and I wouldn't beg out of it.

"It's me, October! You're safe here. We're in the hospital, and everything's going to be alright," Mason assured me.

Von's voice made me ache. "Breathe through the pain, darling. Come back to us."

More warmth. More honey. More love that only made me feel sick inside that someone so wonderful was wasting his love on me. Two someones I didn't deserve.

When I was sat up, I found myself in the same hospital room as Allie. Through the too many bodies jammed into the space, I could see her still lying motionless in her bed. She'd done nothing wrong, but I was the one who got to live. I couldn't think of a worse injustice.

I STAYED AS QUIET AS I COULD THROUGHOUT THE examination performed by too many doctors and nurses, answering the bare minimum and staying in the bed while my limbs tried to figure out what the crap was going on. Ollie, Mason, Levi, Ezra and Von stayed with me throughout, asking plenty of questions that I didn't care about the answers to.

"A coma?" I asked in disbelief. I fiddled with the thin blanket that covered my lap. The hospital gown was drafty, but I welcomed the discomfort of the chill. "Are you sure?"

"For a week," Ollie confirmed. He had a haunted look in his eyes, his hair was sticking up in the back, and he smelled like he hadn't showered in days. He was sitting in the chair next to my bed, leaning forward to face me with his elbows on the edge of my mattress.

"Oh, Ollie. I'm sorry!" My heart broke for my brother, who'd buried his mother and had to watch both his sisters lie lifelessly in the same hospital room. I was encumbered by an IV sticking out of my hand, but somehow I managed to hug him when he stood to grip me.

Ollie's rare display of tears fell into my hair, his words coming out angrily through gritted teeth. "Don't you ever put me through that again! You left in the dead of night, and no one knew where you'd gone! Then you come back half dead? I don't deserve that!" His hug shook my body so I could feel his frustration with the cards I'd dealt him.

"I'm sorry, Ollie! I needed it to be over. I couldn't take one more day of it!"

"Then you take me with you. You never go off on your own like that! This is just like you, always crossing the street without holding our hands! Allie and I are here for a reason. You have to stop running headfirst into traffic. You have to stop throwing yourself away!"

I let my pride fall by the wayside and clung to my brother, sobbing incoherently into his unwashed polo. He held onto me with trembling arms, and I began to regret each minute I spent wallowing and hiding in my dark escape. "I'm sorry, Ollie." Then my brain flicked to a point of urgency that resurfaced as I started putting things in proper order again. "September," I insisted, clawing with weighted hands at my brother. "Sama had her bones!"

Ollie shook his head, trying to fake his way to calm, so I would follow suit. "That Levi guy burned her bones, so no one would try to reanimate her again." Before I could protest in panic, Ollie said, "Ezra agreed that there's no way Sama could have given you your daughter back. It was only a shell that was left, so Levi burned it, and then buried the ashes on the island. It's over." He squeezed my biceps until my chest began to expand with emotion. "It's over."

I slumped into my brother's arms, letting out a loud cry of anguish at the hope that was now dashed to pieces. I knew in the back of my mind that it had been a fragile wisp of a chance. I'd wanted it to be true, though. Ollie held me for a solid two minutes, while I unloaded what I'm sure wouldn't be the last tears shed for my daughter.

"I'm freaking out!" Ollie admitted after I pulled away to reach for a tissue. Then remembering we weren't alone, he barked at the men in the room. "Get out of here! Can't you see we're having a moment?" Ollie was never great at breaking down in public. He usually got surly to cope with his vulnerability, hence his many forays into Anger Management support groups.

Mason kissed my forehead, then Ezra followed suit before they exited. Levi bowed his head respectfully and brushed his knuckles to mine before he ducked out of the room, but Von didn't budge. In fact, he pulled up the chair Ollie had occupied and crossed his arms over his chest. "Carry on. I'll not stop you from yelling at her. But she's also not allowed out of my sight. Ezra's orders are that either Mason or I are watching her at all times. You know the rules."

Ollie grumbled and went back to hugging me. "You brought back that guy, that dad guy. Levi? What's his deal?" I could tell Ollie was trying to move on from his tears, but a few still leaked out.

"I saw him, Ollie. I watched him transform from Sandy into that dude. Sandy's been with us our whole lives. He tried to kill Sama to save me." Ollie released me and sat on the side of the bed, leaning his elbows on his knees. He was patient with me while I laid out the entire story as I remembered it, from the moment I decided I was fed up waiting for Sama to mind-warp me, to waking up in the hospital bed.

I stared at my knees as I muscled my way through the admission of everything that had happened with Finn, not sugarcoating it for the two viewers, who both hissed through clenched teeth at all the right parts. I expected Von to get up and leave, but he didn't. He sat with his hands folded over his stomach, taking in the story that punched him in his sore spots with nary a word.

I couldn't believe how much we'd both grown. I wasn't running from the truth and hiding it, and he wasn't running from me. We sat in the room after I'd finished the retelling, too shaken for eye contact.

"Is that everything, then?" Von's voice was cool, which meant he was furious.

I swallowed hard, and I sorely wished I had let Bruce Campbell chop me to bits with his chainsaw. "What else could there possibly be?" I couldn't look away from my hands that were too clean now. They deserved to be filthy, still coated in Finn's blood, but the spotlessness mocked me. *I* was the filthy one.

Ollie leaned over and kissed the top of my head. "I love you, kid." When he stood, I panicked that I'd finally pushed Ollie too far, and somehow I'd managed to max out his infinite patience.

"No, Ollie! I'm sorry. I'm so sorry! Please don't walk out. Please don't leave me!"

Ollie paused, tapping his hand to his heart like I'd shot an arrow through him. Then he patted my arm gently to reassure me that he was my brother, and he wasn't going anywhere. "I'm just going into the hallway to tell Ezra and the guys everything. This way you don't have to relive it all.

I'll give you two a minute." He slapped Von on the shoulder twice before shutting us in the room with no witnesses other than Allie, who wasn't exactly a solid buffer.

I wasn't going to be the one to speak first, since there was nothing else for me to say. I'd broken us, and I knew there was nothing I could do to fix it. I deserved to lose the man I loved – both of them.

Von broke our stalemate with a level, yet tense, tone. "I was thinking of going off to find Danny. See if I can't sort him out and get him to give up Mariang."

I kept my eyes lowered. "Okay. Makes sense." Makes sense that he would leave. I deserved it, and had seen it coming. At least he had the decency to tell me to my face this time. It was growth that came when it was too late to make much of a difference.

Then Von said something that shocked the crap outta me. "I think you should come with me. Just the two of us. Give us some time to sort this mess out."

I was sure I'd heard him wrong. My chin lifted slowly to look at him, tilting my head to the side to assess whether or not I'd hallucinated. "Sort this out? You mean us?"

"Who else would I mean?"

"I didn't think you'd want to sort anything out. I thought you'd be gone. I'm kind of surprised you're still in that chair. Thought there'd be a Von-shaped hole in the door by now."

"I'm going to be a married man. Ezra had a good sit-down with me while you were off falling in love with Finn." His words cut us both so badly that we winced in unison. Von licked his lips before continuing. "He said that marriage was in sickness and in health, for better or worse and all that. I can't imagine things getting much worse, but I figure if you can forgive me for running out on you and September before I knew she was mine, and then sleeping with Katrina on top of that, then I can eventually forgive you for Finn." He sighed, shaking his head. "I can't even be truly angry at you both, though I want to be. Finn was more committed to you than I was in the beginning. I'm almost glad for him that he got the girl in the end. Went out a victor."

My face soured. "You don't mean that."

"No, I don't. But I want to be the kind of man who does. I know you resisted him as long as you could. I know you sent him away and stayed faithful until this all blew up in your face." He chewed on his cinnamon stick. "I also know that you went to *him* with this whole Sama business, and didn't come to me."

I scoffed. "You really think I'd let you near Philip? After what he did to you, turning you against me when he stole pieces of your hair? You think I'd let him within a thousand miles of you? You're the one person I would never, ever take with me. You protect what you love, and I love you, Von. I'm just really, really bad at it. Plus, Philip was clear that you weren't invited to his Island of Adventure."

Von was quiet for a minute, his hands still folded over

his stomach. "Occasionally you are quite terrible at loving me, yes. But then other times you're exactly what I need. So here we are."

"Here we are. No one would blame you if you left."

"Do you want me to leave you?"

I looked deep into his crazy gold and blue eyes, knowing that no matter how my heart got twisted, it would always come back to Von. "No. I want you to stay, even when I push you away. I want you to love me, even when you hate me."

The corner of Von's sculpted lips turned upward. "Darling, don't you know? That's our specialty." He leaned forward and scooped up my hand, pressing his lips to the tips of my fingers. He reached into his pocket and pulled out the engagement ring I'd left in Ezra's shirt pocket. "Do you still want to be my wife?"

I nodded so vigorously, my eyeballs felt like they rattled around in my head. "I do. Von, so much. Do you really still want to marry me?"

"Always and only you." With a steady breath, Von slid the giant diamond I didn't deserve onto my finger. "I think we're going to have a lot to talk about on our trip."

36

WORST ROAD TRIP OF MY LIFE

T tapped my thumb against Terence the Taurus' window, not willing to be the first one to speak. I was the one in the doghouse, so I didn't want to make it all worse by saying the wrong thing.

"I know what you're doing," Von informed me, narrowing his eyes as he merged onto the second highway on the map. We were half an hour into our trip to bring Danny home, and so far, we'd not said a word. "You're trying to hold all the power by not speaking first. You forget I've seen you do this with that wanker, Judge."

I turned to look at him, surprised this was what he'd been stewing on for who knows how many miles. "I don't need to play games with you. I already know you hold the power in this. I'm the one who screwed things up. I'm being quiet because I don't want to piss you off. Kinda surprised you haven't dumped me on the side of the road yet. I'm just trying not to rock the boat."

Von deflated. "You really weren't pulling a power play?"

"You can't compete for power if you don't have any to start with. You really think I'd try to manipulate you like that?" I tapped the car door. "And you forget I lost to Judge. He's got a tracker on this very car, plus access to my phone calls. No, I've given up on power games."

"I don't know which way is up anymore. The more I think about you sneaking off to meet up with Finn, of all people, the angrier I get." He held up his hand in case I was going to plead my case, but I assure you, I was not. He'd heard my side of things. He didn't have to take them at face value, and I wasn't about to beg him to understand my craziness. I barely understood it myself. "Before you get all defensive, I know you did it to keep Mason and me safe. But it hurt me, Peach. You going off like that hurt me. You trusted Finn to keep you from harm, but not me. What more do I have to do? Save your life again? How many times until you realize that I'm in this with you?"

This time he waited for a response, but I still didn't give him one. He had every right to be angry at me. I wasn't about to defend myself if I knew I belonged with my nose in the corner.

Von kept on his rant, though it was nothing I hadn't heard before, and nothing he wasn't absolutely right on. True enough, I hadn't trusted him. When he'd left me after I'd gotten pregnant, it was all I could do to let him out of my sight without the nagging feeling coming over me that he might not come back. I didn't bring that up. I knew blame-shifting wouldn't get us anywhere.

It was another hour of that before he even got to the whole me falling in love with Finn part. "You knew he was in love with you. We all knew it, and you went to him anyway. If you know someone's going to try to break us up, you get away from that person. Why do you think I don't muck about with Katrina anymore? Because I know she'd try to break us up. If you love something, you protect it." He shook his head. "You may love me, but you didn't protect our relationship from Finn. You didn't do all you could to make it clear to him that you weren't an option."

Again, I didn't respond, but simply stared out the window and watched the trees fly past as he drove along the freeway. He was right, and the sucky part about it was that I didn't know for sure how I would do things differently if I was given a redo. Part of me had loved Finn. It had just taken me too long to realize it, and in the end, it changed nothing. My love hadn't saved Finn.

"Aren't you going to say anything?" he asked, throwing out his hand in frustration. "It's not going to work if you hide yourself from me yet again. Not sorting this out with me? It's another form of hiding."

I moved my gaze to the license plate of the car in front of us, wishing I hadn't agreed to a road trip to find Danny without a referee to monitor our fight. There was nowhere to run from our many issues. We were trapped in the car, and there was no way out but forward, through the mess. I began to understand Von's brilliance in planning it to be exactly this way. Neither of us could run now.

I cleared my throat. "I'm not saying much because I won't defend myself. You're right on all of it. I should've been more careful. I want to marry you, and I was leaving part of myself open to Finn. If I hadn't gone to him, he'd still be alive. You think I don't regret going to him every single minute of every day? I got to live, and he didn't. I mean, where's the logic in that? Why do I get to live and he doesn't? It was my stupid idea, and he tried to talk me out of it. He wanted to go to the council. He wanted to take me back to Ezra. He followed me to the end because we loved each other." Admitting our love to Von was nearly impossible, but I managed the feat, owning up to the awful things I'd done to all three of us. "A great warrior died because he was stupid enough to fall in love with me. So, you know, I'd invest in life insurance now, if I was you."

Von deflated, and then choked the steering wheel to redirect his rage so he could be kind. I don't know where he found the strength to be good to me, but it was never clearer that I didn't deserve him than when he replied with a simple, "You didn't kill Finn; Sama did. Finn loved you enough not to let you murder the man who'd tortured your mind so much. Even if you never gave him a second look, he would've kept trying to keep you safe and win your heart till the very end – even if there was no hope of a victory."

"You can't know that."

"Of course I can. I recognize it in him because that same madness is in me. I'll fight with you and for you until the end, even if you're gazing at another man while I'm bleeding and dying for you."

I turned my head to look out the window so Von didn't see my eyes mist over. "I'm so sorry I did this to us. I'm sorry I got Finn killed. I'm sorry for Bishop, for Garrick, for Mariang and Bev. For September. I'm sorry for all of it."

"I know, love. It's survivor's guilt, and it'll pass." His nose scrunched. "What could you have possibly done to feel guilt over Mariang's death? You actually gave our sister a peaceful passing. That's more than any of us could do for her."

"Mariang might not have wanted to get pregnant so soon if she hadn't had to help me with my pregnancy so much. I was the one who suggested it to her in the first place while I was taking that stupid pregnancy test. It was right after the healing waters made her all better. I'm the one who pointed out that she should get a little crawler of her own. Philip warned me that it was harder for an Omen to carry a baby, but I didn't realize he was real at the time, so I didn't take it seriously. If I hadn't told her she should talk to Danny about having a baby, then she might not've..."

Von surprised me by laughing. "I hope you're joking. Mariang wanted buckets of children with Danny from the very beginning. She only told him no and wouldn't marry him for so long because she was ill. Either way, she would've died. It's horrible, but it's not your fault. None of it was your fault. You cheated on me and fell in love with another man. *That's* your fault. Only that."

I was quiet for a few moments. "Even if that was true, it's enough to sink me. I should've stayed away from Finn."

"Yes, you should've." Von turned off the freeway and pulled into a hotel. He cut the engine and reached over to hold my hand. "Let's be done with it now."

KABAYO IN A BLOND WIG

I awoke to Von wrapped around me, using my hip like a body pillow he'd decided sometime in the night to sling his leg over. Though I was caged in and twisted in his unconscious grip, I didn't dare move. I didn't trust that he wouldn't run the second he woke up. So I stayed hemmed in by Von's arm and leg, his breath on my neck and his lips resting open against my skin.

When half an hour went by and I couldn't hold my bladder anymore, I carefully extricated myself from him and got ready for the day. I quietly headed down to the continental breakfast I'd seen advertised in the lobby.

I loaded up on all the staples, though I was eating more for fuel than desire. I assembled a tray and brought it up to the room for us to enjoy together, hoping I'd selected enough of whatever Von happened to wake up craving.

I expected him to be asleep still; I hadn't been gone

that long. When I opened the door, Von was sitting on the edge of the bed, holding his phone with a hopeless expression. His shoulders relaxed when I came in, and set the tray on the desk that was too narrow to do any actual work on. "You alright?"

Von shook his head, not bothering to hide his confusion. "Is this what I did to you? When I left after I found out you were pregnant, did it feel like this?"

I blinked at him, a little bowled over at the plunge into the serious first thing in the morning. "I don't know. How do you feel?"

"Anxious when I wake up and you're not there. Rolling over expecting you to be in bed with me, but being completely alone. Wondering why you left, what I did to push you away, and not sure if you're ever coming back."

"Jeez, Von. I was just getting you breakfast."

"Last time I went to sleep with you in my arms and woke up alone, you were in an entire other world, snogging another man while I searched for you like a bloody fool." He rubbed his chest to soothe the ache there. "I guess it's going to take me some time."

The waffles I'd heated for us didn't look quite so appetizing anymore. "Is this what it's like to be in love?" My melancholy was palpable as I leaned my hip to the side of the desk.

"No. This is what it's like to love poorly. I shouldn't have left you, November."

I folded my arms over my chest. "Back atcha. I know

this is too little too late, but I won't leave you out of my plans anymore. We're going to be married. I think there's some kind of rule about that."

Von tilted his head up at me and smiled. I don't know how he mustered up a smile for me, but there it was, gorgeous as the morning sunshine that I desperately needed, so I could feel goodness in my bones again. "We are going to be married. Maybe we should set a date for it, yeah? Make it all official. Mum informed me that a woman doesn't feel settled in the engagement until there's a date set."

"Please always start off conversations about our future together with 'my mum said'. It's dead sexy."

Von chuckled, standing up to stretch. He tossed his phone on the bed and made his way over to me, looking far too good in such simple clothing. Boxer briefs and a t-shirt, and I was ogling like a star-struck teenager. "When do you want to be married, love?"

"Today, tomorrow. Makes no difference to me." My mouth drew to the side as I thought through my answer.

"Tell me what you're thinking. I know when you're holding yourself back. Be honest."

I shrugged, looking down as he tucked a lock of hair behind my ear. He made me feel precious, even when I knew I was bumbling one of our few good moments. "If I get a say in it, then I'd want Allie to stand up with me. I'd want Ollie to walk me down the aisle." I cleared my throat.

"I'd want Ezra and Mason there. And Levi. Is it okay to want Ollie to walk me down the aisle if Levi's there? Or should I just..." I crossed my arms over my chest and chewed on the inside of my lip. "It doesn't matter to me. Let's just go to city hall and be done with it. We can do it on the way to bringing Danny home. A couple of signatures, and blammo. Eternal bliss."

Von tsked me, tracing my lower lip with his thumb. "You little liar. You want a wedding. You want Ollie to walk you down the aisle and all your family to be there."

"Oh, hush. It's fine. Like I said, whatever's easiest. I just don't want any blowback from Ollie if I get married without him there to see it."

Von's teasing smile toyed with me. "You want to wear a white dress, and have everyone adore you for the virginal beauty you are."

I bent my head down, my arms banded around my stomach. "I don't feel virginal. I feel dirty. My body's different now. I mean, I've had a baby already. Let's just sign the marriage certificate and be done with it. I don't need the charade."

Von drew my hair back into his fist, tugging my head up so I couldn't stare at my shoes anymore. "Don't talk about my bride like that. Now tell me what you want."

"Just you. Everything else is whipped cream. Nice, but I don't need it."

He shook his head at me, an impish smile playing on

his lips. "What do you want? In twenty years, after life's been positively boring for two decades for us, you'll be sitting in a nail salon and talking to our daughter. She'll ask you what our wedding was like, and you'll say… You'll say you went with whatever's easiest? What are you going to tell our daughter about our wedding day?" He brought his cheek to mine, letting my hair fall down over my shoulders. He slid my hand into his and coiled his other arm around my waist, slowly turning us to a melody only he heard. "Close your eyes, Peach."

I humored him, grateful he was willing to clear the gap between us, and that he wanted me near him. We turned slowly, his hips leading me in uncomplicated steps. My feet trusted him, so my heart started to let go of its fear, too. I'd been married to my worry, and I knew that if I truly wanted to marry Von, I'd have to divorce myself from my first obsession.

"Close your eyes and tell me what you see on our wedding day. Tell me what you'll say to our daughter."

Insecurity threatened to overtake me, but I ventured on, trusting that Von wouldn't leave if I asked for too much. My admission came out in a whisper I prayed he wouldn't make me repeat. "There's lilies. White lilies tied with a blue ribbon."

I could feel his cheek lifting to smile against mine. "I like lilies. Tell me more. Who's there?"

"Ollie's friends. Darius. Terence. Brenden. The warden. The council. Mariang. My family. Your family. Levi giving me fatherly advice before the vows. Ollie walking me down the aisle, but not a big aisle. Just a small church." I dug deep for the things I really wanted, but didn't want to say to anyone. "Ezra marries us." I swallowed hard. "I'd want Judge there. I'd want him to see me walk down the aisle and be proud of me." I squeezed Von's hand through the painful admission that after all these years, I still had a little sister complex that made me seek out Judge's approval. "But that wouldn't happen. Judge thinks falling in love is stupid. He would never come to a wedding, least of all mine."

"Go on. I'm listening." Von was gentle with me when I was fragile, stepping out on a limb I was unsure could hold all my hopes and dreams.

"Penny and Anastasia wearing matching dresses. Allie in a gorgeous yellow dress that she'll make herself, because she's just that good. Maybe she could make my wedding dress." My eyes opened on that last note, and I dropped Von's hands, stepping back to break us from our dance. "But it's not real, Von. I can't have those things."

"Says who? I can find you white lilies easy enough."

"Kabayo can't pal around with Ollie's friends, for one. He looks like a horse. They'd freak out. Ollie's only known Levi for a week? Week and a half? And he's barely able to look at him. He's got some man of the house thing he's holding over Levi, and I get it, but the two of them working together for a whole day? I don't see that happening any time soon." I ran my fingers through my hair, trying to hold myself together. "And Allie's in a coma. No matter what kind of wedding we have, my sister won't be there for it. Neither of my sisters can be there. I'd finally be in a dress, and Mariang wouldn't get to see it."

"Then we'll wait," Von replied, as if this was a simple fix. "Sure, we can't bring people back from the dead, but we can get most of those people there. Penny and Anastasia would look smashing in matching dresses. I didn't even think about that. Ollie and Levi will sort things out. It's not even been two weeks, remember. Ollie doesn't trust easily, so it'll take him some time. And as for Judge? Well, he might intimidate with guns, but he doesn't know how truly terrifying fangs can be. I think it's time he gets to know my true nature."

I let out an incredulous chuckle at the thought of introducing Judge to Terraway. "What about the other stuff?"

"Easy. We'll throw a blond wig on Kabayo. No one will ever be able to tell he's not human."

I snorted at the mental image. "Wow, you totally solved it." I cupped his face and kissed his lips, taking a chance on tenderness, since he was being so sweet. "Thanks for making a joke."

"I'm serious about the blond wig." Von leaned his forehead to mine, resuming our slow dance. "As for Allie, I say we wait until she wakes up. You're right; Allie deserves to see you get married, and you deserve to be able to have as much family there as you can get."

We turned a few more beats before I rested my head against his chest. "Von?"

"November?"

"I stinking love you, you know."

He grinned, and the light in his eyes was genuine, giving me hope that one day the world wouldn't be filled with such dark limitations. "And right you are to love me. I'm only standing here in my knickers, promising you the wedding of your dreams."

"You and your sexy British words. You know how that gets me all hot and bothered. Say it again."

I meant it as a joke, but Von yanked me closer and whispered in my ear, "Knickers." Then he lowered me to the bed and climbed atop me, kissing his way up my torso until his lips made themselves at home in my neck. My eyes rolled back in my head when he whispered, "Bangers and mash."

I snorted, but was quickly brought back to the moment when his lips sucked on my neck again, harder this time. His lips controlled every nerve ending on my body, turning me into a live wire that sparked easily for him. He waited for my back to arch before saying in a seductive voice, "Let's take a ride on the tube and watch the telly."

"Oh, shut up and kiss me, you dork!"

Von sat up, his knees on either side of my thighs as he looked down at me with a smirk that had too much smug seduction laced into the edges. He lifted my left hand and kissed the ring he'd given me. "Cheers, Mrs. Vandershot."

That was about all I could take. I reached out and yanked him down by the front of his t-shirt, tearing it over his head and throwing it across the room, as if the material offended me. My hands were magnets to his warm skin, and though he wanted to make light of the sweetness blooming between us, I wanted to make a mess of the sheets, which is exactly what we did until checkout.

DANNY'S CRACK HOUSE

*V*on was far more chipper on the rest of the drive to the mystery destination only he knew. "If I told you, you might sneak off to find Danny without me. Then we'd be right back at square one, and I honestly can't handle another serious conversation." He lifted his right hand off the steering wheel and pointed to his lips. "This face is far better put to use with the levity."

"Would it help if I whined and asked how many minutes until we get there?"

"You have too many layers of clothing on for me to find that charming."

I chuckled at his attempt to lighten the mood. "Thinking about our honeymoon already?"

"Darling, I never stop thinking about it. In fact, I was debating whether or not I should add something about your glorious naked body into my wedding vows."

"Sure, I think Ollie could use a heart attack on my wedding day."

Von kept his eyes on the road while he reached over and picked up my hand to kiss my knuckles. "We'll be there in five minutes, love."

"Oh, that's not bad."

"It's not, but five minutes is code for two more hours. Rest a bit, November. We reaped too many people this morning, and you'll need your strength for this."

"Six people isn't too many. I can handle it. Plus, we need to stay on top of the count."

"I know, I know. Still, it's a good thing we're on a long drive. Take the break while we have it."

I settled into the seat as Von drove, giving me full control of the radio and the flow of the banter until he pulled onto a dead-end street with only dilapidated houses I didn't want to go searching through. "Danny's not here. He's used to the mansion. He wouldn't stay in any of these. They're completely falling apart. I mean, look at that one. The windows are all busted out and boarded up. He's not in there."

Von took out his cell phone and tapped the screen a few times. "Courtesy of your fairy godfather."

"Huh?"

"Judge gave me the idea. I put a tracker in Danny's cell phone after Mariang died. I was worried he'd take off, and we wouldn't be able to find him. Of course, I didn't imagine he'd bring a Woman in White along for the ride, but to each his own."

"You've had a tracker on Danny this entire time? Why are we only just now looking for him?"

"It only works if his phone's turned on. I suggested the road trip the very day I saw it. Sure, we had to wait for the clean bill of health from your doctors, but we left right after that."

I gaped at him. "I can't believe you've been sitting on information like that this entire time! Seriously?"

"You want I should say something adorably British to charm my way out of your wrath?"

"Maybe after we get Danny in the car. Try to work the word 'water' into your seduction. I love the way you say it – like James Bond on a mission. Melts me every time."

Von chuckled. "Truly? The way I say 'water' does it for you? I'll have to remember that one."

"Stop trying to seduce me. We're on a mission."

"Okay. Now remember, I'm dealing with Mariang, and you're to get Danny out of there. Get him to give you her finger, if you can. Then I'll burn the finger, and she'll be able to rest."

"Why can't I just burn the finger if I'm the one getting it from Danny?" I grimaced. "I hope that's the most terrible sentence I've ever had to say."

Von stared ahead at the once-green house that was half burned to black on the outside. "Because Danny already hates me. There's no point in you taking Mariang away from him. Then he'd blame you for all of eternity. You saw what happened when I made sure our dad never came back. He never forgave me for that. Danny adores you. I don't want to take you away from him. You're good for my surly brother. He needs someone he trusts. I've seen it; Danny loves you – and he doesn't indulge in that emotion often."

"You're too good to him."

Von cast me half a smile. "That's the thing about being the older brother. You take the blame if it'll make things easier on your family. Remember that and be patient with Ollie the next time you two have a row." He took a steadying breath and placed his hand on the car door. "Find the finger as quick as you can. I don't fancy stabbing our sweet Mariang through the heart."

"Huh?"

He punched his fist to his chest. "Silver blade through the heart. That's the only way to kill a Woman in White without burning the piece of flesh she's tied to. So best find the finger quick. Are you ready?"

"I'm not sure that really matters, does it?"

"That's the spirit. Hold tight to me for now. I've got this."

Von and I both drew our knives, holding them to our sides as we trotted down the sidewalk that had no doubt seen its fair share of illegal weaponry. The forgotten buildings almost looked haunted by the violence they'd had to witness, weary from their broken windows and the gaping holes in the dulled siding. Von's eyebrows rose when he tried the knob to the busted-up front door, and it actually opened for us. "Danny? Danny boy, it's me. November and I've come to take you home. Miss your cheery smile, we do."

I heard a weak groan that made my heart race. Without waiting for Von, I bolted over the creaky floorboards, ignoring the spider webs, and the holes in the walls and the ceilings as I ran through the house. "Danny?"

I turned the corner and gasped at the sight I didn't expect to smack me in the face with its brutality. Danny was lying on the warped wooden floor, his naked torso covered in bloody slashes. He had a black eye, bruises peppering his ribs, and looked like he hadn't eaten in days. "Danny!" I ran to him, falling to my knees as my fingers flitted over his body to assess the damage. "We've got to get you out of here. Did you get jumped? What happened?"

His left eye was swollen shut, but his right one took in my form in the room that was lit only by the sunlight filtering through a smashed-out window. "October? What are you doing here?"

"I'm freaking out, is what I'm doing here! Can I sit you up? Do you think anything's broken?"

"You have to go," Danny choked out, holding his side in pain when he tried to budge enough to sit up. "She'll see you and come after you."

"Mariang? Oh, honey. We've got to take you home."

"Just leave me. It's too late."

I pressed on a few points to check his organs for signs of internal distress, assessing his pallor and heartrate that was surprisingly steady. "You'll heal from this beating. I don't think anything vital's been hit. But we need to get you to a hospital."

"I don't want to go home," he admitted, his voice scratchy. "Life. All of it. It's too late for me. I did everything I could, and I still failed. She still died."

My heart broke for the solid man who truly had sacrificed his life so Mariang could have one. "Sweetheart, I'm taking you home now. You aren't going to die in here like this, all alone. You've got a daughter back home waiting for you. You've got a whole family who loves you and needs looking after. You're not done guarding the things you love. We're still here, and we need you." I managed to find an unbeaten part of his face, and dragged my thumb across the crest of his cheekbone to remind him that the world still had gentle parts to it; not everything would be war and loss. I think we both needed that little reminder. "*I* need you, Danny. You're my big brother. Aren't you going to come home and look after me? Let me look after you?"

Danny sucked in a panicked breath when he took in my face more fully as I shifted into the sliver of light. "You have to go! You can't be here. If she sees, she'll come after you."

"Where's the finger, Danny?"

He slowly shook his head, still lying on his side holding his ribs. "I can't give it to you. It's fixable. She's fixable. I know her, and she'd never hurt me. Just give me some time. She's in there, I know it."

"This can't be how your life turns out. Mariang wouldn't want this for you. She loved you, honey. She wouldn't want you bleeding on the floor of an abandoned crack house, trying to put together a puzzle that's only half there. She's gone, and you have to let her go."

"You don't understand! No one understands!" He lifted a hand with dried blood caking the knuckles and pushed it to his chest. "It hurts too much. Being so tied to someone and then have them ripped away from you? I had to bring her back! Everyone was just giving up. I would never give up on her! She's my w-wife." His voice quavered on the last note, but then stopped with a loud gasp. "Run!"

I didn't have time to turn around. The next thing I knew, I was being launched through the air toward a wall with an aged blood splatter. My shoulder broke through the wood, separating me from Finn's balisong blade before I smacked to the ground.

GIVING ME THE FINGER

"Don't take what's mine!" Mariang screeched.

I thought I was prepared for freaky. I mean, I've seen every episode of the X-Files at least once – twice, if the Smoking Man made an appearance. But nothing Bruce Campbell or David Duchovny tried to prepare me for compared to the translucent shape of Mariang. Her once serene face was twisted in malice that looked unnatural on the beautiful ballerina. She had holes in her blue-white skin now that looked like leprosy, and her eyes were glaring at me with boiling rage.

I held up shaking hands to show her I wasn't about to take anything that belonged to her.

Except her finger. She got me there.

"Hey, Mariang. You look great. You and Danny decide to move out on your own?" I tried to be conversational to hide my terror, but I knew it was a bad act. My hands were shaking as I sat up and leaned against the wall she'd thrown me into.

Mariang was levitating five inches off the ground, which made her rage seem all the more terrifying. "This is our house, not yours! You're trying to steal Danny away from me!"

"No!" Danny shouted, somehow crawling towards me through his haze of pain, and collapsing twice on his face along the way. "Don't hurt her. October just came to visit. I thought you'd be happy to see her again."

The force of Mariang's shrill screams shook my insides, reverberating agony of all sorts through my chest. "I don't want to see her! Did I ask you to bring her here? When were you making phone calls without me? Who else have you been calling?"

This wasn't Mariang. This was a woman possessed. The real Mariang would be horrified to hear such cruel and possessive words coming out of her mouth. I fumbled around in the dim light for my knife, but it was too far away.

"Then she'll leave right now. I thought you'd like to see your family, but if you don't, they can go. Go on, October." Danny jerked his head toward the door and lowered his voice. "This is my fight. I won't see you die like this."

"I won't see you die at all," I argued, seeing Von inching toward Mariang from behind. "I need her finger, Danny."

"Give me more time to fix her. I need more time."

"She won't give you more time! Don't you get that? You're going to die in here if we don't get you out."

Mariang moved from floating in the entryway to standing in front of us, towering over us with her diminutive form, arms akimbo. "Danny's not going anywhere. You want a finger?" She reached down and grabbed his cast aside shirt, using it to shield her hand from the silver as she bent to pick up my knife. "I'll give you a finger."

She turned on a dime and whirled on Von, slashing him across the chest and ignoring my scream. Then she jerked Danny forward with such surprising strength, I couldn't make sense of it all. She dragged Danny so he was face-down on the floor, flattened his hand to the ground and brought the knife down hard on his pinky finger.

I'm not sure whose howls were louder – the three of us were all losing our minds. Mariang smiled darkly as she tossed Danny's pinky finger at me, smacking me in the cheek with it. Disgust and horror rang through my body. Without a doubt, I knew that no matter how much time we gave Danny, he would never be able to reason with the unstable spirit he'd brought back. My heart broke for Danny. He'd given up everything to save her, and now he was donating his own body parts to the cause.

It was enough.

Though Von was injured, something ferocious rallied in him at the sight of his little brother so thoroughly destroyed. He ignored his bleeding chest and lunged for Mariang, tackling her to the ground.

I rolled Danny's little finger in the hem of the forgotten shirt next to my balisong blade, and ran to Danny's side, using the filthy material to stem the bleeding from his hand. He yelled his agony into the floor, not paying attention to my pat down. I shoved my hand into the front pocket of his jeans and pulled out a plastic bag with a zip seal. I didn't need any light to tell me I'd found Mariang's rotting finger.

"Von, the lighter!" I shouted into the chaos.

Von was wrestling the dainty Mariang on the floor – and losing. I tossed my conscience aside completely and ran over to the fray, catching her jaw with my shoe. "I'm sorry!" I cried as my sweet ballerina went flying backwards. "Von, I need the lighter!"

Von's hands were unsteady as he fumbled in the pocket of his jeans for the gold rectangle that we needed to end the madness. I ran to Danny to act as sentry for my brother and flipped open the lighter, clicking up the flame. The dancing yellow and white heat clung to the plastic. I rested the carnage on the floor, lighting all four corners of the bag in hopes it would burn before Mariang could rally.

Von stood to his feet, tears in his eyes and a knife in his hand. "I love you, little sister. It's time to rest now." He shot forward, but she was ready, throwing him off of her as if he was merely the family pet – nothing more than a nuisance.

She hissed at the small nick Von's silver blade had managed to cut into her arm.

I silently urged the flame on, holding the lighter to her severed finger through the plastic to speed things along. The stench of melting Ziploc and flesh made vomit churn in my gut, but I muscled through the horror as best I could.

Mariang screeched, and the sound had a metallic bite to it as she flew at Von.

I saw the fear in his eyes that was mingled with agony at having to play such an instrumental role in his sister's final moments. I saw the unending craze of malice in her expression as her fingers wrapped around his neck, choking the man I loved above all others.

"No!" I didn't think it through; I simply acted. With my balisong blade clutched in my hand, I charged Mariang, wrapping my arm around her throat and jerking her backward. Finn's blade protected me once more – his love for me extending well past his shortened lifespan. I sacrificed what was left of my youth and plunged the dagger into Mariang's heart through her back.

I closed my eyes as my bearings and my soul crumbled at Mariang's dainty cry. It sounded too human, too distressed. I would've done anything to save her if she was actually alive. I realized that no matter what distractions and barriers separated me from Von, I had no limits when it came to him. I would stab my own sister in the back if it would help him breathe easier.

I was the worst kind of person.

I stumbled back in horror at what I'd done, dropping the knife to the floor with a clatter as I bolted out the door. I didn't know how far I had to go to outrun myself, but I knew I couldn't face my actions.

So I ran, leaving Von to clean up my mess, as Mariang's severed finger burned away.

40

CHECKING IN AND CHECKING OUT

Danny was a bloody and bruised mess by the time Von dragged his brother to the car, found his severed finger, and located me four blocks away. He'd tried to coax me into the car with assurances that it wasn't my fault, that I'd saved his life and Danny's. The ticket that finally worked was when he said that Danny might not make it to the hospital, that he needed a nurse to keep him stable.

I held an unconscious Danny upright in the backseat of the car, bracing myself on the door when Von drove through the streets like a maniac to the nearest hospital. I helped Von get his besotted brother into a wheelchair and checked him in.

Then something happened to me. Something valuable and precious to my sanity shattered in my psyche. I snapped as I handed over Danny's manky finger that was wrapped in the bloodied shirt. My ears felt like they had cotton inside them, and my mouth went dry. My legs didn't have a thought to them when I started walking. My feet moved on autopilot as I stumbled unblinking out of the emergency room and into the parking lot. Von was tending to Danny and answering the doctors' questions as I ambled toward the main street, moving along the side of the road that led to the freeway. Slowly my legs climbed up the embankment toward the steady flow of post-rush hour traffic.

I'd lost Finn, and now I'd murdered Mariang. There was no glossing over that one, as everyone tried to do with Finn's death at my hands. I'd stabbed my sister, who had only ever loved me in her shortened life.

My feet dragged along the pebbled ground as I walked along the freeway, in the throes of shock. I couldn't blink or think beyond putting one foot in front of the other. The steady forward motion was all I could do, and I had no idea why I was even doing it. Like the numbed souls in Terraway who made their pilgrimage to Sombi, I was dead inside. I wanted to go to Von, and though part of me knew he was back at the hospital, I moved forward, as if he was somehow ahead of me.

I tripped on a crack in the pavement and pitched forward. The pain of smacking my hands and knees on the ground ricocheted up my limbs. Still it did nothing to bring me back to sanity. I picked myself up and moved forward, ignoring the trickle of blood that slowly oozed from my left kneecap. I couldn't bring myself to care about the spots of red that wept from the heel of my hand, and dripped down through my filthy fingers.

I wasn't sure where I was going; I only knew I couldn't go back to the person I'd once been.

~

I DON'T KNOW HOW LONG I WALKED BEFORE A CAR PULLED TO the side of the road ahead of me, blocking my steady path. Von got out and charged at me, his face a mix of worry and fury. "October! What are you doing out here? Are you so desperate to run out on me that you'd hitchhike home? Are you completely mental?"

Von was livid, but I didn't feel myself rise up in defense. In fact, I didn't feel anything. Von ran to me, angry and afraid, but I had no emotional response to his pain. I'd somehow finally reached some sort of pain maximum, and was numb to it all. Mariang, Finn, September, Bishop, Bev – all of it was white noise, blurring my vision and keeping me from processing the rant Von was spewing at me.

"I had to call Judge – Judge! I phoned that tosser to get him to use the tracker on your cell to find you." Von jerked my chin up, snapping his fingers in front of my vision, his eyes widening in sudden alarm. "Can you hear me at all?"

I could hear him, but it made no difference. Everyone was still dead. Allie was still in a coma. I'd slept with the king of all the bad guys. I was dirty. I was filthy.

I was trash, as I'd always suspected.

My feet left the ground, and I was carried past the rushing cars, who all had better things to do that morning. Von buckled me into the car, holding my hand as he chanted panicked oaths of loyalty over and over that I couldn't hear, and couldn't feel.

Suddenly we were back at the hospital, and I was put onto a gurney next to Danny, who looked more dead than alive.

Danny was wheeled away, I'm guessing to sew his finger back on, and I was left staring at the ceiling. "I have to go with Danny, but I can't leave you to wander off." Von looked torn, and at the utter end of his rope. "Forgive me, love, but you need to go to sleep. I'll be back for you just as soon as Danny's out of surgery."

I knew I was looking straight into his face, his one golden eye and one blue eye taking in my blank expression with unswerving devotion. I guessed he was waiting for me to say something, but there were no words.

"Go to sleep, darling." Von placed his hand on mine and pressed his lips to my forehead. I felt the gentle waves of pulling relax my limbs, melting me to the thin mattress and taking me away from the coldness of my world.

41

WAKING UP TO HOME

I awoke in the mansion, blinking up at the ceiling in confusion. I didn't know how I'd gotten there, or even when I'd been driven home. I didn't know what day it was, or anything that might clue me in to the shifting life I somehow still had ownership of. I turned my head and saw Levi sitting in a chair at the side of my bed, his head bowed. Mason was next to him, his eyes closed and his hands folded over his lap.

My limbs ached and creaked like the Tin Man as I sat up on my elbows, frowning at the too many questions that didn't have solid answers. "Levi?" I whispered, unsure if I was allowed to call him by his first name, or if he preferred Sandy or Dad.

Levi's head shot up, and in the next breath, he was standing, bent over me to help me sit upright against the headboard. "You're awake? You're finally awake?" He slapped Mason across the stomach, jerking him to consciousness. "October's awake."

Mason was at my other side in the next instant, pressing a glass of water to my lips. After I took a few sips, he set the glass on the nightstand. Mason's arms wrapped around me a cocoon of the safest love. I breathed in and out, inhaling the shelter I never wanted to live another second without. "Don't do that ever again. I don't know if Von pulled too hard, or if you were just that far gone, but you're not allowed to check out like that."

"How long was I out?"

"Two days," Levi informed me, taking in my pallor and feeling my forehead.

"Whoa, seriously?" I watched him check me from head to toe, enraptured that I had a dad who'd stayed with me, taking care of me when I couldn't. The skin on his fingers was rough, the knuckles cracked from what looked like manual labor. They were dad hands, and I studied every crevice carefully. "You're here," I observed, sounding like a dummy for stating the obvious.

"Of course I am. Where else would I be? Oliver and I have been taking shifts, switching between you and Allison."

My arms were weak, but they had just enough oomph in them to lift up and wrap around his neck, pausing his examination for the hug that couldn't be delayed. I didn't have the right words, so I stuck with confessing my sins, testing to see which one would be so big that it pushed him away. "I murdered Mariang," I choked out, ashamed. "I know she was a ghost or whatever, so I didn't expect it to feel like I was actually killing her, but it did. I stabbed her in the back."

Levi's arms engulfed me in acceptance I couldn't fathom the depths of. "You did Danny and the world a favor, and put down a Woman in White. Lady Mariang has been dead for weeks; you aren't what killed her."

I didn't have a valid argument to this, but I didn't feel any more at peace about the whole thing. So Levi continued to hold me, letting me hand over my heaviness into arms that were strong enough to shoulder anything I could hurl at him. I guess that's the thing about good dads. "I've done terrible things. I may not be a good person," I warned him.

Of all things, Levi chuckled. "Yes, what a rotten girl you are. Taking care of a dog who wasn't even yours throughout your entire childhood. You can tell a lot about a person by the way they treat animals. I've known your quality for ages. No matter how you try to convince me that you're a lost cause, I won't believe it. You're mine, and I love you."

I squinched my eyes shut, unable to understand how he could claim me as his after knowing the horrible things I'd done, and the mess of a person I now was. I didn't understand it, but I needed it.

Levi and I held onto each other for as many minutes as it took for me to gather my bearings, and for him to feel like I was stable enough to release back onto the bed. "I'll get you some juice." Levi jabbed a finger at Mason. "I'll go get Von and Ezra. Don't let her fall asleep again, son. I mean it. No pulling at all."

"Yes, sir." Mason waited until Levi was gone before he slid into the bed next to me. He sat against the headboard, scooping me to him so I could lean my head in the crook of his shoulder. He sighed contentedly, as if the separation had been painful. I knew that desire well. "That's much better. I didn't feel right lying in bed with you with your father in the room. I'm having a hard time getting a read on that guy."

"I'm so glad you're here," I admitted.

"You scared me. We couldn't wake you up. If it wasn't for you talking in your sleep, I would've thought you'd slipped back into your coma."

"Talking in my sleep? Did I say anything awesome? Solve world hunger? Lay out plans to patch that pesky old hole in the ozone layer?"

Mason chuckled, and the sound warmed us both, cuddling us closer together. "You weren't all that eloquent. Mostly just called out for Ollie, Allie and Bruce Campbell. Screamed for me and Von a few times, like you were afraid someone was hurting us. You had a few nightmares that sounded decently graphic. You cried for Judge a few times, begged him not to leave you. Ripped my heart right out."

I tangled my fingers in his shirt over his chest. "I don't

want to know any more. I don't remember them, so I'm counting that as a good thing."

"Maybe that's best." Mason squeezed me, kissing my forehead before tucking my head under his chin. "Lang built you another porch swing. It's for the mansion, to match the one at your house. When you're feeling better, we can go sit in it. Built it with his own hands."

"Aw, really? He didn't have to do that. He's got a whole kingdom to worry about now."

"Yes, well, Kabayo and Lang stopped by more than a few times to check on you while you were out. They love you, kid."

I snuggled into Mason, indulging in his patchouli scent. "I love them, too."

I could feel Mason's body radiating with pride and affection when he squeezed me again. "You did it, *hani*. Danny's home safe. He's recovering, though who knows how long that'll take."

"Were they able to reattach his finger?"

"They were. Though it'll take some time before it's even a little functional."

"I'll take what I can get." I huddled closer in his nook, wishing anyone or anything in my life was big enough, strong enough to keep me safe.

"Do you want to talk about Mariang?"

"No. I don't even want to think about that. It was too terrible. Too brutal. I didn't know I was capable of that.

Scares me a little that I could just... No, I don't need to talk about it."

Mason kissed my forehead again and thumbed my hip that his arm was wrapped around. "What about Finn? You ready to talk about that?"

"I'll never want to talk about that. Not ever."

"I'm not Von, you know. You can tell me things. Private things about the men in your life. It won't send me over the edge."

I mulled this over, reasoning that he was probably right, but it was still too soon. "You're a good man."

He leaned down and pressed a closed-mouth kiss to my lips, a lazy smile coming over his unshaven features. "I'm *your* good man, so stop running out on me. I could've helped you with Sama. I could've taken you there."

"But then you'd be dead, and I couldn't live with that." I tapped my heart to let him know where his home truly was. "I love you too much to risk your safety even a little bit."

Mason looked like he wanted to protest, to make a new case for his point that we were tied by unbreakable bonds I should've trusted, but he kept his mouth shut about it. "I love you, too. And I know how much you cared for Finn."

"I said I don't want to talk about it."

The door opened, and Mason shot up from the bed to stand at attention, but then relaxed when he saw it was only Von coming in with Anastasia tucked in his arms. "Oh, I thought you were Levi." He sat back down in the bed, his arm draping around me as Von leaned down to kiss my cheek.

"You alright, love?"

"Better, now that you're here." We shared a smile that had a sigh of contentment to it, our hearts beating more easily, now that we were in the same room.

The left side of his mouth tugged upward in a half-smile that endeared me to him. "Had enough beauty sleep? You know, I think I'm going to schedule a bout of shock so I can sleep for a solid forty-eight hours. Brilliant plan, that."

"You know me, always laying down on the job. Can I hold Ana?"

"Please. She only sleeps for us and Mum. Even Ollie's losing his touch."

I glanced over at Mason. "You alright, wolf boy? You're not going to go all Matruculan and Hulk out on me, are you?"

"Nah. She's well over a month old. My stomach barely even growls anymore when she's near."

"I love you and your totally gross ways," I commented, taking Anastasia from Von. I cradled her in my arms so he could sit in the bed on my other side. "No way is she this big. I mean, I know your mama's had her since we got back from the funeral and came here, but it's only been, what, a few weeks since I've seen her? That can't be right. She's giant!"

"Giant, and taking a bottle from Ezra now. Took some

coaxing, but we tried the spit trick, and it worked like a charm."

"Spit trick? Tell me that's not something to do with actually spitting on my niece." I nuzzled my cheek to hers, taking in the inherent baby smell that made me think of pink bubblegum and fresh linen.

"Yeah, you know. You spit on your thumb, rub it on the baby's belly, and they don't resist you as much. 'As much' is the key there. She's still got a lot to say about the state of the union when she gets riled up."

My nose crinkled. "What the crap kind of baby book have you been reading? That's not a thing."

Von chuckled, leaning his head back on the headboard. "It is in Terraway. I had to do it with the twins when Mum went back to work and they were still babies. They wouldn't take a bottle from me at first, but after the spit trick, they calmed down."

"I'm not going to comment on the ridiculousness of that, or the total lack of medical backing for it."

"That's probably best. I'm much smarter than you. It's such a chore having to constantly prove it."

I reared back, nearly raising my voice in indignation, but catching myself just in time, so I didn't disturb Ana. "What? Oh, man. You've gone crazy on me. You finally cracked."

Von grinned, his smile tired as he rested his temple to mine. The three of us admired Ana for the princess she was. Mason even managed to cup her tiny head in his massive mitt without his stomach rumbling.

"I think we should be boring for a while," I announced. I was riding the high of feeling surrounded by love and acceptance. Even when I fell apart, they were there. Mason and Von didn't judge me, didn't run from my crazy, and didn't turn on me even when I pushed them away. "We've had too much adventure, and not enough television."

Mason pulled up the covers and straightened them over our laps. "I've been missing this bed. Never thought I'd get used to sleeping with two other people, but now I can't seem to relax without you."

Von blew Mason a kiss over my head. "I knew you were hot for me. Can't say I blame you." Von handed me the remote for the TV. "Pick something without a love story in it. I can't take anymore drama."

I flipped through the channels, hoping for the perfect rerun. The remote flopped on the bed when the grin spread over my face. "Mrs. Brady knows how to stop the drama dead in its tracks. This is a great episode. Oh, you are so lucky."

Von groaned. "I should've been more specific. Something from this century."

"Shh. You don't want to wake Ana, do you?" I giggled when he blew a raspberry onto my cheek in lieu of a kiss.

Mason tapped his leg to mine under the covers. "Boring sounds nice. I think Ollie could use a little boring when he gets home from sitting with Allie."

A niggling thought that had been tugging in my mind could not be ignored any longer. "Hey guys? I think boring might have to wait just one more day. I have an idea."

Von and Mason both started snoring in unison, feigning sleep to escape being caught up in another one of my plans.

42

I LOVE YOU, JUDGE

"I still maintain that we should not get our hopes up," Graham repeated as we rose in the elevator our group was packed into. It had taken a whole day to convince the Vandershot boys and the rest that my plan was worth a shot. Each hour passing felt like a hundred years.

Well, in my opinion, it was worth more than a shot. It was worth a friggin' parade. Von, Mason, Graham, Boston and I stepped out into the wing my sister was being kept in, while Ollie wheeled our prisoner who'd been blissed out for the occasion. We'd put a baseball cap on his lolling head so he didn't look quite so out of it. King Geon had been rotting away, biding his time in Kabayo's prison for over a year, tried for his long list of crimes one by one. Apparently, Kabayo had also kept him alive for sport – a topic he and I went back and forth on heatedly when I found out the previous night. I thought I'd been asking for a death row prisoner, not uncovering a whole mess of corrupt political crap that needed straightening out.

One problem at a time. Today, Allie was top priority.

Kabayo had made it clear that there would surely be an "accident" if the dethroned King Geon was let back into society, so dude was doomed either way. Kabayo didn't even ask any questions when I'd requested a prisoner in need of executing. He had Geon bound, beaten and blissed out, and then delivered to my doorstep with a bow on his chest. An actual red bow.

Mason shook his head. "I don't like that we kept this a secret from Ezra. And it took forever to shake Levi. Are you sure you don't want him here for this? Seems like the kind of thing you might want both your dads for."

"It's called plausible deniability. When I was awakened, it was done on the fly. This is planned out. If Ezra's in on it, he'll have to call on the top graduate from the Academy. I won't gamble my sister's safety on a stranger. This way when the Academy's pissed, or the council questions Ezra, he'll be able to answer honestly that he had no idea what we were up to." I glanced to my brother. "And Ollie doesn't trust Levi just yet."

Ollie harrumphed like the old man he was at heart. "I trust him fine. I'm not ready to call him 'Dad' or anything yet, but I've got no problem with him."

It was a total lie. Ollie had already started two arguments this morning alone. Levi had played the role of the adult and refused to participate in the childishness. We both knew it was Ollie's way of defending his own parental territory, while also trying to push Levi away to see if the dude would actually stick around when there was opposition.

"Well, I don't want Levi here for this either, because I don't want him mentioned if it goes south. People are already freaking out that another immortal exists. Can't have him too near a scandal, or Terraway will go on a witch hunt."

"Are we sure about this?" Graham asked again. "I mean absolutely sure there's no other way?"

Boston rolled his eyes, though I knew by his excessive throat-clearing that he was just as nervous. "It'll be fine, Graham. You're not expecting me to propose to your sister though, are you, Cherry?" he asked me with a grim expression. "I'm sure she's great and all, but I don't want anything to do with what you and Von went through to get where you are – wherever that is. I've seen how falling for his charge destroyed Danny, and I don't want that. I want to be able to have a life that doesn't revolve around opening doors for her."

I shot Boston a simpering look. "How she's not going to fall in love with you is beyond me. And it's not a given that she'll end up with either of you. We just know that Omens last longer if we have two Reapers. That's all we're asking you to do. So be cool and do what you went to school for. Polish off that nice, shiny degree and make yourself useful." When Boston looked like he wanted to argue, I held up my hand. "It's either reaping or babysitting. Which do you think you'll be better at?"

Von snorted. "Boston's never changed a nappy in his life."

"Yeah, yeah." Boston shoved his hands in his pockets and bumped his hip to mine, letting me know that I'd won. He caught my eye and nodded to let me know that eventually he'd wrap his mind around being a team player – instead of just, you know, being a player.

I reached out and held Graham's sweaty hand, offering him a small smile that still felt unnatural after all I'd been through. "You'll do fine."

"Or I'll screw it up, and your sister will die. You understand that it's pretty much fifty/fifty, yeah?"

"It is not. This is the closest chance we have to a sure thing. When you all had me reap someone when I was in my coma, it woke me up. Same thing here."

"Yeah, except that Allie's not actually been awakened yet. She doesn't know how to let go of the life force, as you've been trained to do. She could freeze from the inside out, and I'd be responsible for killing a potential Omen."

Von was on Graham's other side, his hand on his younger brother's shoulder. "I have faith in you, mate. No one's better suited for the job than you."

I nodded as we plodded down the sterile hallway. "We can't trust anyone else until word gets out that Philip died."

"Sama," Von and Mason corrected me.

"Oh, right. Sorry."

"It's alright, love." Von inclined his head to me behind Graham with a polite smile. We were very polite now, and it was killing us softly.

"Would you rather we call Alton? I'm sure he could handle it."

"No, no. I can do it."

I smirked at Graham's unwillingness to let anyone take up the position of watching over Allie.

When we reached the room that was guarded by one of Judge's goons, Graham hesitated, fists clenching apprehensively. Graham had been drafted, and he was nervous to start this new chapter, which would surely define his life. He'd asked nonstop about my preferences when it came to Omen duties, our childhood and Allie specifically every second we were together. Then he wrote down more questions when I confessed that I couldn't talk about our jagged beginnings anymore that night. Now that the day was here for me to try out my experiment, Graham was scared, and the others were anxious. I took this as a good sign. I'm not sure why.

I signed us in and asked for us not to be disturbed by the hospital staff. The redheaded nurse behind the desk gave me a polite smile. "If you could wait just a few minutes, Allison's linens are being changed, and she's getting her sponge bath."

"Sure. We'll wait over here, then." I didn't like the idea of standing around in the hallway with a beaten and blissed out former king of Terraway. The brim of the baseball cap could only hide so much. "Guys, why don't you take Geon into the bathroom while we wait." I motioned down the hall to the handicap-sized bathroom that would be a more concealed place. Mason, Ollie and Boston took Geon, but Von remained at my side with Graham, who was visibly sweating.

Von pointed to the hired hand Judge had sent to stand guard outside Allie's door. "Is he going to be a problem?"

"Oh, right. Give me a second. I'll take care of it." I pulled out my phone and dialed Judge, knowing his posted goon wouldn't take orders from me. "Judge?"

"If it isn't the girl who beat the odds. In a coma, and then walking around in the daylight again. How'd we get so lucky?"

"I chased down a leprechaun and found where he keeps his Lucky Charms."

"How are you feeling, baby girl?"

"Grateful. Thank you for the flowers. They were so pretty, I didn't even consider sending them back to you this time."

Judge chuckled while Graham gulped next to me. He stared at the door, as if he expected a horror movie clown to pop out of it any second. Judge's voice was warm, so either he'd had a successful day, or he was happy to hear from me. I pretended it was the latter. "I'm glad you're upright. Waste of a pretty face to have you not be able to talk back to me all the time. Coma doesn't suit you. Did you get the necklace?"

"I did. Expect it to be sent back tomorrow. I was too busy to put it in the mail to you today."

"Wear the necklace. It's not every day the girl who gets under my skin wakes up from her coma. Did you get the offer to take your lucky fiancé to La Luna to eat at my table? Reservations are six months out usually. Thought you two could use an evening to celebrate."

"The flowers are plenty, and they're all I'll accept. But thank you. Really, Judge. You're a drug dealer with a heart of gold."

Von snorted at my joke, and listened in closer to hear our conversation. It was a little intrusive, but I'd made Von worry too much lately, so I allowed him to hover.

My little quip made Judge laugh in that deep, abdominal way that echoed up through his whole body. He didn't often indulge in such levity, so I made it a point to draw the sweet sound out of him as often as I could. "'Drug dealer with a heart of gold.' Priceless. I'll have to remember that one," Judge said.

"I know I usually want to punch you in your smug face, but you're starting to grow on me. Lately life's been... rough. The flowers helped with that."

"So would the necklace. Wear it when you go to La

Luna." He paused, and then added, "I bought it with money pulled in from one of my restaurants. I knew you wouldn't accept it unless everything was aboveboard. See? I'm learning."

"I wondered what that weather report about icicles forming in Hell was all about."

"Wear the necklace, October."

"Maybe I will," I conceded.

"That's my girl."

I smirked, cradling the phone on my shoulder so I could squeeze Graham's sweaty hand. "I'm calling because we're trying a new treatment today for Allie. The same one they used that woke me up. It's pretty aggressive, so Allie might wake up in a couple hours."

Graham whimpered, "Or she might die!"

I brought Graham closer to my side and wrapped an arm around his waist. "So thank you for the protection detail on Allie, but it's not necessary anymore." Before he could protest, I added, "I know I still owe you for all the help you've given, having someone watch Allie when I couldn't. I'll still be the unofficial nurse for you and your brothers, but I can't go down to the prison anymore. My new job won't allow it."

Von gave me a grateful nod. He was no doubt over the moon that I was turning away from danger this time, instead of running headfirst into the pile of broken glass while pretending it didn't exist.

Judge's tone turned sharp, but his words didn't come

out hurried. "This ends when *I* say it ends, not you. You'll keep the tracker on your car, young lady." His voice dropped to barely above a whisper. He sounded younger, and a touch unsure of himself. "I've heard things in your phone calls. Things I want explained. Who's Kabayo, and why's he bringing you prisoners? What are you mixed up in this time?"

My spine stiffened at having Judge anywhere near the world that had imploded my carefully constructed life. I closed my eyes. "Nothing. And you shouldn't be listening in on my phone calls. You'll spoil the surprise of the elephant I bought you. I was going to giftwrap it and everything. Now I have to send it back."

Judge wasn't derailed by my shtick. He was too smart for that. "What's an Omen, and why does Ollie think you should stay away from windows?"

Ollie had gone a little nuts, triple-checking the locks on all the doors and windows in the mansion, hiding my car keys, taking my shoes – all things to ensure I didn't go running off again. It was sweet, if not a tad overbearing. I guess I'd driven him over the edge, so I tried to be patient while he sorted out his fear.

I sighed, not sure how much about Terraway Judge had heard, and how much I could brush off. "Ollie's got a lot on his mind these days." I cleared my throat. "The tracker you put in my cell phone actually did help Von find me when... Just thanks. It's been a long one. You... I..." Von squeezed my hand for moral support when I tripped over my words. "Judge?"

"Yeah, baby girl?"

I swallowed the lump in my throat. "Maybe I was..." I chewed on my lower lip. "This is probably neither here nor there at this point, but just so you know, I really do love you."

Judge was quiet a few beats. "Does someone have a gun to your head?"

I let out a nervous laugh in time with Von's snort. "No. I've been thinking about everything lately. You and I have put each other through too much." I inhaled a long breath before stealing myself to push into my personal life – giving Judge a little bit of myself, instead of constantly pushing him away. "My dad recently came back into the picture." I couldn't hide the hopefulness that crept into my voice. "He came back for me, Judge."

"No kidding. I'd like to meet the lowlife who abandoned you." I could practically feel him wincing at his own words. "If you tell me to go look in a mirror, I'm hanging up on you."

"I wasn't going to say a thing." I sniggered. "'Look in a mirror.' I'm funny."

"Ask your dad where he was when *I* taught you how to tie your shoes. I want a complete play-by-play of what he was up to when you were stuck with Bev all those years, and escaped to my house just to get some food in you."

"He didn't know about me," I lied, going with the most

believable explanation that didn't involve warlocks and immortals.

Judge grumbled at this, but eventually switched to his next concern. "So tell me about why you went missing. Why your fiancé called me to help track you down. That takes some balls, I'll hand it to him."

"Oh, that?" I started to wish Von and Graham weren't right next to me. "I sort of had a little breakdown. My new stepsister? She passed away. I think it was one too many things, so I sort of lost it for a bit." I leaned into Graham, who reached past his own anxiety to kiss my temple.

"I'll schedule you some time at the spa I send Sherita to every year for her Christmas gift. Would that help?" When I didn't answer, he sighed. "I'll even pay for it with one of my legitimate businesses, so you don't have to come near drug money. In fact, it goes without saying that anything I give you from here on out will be bought that way. I know that's important to you."

"You love me," I marveled, softening at the generosity that finally started not to feel so tainted. It wasn't the spa offering that did it, it wasn't even him who'd changed all that much; it was me. After all the loss I'd endured, the love that managed to survive around me was somehow easier to see.

Judge scoffed. "Are you really just now getting that? After all this time?"

"I love you, too."

Judge paused, and for a few weighted seconds, we said

nothing. We allowed a moment of silence while our ancient feud started to crumble. The destruction of all the hurt wasn't something I'd put much hope in as an adult, but now that it was here, I desperately wished I could see his face. I wanted to watch the hardness in his dark eyes melt away; it had been clouding his kindness for too long. When he finally spoke, it was with the air of taking charge. "I don't like that the only time we see each other is when you stop by the restaurant to ruin my meetings. I want to come over for a real family dinner, with Ollie, Allie, Darius, and T, when he gets out." His next words came out a grumble. "And your fiancé, I guess. It's about time I meet him."

I chewed on my lower lip. "But you already know him. The Eastside Strangler? I thought everyone had heard of him by now."

"Hilarious. I'm meeting your fiancé, your stupid new dad, and all of us are going to be one big, happy family. Understood?"

"Yes, Judge." I giggled at the back and forth. I loved provoking him, because when he got all riled up, I could see that he actually did care about me. Some days I needed someone to give a crap.

"I've been trying to call you, you know."

"What's up?"

"Darius has been different since he started seeing Ollie's friends again."

I rolled my eyes, wishing I could just go into the

hospital room with Allie already. The nurse was still in there with her, though. "It's called smiling. You should try it sometime."

"You can pay me back for all you owe me by making sure Darius gets back into step with your social life, back in tight with Ollie's friends. I'm starting to realize that my brothers need more than my life – otherwise they get restless. Then they're no good to anyone."

A gentle smile swept across my face as Von pulled me closer so I was completely engulfed in his hug. "I can make sure that happens. Terence can come by when he gets out, if he'd like." I cleared my throat and then took a deep breath. "If you promise to make Big Mike wear a pink party hat, you can stop by too, Judge. No guns, though."

I could hear the grin in Judge's tone. "Always trying to rehabilitate me."

"I want you to stay out of trouble, understand? Mama McCray wanted better for Darius and Terence. She wanted better for you, too."

"Yes, ma'am," Judge chuckled. I could picture him smiling with his head tilted back, the way he often did when I scolded him. "I'm sure I'll be seeing you around. Call if you need anything. I'll be listening in to hear more about this Terraway that seems to be causing you so much trouble."

Before I could toss him a tart response, he'd already hung up, besting me by getting in the last word. "Doggone! I hate when he wins."

Boston poked his head out of the bathroom as the guard's cell phone chirped. Right on cue, the nurse inside vacated to give us our privacy. "Shall we?"

I nodded, closing myself in Allie's hospital room with our grim crew.

43

TEARING AND RIPPING

"This is mad," Graham warned, his eyes still on me.

"If it were you in that bed, no way would I shy away from an opportunity just because it was nuts."

"You're nuts, little sister." He thumbed the engagement ring on my finger, reminding me that I had narrowly escaped losing not just Von, but all the Vandershots. I wouldn't be so careless again.

"You can do this, Graham." I pulled Finn's jagged balisong blade from the hook on my belt that I had tucked under my thin lavender jacket. I carefully flicked the blade out, and turned it over in my hand. I waited until Graham tore his eyes from Allie, which was a solid minute later. A holy hush had fallen while we all watched with rapture as Graham studied Allie's face. He was scared, sure, but beneath the nerves there was a tenderness – that same tenderness that drove him to sit with Allie when I hadn't been able to get there.

He would be a good partner for my sister; I was sure of it.

Finally I broke the silence. "I think we should get to it." I handed Graham my blade, standing aside as I waited for my sister to come back to me. I'd waited long enough. Another minute was just plain asking too much.

Graham was careful as he lifted her hand, caressing the back that was smooth and delicate from years of disuse. He wrapped her fingers around the hilt of my knife, motioning for Mason to wheel King Geon closer. Normally I wouldn't condone murdering an inmate on the fly, but as it turns out, I had very little qualms about anything moral when it came to giving Allie a better life, like she'd tried to give me. Once Lang gave his permission and confirmed there were traces of human in his ancestry, it was a done deal.

We all backed away and watched as Graham tried to get the perfect angle that wouldn't produce too much blood from our victim.

Boston was scared to touch Allie; she looked so fragile. Mason and Von moved to either side of the head of her bed and carefully lifted her to sit up. Mason rested Allie's head to his shoulder, his arm stretching behind her to keep her steady.

They took painstaking care to be gentle with Allie, knowing she was my treasure. Ollie's mouth kept opening and closing as he made several stops and starts about how our sister should be supported. Though I'd always thought of the two of them as equals, Ollie was forever a father, anxious whenever either of us skinned a knee.

It wasn't a fair fight. It wasn't even a fight. With his fingers wrapping Allie's hand around the hilt of Finn's blade, Graham thrust the steel through Geon's chest. He hit the heart and twisted the knife before retracting it. Geon made a terrible gulping noise as he tried to rouse from his blissed-out state, but the small disturbance was the most fight he had left in him. It was clear Kabayo's warden hadn't been feeding or caring for his high-profile prisoner. He'd had a round Santa face and belly when I'd seen him last, but he was gaunt now. When I'd asked Lang permission to push up his father's impending death for this cause, he'd been all too eager to see his father's torment ended swiftly.

Ollie pushed the wheelchair closer, and Graham was ready with Allie's wrist clutched in his hand. "Now back up, Von. Mason, don't touch her. It won't do for the soul to split and run into you lot again."

Boston edged Mason out from behind Allie, supporting her with a look of let's-do-this about him. "We're not taking chances with this one. Mason, you and Von stay far over there." He motioned with his chin to the opposite end of the room. The bold determination in Boston's eyes belied his insistence that he didn't want to be tied to such an adult responsibility. Boston clutched Allie's shoulders, looking more like a man and less like the assjack party boy I'd grown to love. "Do it, Graham!"

"Steady now!" I yelped as Graham shoved Allie's hand to rest on Geon's arm. My hands covered my face with my fingers parted for me to peek through. It was a historic event, awakening an Omen, and we were the only witnesses. I half-expected light beams to shoot from Allie's arm, for songs to play on harps from the heavens, or for aliens to touch down after getting the strong signal that something monumental was taking place in Room 43C.

But the aliens didn't come.

In fact, nothing at all seemed to be happening. "Is it working?" I asked when Graham and Boston were only gritting their teeth.

"I can't find it!" Boston growled, one hand around Allie's shoulders and the other cupping her forehead. "It's cold, right? The soul's supposed to be cold, and slide into us. I don't feel anything."

"Don't bruise her!" Ollie barked when Boston squeezed her shoulder. "I don't like this. This was a bad idea. Tell them to stop, October."

"Keep searching!" Graham urged, clutching Allie's wrist and knee. "I felt it dart in through her hand, but it slipped past me. It's in her, Bos, we just have to find it."

I thrilled that at least phase one of my plan was working. I stood on my toes in trepidation, scared that they might not be able to get it out before serious scarring set in. I swallowed hard when I considered the bleak possibility that the cold might remain stuck in her forever, freezing her from the inside out.

Mason smacked his forehead in frustration. "You can't wait for it to come to you, you have to tug it into your hand. Find the cold and rip it out of her." He smacked his bicep, growing anxious that they weren't performing quick enough. "Yank harder, guys. It doesn't know it's supposed to find its way to you. Allie can't tell it where to go. Even when October tried to give us that first soul, it didn't want to come to us. We had to tear it out of her." Mason lightly slapped my stomach a few times, and mimed ripping out an invisible force from my core, shaking it in his grip. "You're not being aggressive enough."

"Stop it!" Ollie shouted. "You're going to hurt her! Just leave her be."

Von intervened before a nurse could respond to the ruckus. He cast me an apologetic look as he placed his hand on Ollie's shoulder, pushing him down as he pulled a portion of the fight out of my brother. Mason helped Von lower Ollie to the floor, though my brother wasn't out completely. "Sorry, mate. It's already in motion. We explained this to you. Once she reaps a civilian of Terraway, she's got the rotting soul inside of her. It has to come out, and it has to be now."

"Von!" I admonished him with a glare he didn't seem to care about. I dropped to my knees and wrapped my arms around Ollie to ensure he stayed upright. "It's okay, Ollie. They'll find it. They won't hurt Allie."

"Allie!" he moaned softly, though that was the most he could do. As much as I was tied to Von and Mason – Allie, Ollie and I were just as much bound to each other. When one of us felt pain, we all got dinged. I held onto Ollie's hand and tried to be brave through my fear that they wouldn't get it out before she froze over.

I called out from our corner in a high-pitched command. "Remember, now. Don't pull the soul completely out until she wakes up. Wait for her to open her eyes." I silently chanted over and over, *Come on, Allie! Come on, girl! Open your eyes! Wake up!*

Von and Mason each picked a brother and coached them, encouraging them where to look for the cold and how to catch it. "It's too slippery!" Graham protested. "It's like a fish."

Boston huffed, his brows knit together. "How come I can't feel it? I mean, I can't feel it at all. Nothing."

"I've got hold of it!" Graham shouted, letting out a bray of relief.

Mason picked up Boston's hand and moved it from Allie's forehead down to where Graham's hand was at her wrist. "Try here."

Boston's eyebrows lifted. "Oh! That's incredible! Okay Graham, I'm ready."

"Not yet!" I screeched. "Wait for her to wake up! Come on, Allie!" I left Ollie's side to stand at Allie's, smoothing her hair back from her face and kissing her cheek. "Wake up! Open your eyes! Don't you see me? I need you here!"

My eyes watered, and when I blinked, whole tears splashed onto my sister's face. "It's my turn to take care of you now. I'll make sure no one hurts you ever again. Just open your eyes for me." When nothing happened, I shook her shoulders, unable to hold back any longer. I needed my sister to come home to us, and I wouldn't stop breaking rules until she was looking up at me with that unshakeable love she'd always held tight to. I shook her again, desperate to get my sister back, to right the wrongs done to our family, and end the madness for her.

"Her skin's turning cold," Boston warned me. "We have to get it out soon!"

I shook her harder, angry at all of Terraway for keeping my sister from me for so long. "Dammit, Allie! Open your eyes!"

Though I'd demanded it, I nearly fainted when Allie's lashes fluttered, slowly opening to reveal unfocused pupils. She blinked three times, and I almost dropped her shoulders. "Allie? Allie? Allie, I'm here!"

Von and Mason heard the hope in my voice, gasping and swearing when they saw the miracle I was holding in my arms. "She's awake?" Mason needed confirmation, though he could see plain as day that Allie's eyes were open.

"Yes! Allie, you're okay! I've got you!" I choked out a sob as I gathered her rapidly stiffening body to me in a hug. Her breaths were ragged and growing more uneven as the seconds added up. The corroding soul was freezing her more fully with every breath. Her eyes went from unfocused to panicked at the sudden pain of the ice.

Mason held Boston's hand in place on Allie's wrist. "Tear it out of her now!"

"Hurry!" Von commanded, bracing Graham so he didn't fall away from his goal.

Boston met Graham's eyes and nodded. "I'm with you, brother. On three."

44

FOUR

Mason's hand was still on Boston's arm to keep it affixed to Allie's wrist, and Von was clutching Graham's shoulders like a boxing coach. Von counted down from three, and though I felt the instinct to close my eyes, I couldn't look away when Von belted out the final one. "Now, pull!"

All four men shouted out with varying degrees of surprise and confusion, each falling back after a belabored pause. Mason and Von shot back the farthest, and Von smacked his back against the wall. His hands fluttered over his chest in panic, as if searching for his cigar. "Oh no! No, no, no! I didn't touch her! How could... No!" Von dropped to his knees and clutched the back of his head, bowing down to the floor with so much angst, I didn't know how to help him.

"What's wrong? What happened?" My head whipped

around the room, surveying the multiple shades of befuddlement, amazement and horror as I watched the four men each drop to their knees.

"I didn't do it! I didn't pull from her, I swear!" Mason wore a similar expression of horror to Von's, looking to Von and then gazing up with shame and desperation at me. "I didn't touch her! You saw me, right?"

I made sure Allie was securely laid back down on the pillow before I stood, running to Von and placing my hand on his back. "What happened? Why are you freaking out?"

Von banged his head to the floor in self-flagellation as he swore on repeat, giving me no useful information.

The door popped open, and I saw that Ollie had managed to drag his body over to the entrance. "Help!" he bellowed down the hallway to the nurses' station. "She's awake!"

I snatched up Finn's bloody knife and slid it into the hook on my belt. Then I quickly threw a blanket over Geon. I tucked the cloth into his shirt like a bib, and tugged down the brim of his hat so the obviously dead guy wouldn't be noticed.

Mere seconds after Ollie called out the herald, a nurse came running into the room, ignoring everyone on their knees and zeroing in on Allie.

A minute later, the room was swarming with several nurses and two doctors, who asked Allie any number of questions she didn't have the ability to answer yet, while they checked her from head to toe.

It was when a third doctor showed up that we were ordered out of the room. I wheeled out Geon into the hallway, my hands shaking and my knees barely supporting my weight. Boston and Graham hoisted Ollie off the floor and dragged him out to sit on a bench in the hall.

Boston pried my grip from the wheelchair and gingerly lowered me to the bench next to Ollie. "I'll go get rid of the body. Stay here and make sure to pay attention to everything they tell you about her." His normally blasé eyes danced with excitement. "We did it! She woke up, and I felt the life force go into me. It was incredible! You're brilliant. I can't believe it actually worked." He clenched and loosened his hand before shaking it out. He stood up straight, beaming with pride. "I did it!"

"You were amazing, Bos." It was all I could manage as the shock continued to hit me in waves.

"Be back in a few."

Boston wheeled Geon down the hall and into the elevator, grinning like he'd just won the lottery.

It was quite a different story for Von and Mason, who were on their knees in the hallway at my feet, facing Allie's door with me. I ruffled my hands through their hair, but jumped when they both gripped my wrists in fear. "Something's wrong," Von whispered mournfully. His black t-shirt was twisted around his torso. "I didn't mean to do it!"

Mason turned to face me, burying his forehead to my thigh in supplication, like a dog. "I didn't touch her! I swear I didn't put a hand on her when the countdown started!"

I took in the fear that coated both of them, my heart racing anew. "What? What's wrong? What'd I miss?"

Von turned and ground his forehead to my other thigh. He slammed his fist against the wall the bench was pushed up to, making me jump. "The soul split!"

I nodded, looking on their distress with confusion. "I know. It worked. Thanks for helping Graham and Boston. Boston seems happy, and Graham, well..." I motioned to Graham, who had already sneaked back into the room to be a fly on the wall, so he didn't have to be separated from his new charge. I kinda loved Graham in that moment.

Von was uttering a constant stream of curses as he pounded on the wall with the side of his fist, still not looking up at me, his face buried on the outside of my thigh. Finally Mason picked up his head, gazing up at me with distraught eyes. I didn't like him so upset. "Mason, what's wrong?"

Mason slowly cradled my hand in both of his, smoothing the skin on the back and massaging my forearm as if to soothe my ache. I didn't have any aches, though. My sister was awake, so I was pretty much living at Party Central in my mind, brought down only by the two great men in my life acting like their puppy died. "The soul didn't split two ways, *hani*. It split four ways. I don't know how, but part of it went into Von and part of it went into me after Boston and Graham. Allie doesn't have just two Reapers. She's got four."

Von let out a frustrated shout into my thigh that was muffled by my jeans, and banged his fist to the wall again. My brow wrinkled in confusion while my free hand drifted to rest atop Von's head, stroking his short hair lovingly to calm him. "I don't understand. I thought you had to be touching her."

Mason hung his head. "I didn't touch her when the soul split. I promise. I don't know how it happened, all I know is that it's happened." He punched his fist to his chest. "I already feel her. It's the same way I felt you from the beginning."

"You mean... You're telling me that you're my sister's Puller now?" The shock of the impossible coming to fruition before me made my mouth drop open. "But you're *my* Reaper. You're my Puller. You can't reap for two Omens. Is that even possible?"

"I guess it is now. I mean, it has to be." Mason sat back on his heels. "I didn't want the job in the first place. Me being with you at all is a fluke. Now I'm doubly tied to this job? It's a life sentence!" He hung his head, slicing us both through the heart with the harsh swing of his words.

Von picked up his head from my leg and reached out, cupping Mason's shoulder, his eyes filled with unease. "It always was a life sentence. Now we're just on double duty." I could see him finally puzzling through the mess with methodical reasoning. "Maybe it won't be that bad. I mean,

Graham and Boston are her Reapers, too. They can look after her, keep her healthy, and we can stay on our normal day-to-day with October. Maybe all we are is backup for them if one of them needs a holiday."

"*I* need a holiday!" Mason argued. "I wasn't even on the active duty list when October was awakened. I'm too old for this. I don't want to be scooping two dying women off the pavement, like Danny had to do for Mariang. I'm not built for this. I need to be with the undead, Von! They don't rip my heart out every time they sneeze twice. I can't feel this much! You saw what it did to Danny!" He pounded his chest once with his fist in anguish. "I can already feel her confusion in there! And I know you're mad with me, *hani*, and I don't care right now. I should be in Sombi, burying the undead and living on my own! I'm not meant to be around the living!"

"Oh, shut up," Ollie mumbled, sitting up a little straighter. Von's excessive pulling had started to wear off, so Ollie was marginally more himself.

"Excuse me?" Mason reared his head at Ollie, his face souring.

"You heard me. Reaping's supposed to be this all-important revered position, right?"

"I don't care about any of that. I'm not meant to live Topside. I'm not meant to be in the middle of someone's marriage!" Mason lifted my hand to display my ring.

"So you're extra useful now. Is it really that big a deal that you can help two Omens? The workload isn't the same as it was for Mariang. She was run into the ground because there was no other choice. There was no way she could've kept up. Now there are two Omens with double the Pullers, and far less work demand than ever for them." He shrugged. "Don't pull for Allie."

Mason's bitter attitude came out in his voice. "I don't get a choice in it, Ollie. If we don't pull, they could die, and all of Terraway dies with them."

Ollie jerked his thumb in my direction. "Only pull for this one. Von's right. You can be a backup, sure, but I doubt you'll ever need to do it. October only has to reap one person a day to keep Terraway going. I vote you go on a tear and rip through a dozen bodies a day a piece for a week straight, and then take a month off. Go fight zombies during your time away. Shoot, I might even go with you one of these days."

"Bite your tongue," I snapped. "It's bad enough Mason goes back to that. I won't let you risk your life so you can live out your zombie apocalypse fantasy. You're not Bruce Campbell."

"That's the meanest thing you've ever said to me. I would never tell you that you're not Bruce Campbell." Ollie wrapped his arm around my shoulders, ignoring my warning completely. "Oh, so you're the only one who gets to fight an army of zombies?"

"Yes. That's exactly right. It's me and Bruce Campbell, and the list ends there. You can make us tea when we get tired of kicking butt." Ollie grumbled under his breath, but

I ignored him. I squeezed Mason's hand and slipped my other one into Von's. "If I have my way, Allie won't reap a day in her life. I only wanted her awakened so she could break out of that coma. Graham, Allie and Boston? They're backups. Allie's been through enough. So's Graham and Boston, for that matter."

Von brought my hand to his cheek, leaning into my palm with his eyes closed tight. "That's all well and good, but we can feel her. You've no idea what it's like to feel bullet-taking loyalty to two people like this."

I raised my eyebrow, stiffening. I reached out and snatched at both of their chins roughly, bringing their faces closer so they didn't have any room to look away. I didn't mean for my words to come out in a slow building seethe, but I was too incited by them to talk myself down. "Oh, *I* don't know what it's like to give myself to two people? I do it every stinking day with the two of you, you know. My heart's divided, even when it belongs to you, Von. Even when I was with you in the beginning, Mason. I can feel when Mason walks into a room. I know when Von needs more blood sometimes even before he even does. I can tell when either of you are staring at me without turning around to look. I live with my heart in two places every waking moment. It's hard, but you're both worth it."

Von's mouth dropped open, a thousand unreadable thoughts flickering across his face. "This is what you feel all the time? I hate it already, and it's barely been a minute."

I leaned forward and sunk off of the bench to kneel between them. I kissed Mason's cheek and then Von's, looping an arm around each of their waists. "Yup. And I wouldn't trade either of you for the world."

Though I could feel their nerves, they both leaned their foreheads to my temples, holding onto me even when life turned us on our heads yet again.

ALL YOU NEED

It was an entire week before we were allowed to take Allie home, and even then, there were specific instructions with plenty of physical therapy scheduled. She hadn't used her muscles in three years, so we all knew not to expect her to be jumping around any time soon, though I was jumping enough for the both of us.

"You don't have to make a fuss," Allie insisted. Her voice was the sweetest sound to me. It was gentle and temperate, and filled with a caress of love in everything she uttered. It's hard to explain to people who haven't experienced that kind of acceptance before, but there was a sweetness in everything Allie did.

"This is part of your rehab, Allie. If you want to smoke Ollie in a race anytime soon, your circulation needs to improve. Hence, the foot rub."

"But you don't have to sit on the floor like a dog. My

feet feel just fine. Come sit up here, sweetheart." She patted the empty spot on her right on the King-sized bed, while Graham carefully rubbed her left arm. He'd been attached to her side since the doctors had let him into her room when she'd been in the hospital, and hadn't left her since. Ezra had one of the larger guest rooms remade into a suite for her, Boston and Graham, and though the yellow daisy touches were lovely, she had yet to see the rest of the mansion.

Von sat with his knees open on the chair, chewing on a cinnamon stick. "I don't think it's a good idea to introduce her to the council today."

Levi was leaning on the wall, dressed in the black pants and matching t-shirt that were typical of a Terraway soldier. "I agree with Von. It's too much too soon."

Von grinned up at Levi, the stick hanging from his mouth and bouncing as he spoke. "Aw. Cheers, Daddy. Good to know you've got my back."

Levi groaned and rolled his eyes. "I wish you'd stop calling me that. You're not married yet."

"But you already think of me as your son? You love me."

Levi jerked his thumb at Von and huffed at me. "This guy? Seriously? I could find you a better suitor. I wonder if Uriah's got any great-grandsons I could find for you. He was a good man."

Allie laughed, the light and gentle sound feeling like a butterfly in my heart. "Von's perfect for October."

"Really, any suitor at all would be better than this fool."

Von frowned, and then laid his head to rest on the back of his chair. "So long as I get to have sex with her, she can marry whoever she likes. That's really all I'm in it for."

Levi shot me a warning look that said he wasn't above laying Von flat out for his smart mouth. Von had taken a liking to Levi, taunting him when he grew bored of being cooped up. I think he was venting a little of his own daddy issues, as well. It was better than Ollie, who stiffened every time Levi opened his mouth. Ollie was a bit of a control freak, and wasn't all that gracious over the prospect of being dethroned as the man of the house.

"October," Levi threatened. "Your court jester is testing my patience."

I held up my hand to stem the flow of their ongoing needling. "I'm all set on suitors. Thanks, though. Von's permanent, so best get used to his terrible jokes now. Otherwise it'll be a long ride, if you plan on sticking around for it."

Levi's eyes softened. "Oh, I'm not going anywhere. I've finally got my children all in one place." My new dad had taken Ollie's distance and cautious exchanges in stride, never once flinching away from his son's prickly nature. When new people threatened to infiltrate our family's protective bubble, the barbed wire we kept across our hearts was displayed as a warning for intruders to keep away. I'd given Ezra the same hard time in the beginning. Levi was patient with us, so I knew everything would be okay in the end. He scratched at his cheek, and glared at Von. "Not even the worst decision of your life could keep me away from you kids."

Von clapped his hands and laughed at the ceiling, relishing Levi's blatant hatred for reasons no one understood. "I was thinking of going commando on our wedding day. What do you think, love? You're always trying to charm my knickers off of me. Now you won't have to work so hard to take my virtue."

"That's it! Outside now!" Levi pointed to the door, fuming at Von's wicked grin.

Von stretched his arms over his head in anticipation. "This should be fun. I haven't fought a Matruculan since Mason and I last got into it."

"Knock it off, both of you." My eyebrows furrowed. "Um, the last time you fought a Matruculan? When exactly was that?"

"Oh, last week."

Mason rolled his eyes, cradling Anastasia as he sat on the foot of the bed. "It was barely a fight. Don't worry about it. We never tell you about them because you worry too much. It's good for us to get it out every now and then."

I gaped at my Reapers, appalled. "'Them'? You two have had multiple fights? What the crap? Never again."

Von blew Mason a kiss, which Mason caught midair and cradled to his heart like it was a precious gem, making the two laugh in unison. "See? Now we're all right as rain again."

I switched to Allie's other leg and rubbed the thinned muscle gently, showing Graham so he could mimic the strokes when I wasn't around. He'd been the perfect help to her. Whenever I had to leave the room, I breathed easier knowing he was by her side.

Of course, Allie's face was crimson at a near stranger massaging her calf. Every now and then Graham would look down on her with devotion I hadn't felt for Mason or Von until weeks after I'd been awakened. Allie would look away bashfully, picking a point on the ceiling that was particularly fascinating, but the blush was always ready for him. "I can't get over this mansion. I mean, seriously. We really live here?"

I nodded, working on her forearm. "For now. Our house isn't big enough for the three of us, my two Reapers, plus your two Pullers, Levi, Danny and Ana. You, me and Ollie need to have a sit-down about what we're going to do."

She straightened her cream-colored pillow that had delicate yellow daisy patterns scattered on the edges. "What are the options?"

"We could move in here," Von suggested, stating his preference. "What? It's not like Ezra doesn't have loads of rooms to spare."

I nodded, my brain turning over the possibilities. "Or we could put an addition on our house. The other option is selling our place and buying a bigger one."

Allie shook her head. "Both of those options are out of

the question until I get a few paychecks in on a job. That might take a while, since I can't do much walking yet."

Graham tugged on her big toe to garner her attention. Every time she looked at him, she blushed. It was totally precious. "You already have a job. Reaping is a full-time gig, and pays better than you can imagine."

"It doesn't feel right, taking a paycheck for a job I don't think I'll be able to do. I mean, kill people for a living? You have to know I can't say yes to that."

I swallowed, trying to be patient when delivering the explanation Ezra had already given her, and the one I'd needed to remind myself of over and over. "They're already dying with or without you being there. All you're doing is giving them a peaceful death."

"When you say it like that, it doesn't sound so terrible, but I can't shake the Grim Reaper feeling it gives me. This is all kind of a lot. I mean, when Thomas was in my head, he said he was from Terraway, but I didn't know what that meant. I thought it was like, Narnia or something." She shuddered each time she thought of Sama, who'd intro-duced himself as a Romeo named Thomas. "I can't believe he was real – that I wasn't crazy."

I shook my head. "I can't believe you left us because you thought you were going crazy. We could've helped you."

Allie resituated herself, leaning on her elbow. Graham and Levi rushed to her side and helped her to sit up straight, leaning her to the headboard. Graham's hand lingered on her shoulder, and then fell to his side, like the professional he was trying to be. He glanced furtively at Levi, whose scrutinizing gaze made him nervous.

Allie frowned at me. "I couldn't do that to you and Ollie. After all we went through with Bev? I wasn't about to put a burden like that on you two."

"You're nothing like Bev." I'd explained how the stone had warped Bev's mind, but the whole giant ball of Terraway magic was pretty much crushing Allie with too much information. A lot of the explanations were falling through the cracks in her mind, which wasn't quite healed yet. She often had bouts of spacing out, which the doctors said might happen for the first few weeks. I rubbed lotion into her leg as I carefully chose my words. "I would've taken care of you. I wouldn't turn my back on you just because some madman infiltrated your brain. I love you, Allie."

A meek gentleness touched her lips. "It broke my heart to see you chaining yourself to Bev, looking after her like you did. I wouldn't be that to you. Ollie and I didn't go through all we did so you'd be held back by us. What kind of a life is that for you?"

"You don't get to decide how good I get to be to you. *I* decide that. Don't you dare run out like that again. The next time you think you need to save us from you, that's when you get your head checked for brain-eating ticks."

Von and Mason let out loud barks of bitter laughter. "I

wouldn't believe it if I hadn't heard it myself. She actually listened to us, Von."

My nose crinkled as my head turned to take in their mocking smiles. "What are you talking about?"

"We pretty much say the same thing to you on a daily basis. You spewing the same speech to Allie? Now there's no excuse for you to ever run out on us again."

I glowered at the two. I didn't like them thinking they could team up on me. "Unless you both become insufferable assjacks, which you're on the brink of."

"Only on the brink?" Von scratched his head. "I wonder what it would take to tip me over the edge of being unforgiveable. Ah, well. Plenty of time to test the limits after we're good and married." An evil smirk played on his lips as he held his cinnamon stick like a cigar, his eyes twinkling as they fell on Levi. "I adore playing with limits. I think we should start testing yours on our honeymoon. I bought a pair of handcuffs for the occasion. My safe word is 'Daddy's Little Girl.'"

Levi pointed to the door. "Out you go. The room's too crowded as it is, and I'm afraid if you stay in here a minute longer, I'll knock that smug smile off your face the fun way."

Von clapped his hands at having met his mark by pissing off Levi yet again. I don't even think his sleazy comments were for my benefit, as much as they were fodder for fighting with the dad he never had. He was having too much fun pushing Levi's obvious buttons. "Oh,

Daddy dearest. Not to worry. Your youngest is safe in my bed."

"Out!" Levi insisted. "Make yourself useful mowing the lawn before I murder you."

Von stood, confusing me with his obedience that was so out of character. "Are you sure about that? Whenever I do housework, I get all sweaty, and this one can't keep her hands off me." Then he grinned and slowly started lifting his shirt over his head, doing a sexy dance for me with his flexed abdomen, showing off his stripper-like moves with a wide grin. I catcalled, which I'm guessing didn't help matters any.

Levi shot me a glare, which was covered when Von's shirt was thrown in his face. He extricated the material that no doubt smelled like Von's delicious armpits, and thrust the garment into Von's stomach a little too hard. Von doubled over with an "oof!" His bravado-laced smile fell to the wayside.

"Dad!" I shot to my feet and stood between the two, scolding Levi while comforting Von. "You're not allowed to hit my boyfriend."

"Fiancé," Von corrected me, straightening slowly as he rubbed his stomach. "Which means you've got a whole lifetime of me making babies with your daughter."

Levi's eyes widened in time with his flaring nostrils. "October, I'm warning you. I was never known for keeping my temper, and Von's long surpassed my short fuse."

I cast an exasperated look up at Von. "Out you go, you

monkey. Go check on Danny. Boston probably needs some relief."

"Sure, love." Von gripped my hip and kissed me just to be a jerk and piss off Levi. He seemed to derive some small pleasure from having a dad who gave a crap about his antics. It was so childish, pissing off the dad who stuck around because the one who took off wasn't there to tell you to clean your room and brush your teeth. Von was having a ball breaking in his new family member.

Levi? Not so much. He was up to his ears fielding all of our daddy issues.

Our kiss was broken when Levi shoved Von out the door, shouting behind him all the way through the hallway and down the stairs. Turns out Levi had a bit of a temper, but only when Von was involved. Other than that, he was an absolute puppy – no pun intended.

Mason glanced at the clock on the wall. "It's almost time, *hani*. We should probably get to the conference room first, so they don't see that Allie's not up to going for a run yet."

"Could you give Anastasia to Lynna instead of putting her in her crib? She just screams in there, and patient as the council is, I don't think they'll be too thrilled with that."

"I don't need to be there. Von can go instead. I don't mind holding her a little while longer." Mason smiled down at Anastasia, who gurgled at him contentedly. "Look how happy she is. I think she likes me."

"She's a smart girl, then. You're the representative for Sombi, though. Attendance is nonnegotiable. And I know Ana's being so good for you because you're pulling, which you guys aren't supposed to do," I admonished him.

Mason couldn't take his eyes off Anastasia. "I'm not even a little bit sorry. She needs me."

It was because of my many insistences that Sombi was finally recognized as its own country. Mason was granted royalty status, speaking for the country he'd set his heart out to redeem. He'd insisted he didn't want a formal coronation, but I'd had Ezra get him a crown anyway. Mason was a king if I ever saw one. "Let's get to it, King Mason."

Mason grinned at being reminded of his new title. "Oh, right. I'll take her to Lynna, then."

"Cool. I'll ask one of the guys to help us get Allie down the hall." I poked my head out the door. "Dad!"

When Ezra and Levi both responded, my heart melted. Though the pieces were still shifting, and not everything was perfectly in place, with that simple act I knew that eventually everything would work itself out.

I had a family – a big one, actually. Sometimes we made sense, and other times the dysfunction ran too deep for even the most qualified therapist to muddle through without a road map. But we had each other, and after everything that had tried to tear us apart, I came to understand that the family you don't run from is sometimes all you need.

EPILOGUE

DIRTY HANDS, WHITE DRESS

"Ouch!" I flinched for the third time that morning when Allie jabbed me in the skull with yet another bobby pin.

"I'm sorry, but this curl's just not sticking where I'm putting it. Hand me another pin?"

"Are you sure there are any left in the universe? I mean, my head's half metal now with all the ones you've already used." I handed her a pin from the diminishing pile.

"Just sit still. I'm almost finished. Do you want your hair to fall down in the middle of the ceremony? I don't think so, kid." She jabbed me again, but I think my scalp's nerves had dulled in that quadrant of my head because they knew no amount of fussing would help. "There. I think it's done. Oh, it's perfect! Better than I imagined it. Hold on." She picked up the can of hairspray and went to town, slicing a new hole in the ozone layer and turning my hair to hard plastic not even a Ken doll could rival. "There. Now it'll stay through a hailstorm."

"It's barely even snowing outside."

"But if it hails, you'll thank me. If I haven't told you before, you look incredible." Allie lifted me to stand, checking my makeup and unbuttoning Ollie's flannel I'd worn over my dress to keep from spilling anything on the pure white. I stood, my bare feet digging into the rug of the quaint church's bridal room.

I still couldn't believe I was actually inside of the church. Our friends were all out in the pews, patiently waiting for Hell to freeze over. My heart thudded at the thought that Ezra was standing at the front of the church, clutching a Bible and readying himself to marry us. The thumping organ in my chest nearly stopped when I pictured Von waiting with Levi and Mason at the altar for me.

Me.

The backs of my hands burned to be scratched, but I glued them in place. My stomach was in knots, and the nape of my neck was starting to sweat.

I don't know why they kept the thermostat turned up so high in here. And all those people out there, did they really need to be here? I mean, I could think of at least thirty better things to do with a Sunday afternoon than spending it watching me trip down the aisle.

Tripping. I cringed as I pictured my foot catching on my

way down the aisle. Von would be perfect, and I would be the kid who couldn't walk in a straight line.

I scratched the back of my hand to alleviate a little of my building anxiety. Allie put her fingers on mine to calm me, knowing exactly how to be the mama I needed in that moment.

In the four months since Allie had woken, a lot had changed. No one was trying to kill me anymore, which was a totally new concept. The new ruler of Lumipad had actually done his job and cleaned house, locking up Sama's sympathizers. Lang had taken over his family's throne, and Sakuna had never known such prosperity. Lang had actually taken the day off for my wedding. He'd already poked his head in with Ruiz and Klark to send me their best wishes. They'd showered the dirt off themselves, and even wore suits that Ezra had selected. I barely recognized them without the thick coating of mud.

"What's the holdup in here?" Danny's voice was stern when he let himself into the bridal dressing room.

On pure instinct, I'd reached for my balisong blade in my purse when the door had popped open. I wondered how long it would take before that reaction would start to fade, and I could handle normal surprises without a weapon in hand.

My shoulders deflated that it was only Danny come to check on us. I rested the hilt of the knife back in the bag, my thumb running over the inscription I'd had engraved on the beautiful jade handle. My heart ached each time I metaphorically stabbed myself to alleviate and still endure the pain of that particular loss. I exhaled, my thumb rubbing a second time over the words written in Mer – *If you live, then I breathe.* Finn was gone, so breathing, for me, hadn't been without considerable effort. He'd been given a grand funeral, complete with a full military salute. In Finn's shortened life, he hadn't been granted much of anything that was personal and precious, except the bits of me I'd let him steal.

Ricardo never got his Lissima.

After the funeral, it had been Ezra and me to be the last to leave, since no one had stepped in to be Finn's family at the lowering of the casket. Ezra stayed with me while I whispered my regrets to Finn's grave, willing it all to be one terrible dream. Such a small, private affair for someone who'd played such a large role in my life. I kept his blade with me at all times, as my own strange security blanket. Finn protected me, even after his death, and part of me would always love him for it.

I blinked at the intruder who stood in the bridal room with his usual gruff expression. "Hey, Danny."

Despite what was supposed to be a grand occasion, he remained ever his surly self. "People are starting to get restless. Mason sent me back here to make sure you hadn't bolted on Von." He jabbed his finger in accusation. "That's not what's happening, is it?"

"Sheesh, a girl needs an extra few minutes to primp, and suddenly she's a flight risk. Back off, Danny."

Danny narrowed his eyes at me, taking in my unsteady breathing and the panic in my eyes I'd never been able to hide from him. He shut the door behind him and cleared the gap between us, his voice low. "You need to calm down."

"I am calm!" I yelled, disproving my point.

"Clearly. You said you didn't want pulling, but you're never going to make it through the ceremony without it." He raised his hand to touch my arm, but I batted it away.

"No. I told you all, no one's pulling for Von or me today. If we're doing this, we're doing it in our right minds."

Danny's eyes flickered, and for a second, he looked like a little boy who'd lost his mama in the park. "But it's my responsibility."

I deflated, knowing that he needed the job, whether or not I wanted any pulling done. He watched me like a hawk most days, unable to stop himself from performing the everyday tasks of a Reaper as much as he was able. I reached out and rubbed his arm to soothe the anxious feeling he got whenever I turned down his offers for help. "Oh, Danny. I'm here, hun. You can pull for me first thing after the reception, okay?"

"Promise?"

"My very best promise."

"You're leaving for two weeks," he complained, not for the first time that day. "I feel like I should be there. I don't like you being so unprotected. It's not safe."

"That's the thing about honeymoons. They're built for two, not three."

His eyebrows knit together, letting me know that he was set on being irrational about the whole thing. "I still don't like it."

"I still don't care," I said sweetly. "You worry about me too much, mister."

He nodded, fingering the doorknob as he cast me a parting glance. "You look, you know, like a bride."

I guess that's a compliment. "Thanks, Danny. You, too." I leaned up and planted a kiss to his cheek, letting his arm wrap around my hips in a half-hug I knew he needed, but would never ask for. His cheek brushed against mine, adding to the sweetness that made him exhale contentedly. Everyone was afraid to touch Danny, since he was so volatile. He only let me hug him these days, so I never passed on an opportunity.

I squeezed him tight, earning a sliver of a smile before he remembered he was pissed at me for making everyone wait. "Hurry it up in here. We don't have all day," he said, and then exited with a bang of the door.

Danny's changes had been slow, but steady. He was in therapy three days a week, and was actually starting to take ownership of his daughter, pitching in and not checking out quite as much. He kind of sucked at changing diapers, but part of me thought it might be because that was the least awesome part of the parenting job so far. Danny slept in my arms two nights a week, when Mason went back to Sombi to do his zombie-slaying thing. It was rough hearing Danny stifle his cries throughout the night, but I held him tight through the agony I feared might never fully go away. I'd taken him under my wing because I was the only person he'd let calm him. Somehow I'd become his Puller, and I didn't take that privilege lightly.

"You're scratching your hands, sweetie," Allie informed me gently.

"Oh, sorry. Can we open a window or something? It's too hot in here."

"We could always go into the church, you know," she hinted. "I think it's about time."

I shook my head too quickly. "Not yet. I, um, I just need a few minutes."

She held up her hands in surrender. "Whatever you say, babe. You sure you don't want me to get one of the guys in here to pull for you?"

I scratched the back of my neck. "I need them to turn down the thermostat. No pulling." I gazed up at my sister, who had color in her cheeks and strength in her body again. I was enraptured by her, as I'd been at least once a day since she'd been returned to us. "I'm so glad you're alive. I don't know what I'd do without you."

She smiled at me as if I was the best thing in her life. "Nowhere else I'd rather be."

Allie had worked hard at physical therapy, blooming and coming alive as she learned the ins and outs of Omen duties. Between the two of us, we'd already reaped enough souls for two entire years. Our goal was to reap so many that Anastasia would never have to be awakened. My sister was finding her groove with Graham and Boston, who rose to their posts with surprising grace. Boston stopped being such a jackweed all the time, and had settled into a quieter rhythm of work during the day, and hanging out with Danny and Anastasia in the evening. Boston was actually pretty decent at changing diapers. Who knew?

Things had slowed down for me so much that I didn't know what to do with all the free time when we took days off. Ollie, Allie and I had done a fair bit of house hunting, but finally decided to move in with Ezra. We realized if we got a place of our own that could fit all our Reapers and Levi, it would leave Ezra in an empty house. I couldn't handle leaving Ezra by himself with only Lynna to care for him, so we'd decided to move into the mansion for the time being. The plan after today was supposed to be that Von and I were going to take the house for the first year so we could have a bit of newlywed privacy, with Mason staying with us two weeks out of every month.

I'd very much looked forward to that privacy. Then Danny had thrown the biggest fit about it, claiming we wouldn't have enough security with only Von there to guard the place half the month when Mason was in Sombi. His trump card was that Omens live longer with a double pull at night. It was only when we told him he could bring Anastasia and stay one week out of every month that he calmed down. Danny had been my shadow for a while now, unsure what to do with his life if it didn't revolve around Pulling.

My hands were clammy as Allie placed the bouquet of long-stemmed flowers in them. I worried I would drop the white lilies that were wrapped in their blue bow. Von had planned everything with Ollie and Allie, knowing I would cut and run, or insist on City Hall if I was given too many details to ponder. I blew out a breath of fear and tried to center myself, picturing Bruce Campbell urging me on so I wouldn't chicken out. My liberal use of my favorite super-hero had taken a departure from his original role, but whatever. Bruce is so talented, he could play any part I cast him in.

Allie straightened her cheery yellow cocktail dress, shifting the blue ribbon that wrapped just under her bust, so that the pearl buckle was in the center. She was a vision – exactly how I'd pictured her in the satin dress she'd made.

I felt like a kid playing dress-up in her mother's clothes. The white gown was gorgeous – simple and elegant, showing off my curves on top and swooping down in dramatic fashion to my feet, with probably too many layers of satin. The luxurious material made me feel like a princess, like a woman, which instantly made me consider taking it off. I wasn't a princess or even a real woman. I mean, come on. My nickname is 'Bait'. The tiara affixed atop my head mocked me, telling me I was playing pretend with the delicate piece Ezra insisted was tradition for

Omens. In the bridal store Gabby and Allie dragged me to, this was the dress I'd chosen. Now that it was on me, my hair done, tiara in place, and the piano playing in the small auditorium that was packed with the council and our friends and family, the dress felt too tight, making it hard to breathe. My hands were clammy, and I worried that all of this was just too adult for me. Marriage was a terrifyingly big deal, and my flight mode tapped me on the shoulder like a forbidden lover.

Graham poked his head in, his hand over his eyes. "Anyone still changing, or are we good to go? The natives are getting restless."

My mouth went dry as the panic set in deep, crawling through my veins and spindling around my spine. "I... Um..."

"We're decent, and just about ready." Allie glanced to Graham over her shoulder, smiling demurely at his dropped jaw when he opened his eyes and took in her striking beauty. "And you can tell the natives that the bride will be there when she's good and ready."

"You look incredible," Graham marveled, looking at Allie as he always did – like she was all the suns and all the moons on earth and in Terraway. His eyes flickered to me and his smile fell. "You alright, kid? You look pale."

"I need a minute." I took a step back, spooking when my shoulders hit the wall. "It's hot in here. Maybe I should take a walk." My voice choked to a whisper on the last word, which I knew no real live wife would do. A wife would look confident in a dress. She would strut down the aisle, instead of running away from it.

Graham's eyes widened as he shut himself in the room with us and locked the door. "What's wrong? Did something happen in the last hour since I dropped off the flowers?"

"No, I just... I can't do this! What if I'm too young for this? What if we get married, and Von finds out that I'm a sucky wife? I don't know how to cook salmon, Graham! I don't know how to make a decent cocktail. I don't even know how... I don't..." My ribs expanded and contracted too violently, and I knew I was on the verge of hyperventilating. "This dress is too tight!"

Graham and Allie lowered me to the white chair in front of the giant, mocking mirror. The fancy seat was lined in lace. That was a wedding chair that deserved to be here. It looked the part. I knew that no matter how much I dressed myself up, I was still Bait. I was the kid who'd grown up in trash, and no doubt the people in the pews out there would smell it on me the second I walked down the aisle. Allie knelt in front of me, her gentle expression telling me that she wasn't freaking out, so I didn't need to. Nothing was all that wrong, or she would be on high alert. "Baby, it's alright. I can teach you how to cook salmon."

Graham stood over us, his arms crossed over his chest as he surveyed my impending freak-out. "And Von knows how to make cocktails, so I wouldn't worry about that."

Allie reached out to hold my hands, but I recoiled. "My

hands are dirty!" I shrieked, popping up out of my chair and racing to the bathroom. There wasn't enough soap in the world as I scrubbed my knuckles, recalling all the people I'd killed, the zombies I'd slaughtered. I didn't belong in a white dress.

I ignored Allie's fist on the door as she beckoned me to come back out. Her voice reached me from the other side of the bathroom door I'd slammed shut. "I thought she was cured from this, Graham. The stone's gone, so why is her OCD still here?"

Graham was frustrated as he tried the knob again. "Because she's panicking, that's why. It's learned behavior. I'll go get Ollie."

When Graham returned a minute later with my brother, I was no closer to getting my hands clean. It was all that time I spent not washing my hands while traveling through Terraway. I'd been so cocky, thinking the germs wouldn't get me.

I heard them fiddling with the door's handle, but couldn't take my hands from the water's stream to open it. When the door popped open, I jumped. "What's going on?" Ollie asked, placing the bobby pin he'd used to pick the lock onto the sink.

"I can't get married today. Another day maybe, but not today. My hands are dirty."

Ollie took in my frazzled state and nodded. "Okay. Mine too. Move over."

"What? No. Get your own sink. I was here first."

"I need to wash my hands. They're dirty."

"Your hands don't matter in this equation. You're not the one in the white dress. You don't have to be the perfect wife."

"Neither do you. Life isn't about being the perfect anything." He cast around the small bathroom and picked up the brown eye liner Allie had left on the counter. "See, even with this, I can still walk you down the aisle." He opened up his tuxedo jacket and drew a line with the pencil from his left breast to the waist of his crisp, white shirt.

I gasped, scandalized. "Ollie, why'd you do that? Now I *really* can't get married today! Get it off!"

"Do you want me to go home and miss your wedding?"

"Of course not, but you can't..."

"So you want me to stay, even though I'm not perfect?"

"I just... And you..." I snatched the eyeliner from him and shouted, "Stop mind-gaming me! You have to change your shirt. We can come back tomorrow and try again. Tomorrow is a much better day for a wedding." I scratched the nape of my neck, feeling the sweat beading there. "Why is it so hot in here?" I demanded, sounding like a lunatic.

"I have plans tomorrow."

My wild eyes darted to his. "Oh, you have plans tomorrow? Tell me these all-important plans."

"Well, I have to return this tuxedo, for one. Not sure I'll

get my deposit back. Then I have a lot of TV to get through. It's been a while, and my shows are stacking up."

"You're being a jerk."

"You're being a coward. You said yes to the ring. You said yes to the wedding. Von's actually been an adult about it, too. He did everything you said you wanted, short of getting Kabayo here. Don't do this to him. Don't run out on him. Not like this."

My lower lip quivered, and I knew I was about five seconds away from losing it. "Ollie, what happens when I suck at being a wife? What then?"

Ollie was unperturbed by my question. "Then you learn to be better. You didn't know how to be a nurse, but you learned. You didn't know how to be an Omen, but you're the best one they've ever seen. I know you. If you put your mind to something, you conquer. Put your focus into being good for Von. He's patient. He doesn't have it all together either, but he's willing to gamble on you." Ollie gripped my shoulders and looked me dead in the eye. "I'll always gamble on you. Every single time, kid. You've got this."

The germs that had been stuck to my hands started to fade away as Ollie dried them off with a paper towel. I nodded, sucking in my tears and breathing out my anxiety. "You're sure I won't blow it?"

"More than sure. But hey, if you really want to leave, I'll drive you out of here myself right now." He bent his knees slightly so he could get in my eyeline. "But if I do, we're not coming back. In or out, kid. It's your call."

I leaned my forehead to Ollie's chest, centering myself with closed eyes as I considered walking out on the life I knew I didn't deserve. It was too wonderful, too filled with romance, possibilities and real, actual love. I knew for certain I didn't deserve it... but I wanted it. I wanted it enough to work hard to be the person who deserved a bliss like that.

I wanted to wake up next to Von and make pancakes with him on Sundays. I wanted to watch cheesy horror movies and stay up late playing cards and making love with him. I wanted a future, and I knew that I wanted it all with Von.

Right then I made a vow to myself that I would work to one day be the kind of woman who deserved the gift he'd been to me. He'd been patient with my neurosis and overlooked my glaring flaws that even I couldn't see past. He loved me, plain and simple.

I swallowed hard, rolling my shoulders back. "Okay. Let's do this."

Ollie opened the door with a calm smile that told Graham and Allie not to push me, lest I lose my fragile nerve and bolt again. "Everything good to go, then?" Graham asked, treating me with kid gloves I'd well-earned with my panic attack.

I nodded. "Please don't tell Von. I'm a little more nervous than I thought I'd be."

"You don't say. I'd be nervous too if I was about to get four new older brothers." He extended his arm to Allie. "Shall we?"

I waited in the bridal room with Ollie after Allie left to walk down the aisle. I could hear the piano wafting in with a delicate rendition of *Canon in D*. Von had originally suggested I walk down the aisle to *I'll Make Love to You* by Boyz II Men, but I had a feeling that was only so Levi would turn purple again. Now that it was just me and Ollie in the room, I twiddled the long-stemmed lilies at my side, still feeling like a child in a woman's dress. "Hey Ollie?"

"Yeah, kid?"

"This next phase of life's gotta be easier than the last one, right?"

"I don't know. None of the zombies we invited RSVP'd, so I'd say we're off to a decent start." He straightened his tie and buttoned up his tuxedo jacket. He pulled out a thin box from the inside pocket and handed it to me. "Fair warning, Judge insisted you wear this. Allie picked it out, but he paid for it. Said it was bad luck if you didn't have your something old, something new, something stolen and something blue."

My hand flew to my forehead. "I don't have any of those things! I'm screwing this up already! See? I knew I would suck at this!"

He lifted my bouquet, tapping the ribbon. "Something blue." Then he motioned to the box from Judge. I knew it would have a piece of jewelry that would be too extravagant for me to keep. "Something new. Levi can be your something old. He's like, over a hundred or something." Ollie searched his pockets for something borrowed, pausing when a smile came over his face. "I've got just the thing." He reached under his sleeve and pulled off the rubber band from Anger Management that had seen him through many a difficult moment. He slid it onto my hand, snapping the rubber as it dangled on my wrist. "Something borrowed. Now you're the perfect bride."

His words stuck to the cracks in my heart, reminding me that Von didn't need me to be perfect. He needed me to be present, and I was keeping him waiting, making him sweat it out at the altar.

"But you need that. It's your Anger Management homework."

"Then you'll just have to give it back after the ceremony. It's supposed to be borrowed, isn't it?" He opened the sleek box from Judge and took out a diamond necklace with a matching tennis bracelet. Ollie's fingers fumbled with the necklace, swearing a few times before he got the hook clasped in place. The tennis bracelet draped over the borrowed rubber band I preferred.

I looked down at the sparkles that only made my ring shine more brilliantly. Judge always had good taste in jewelry, but he'd outdone himself this time with the delicate white gold and diamonds that seemed to shine just for me. I'd admired every single piece he'd given me before I'd sent it back. This was wedding jewelry, though, so I swallowed my arguments and permitted myself to keep the two extravagant treasures.

"Don't send this back to him," Ollie said, voicing the thing I'd been debating. "It's a wedding gift, and he's been playing nice. He's sitting out in the pews with Darius, Terence and the whole crew. Didn't think it would be possible to get Judge into a church, but you pulled it off, kid. And look at that, no lightning bolts anywhere in sight."

It warmed my insides that the three McCray boys had showed up to be my family on my special day. Our McCray/Reese/Vandershot/Manaul biweekly family dinners had started out tense, but we were beginning to find our rhythm. We were easing them into the whole Terraway business, which was when Judge outfitted my home with an alarm system. He'd even posted a guard outside the church, just in case. "I can't believe Judge came. He hates churches, and he doesn't believe in marriage," I said, wondering, as I always did, if he was proud of me.

"Our little girl's getting married. Maybe there's hope for the rest of us, if you can find happiness like this." Ollie picked up my hands, admiring them as they rested in his. Something tender shifted in his face, and then his eyebrows furrowed. "Your hands used to be so tiny. You'd let me lead you anywhere. Now that you're all grown, I'm not sure I can let go." He cleared his throat and plastered on a brave face neither of us bought. "So where do you want me to take you today?"

The corners of our mouths lifted in unison. "How about a trip down the aisle?"

"I think I can manage that." Ollie led me out into the narthex of the church, both of us holding our breaths as the dozens of guests all stood in unison, staring at us and taking pictures.

I was frozen in place, the pianist no doubt ready to throttle me for making her play for so long. My chin dipped to the floor, nervous and wishing I'd insisted on City Hall.

Ollie tapped his finger under my chin, lifting my head so I was looking up into his eyes that had only ever loved the mess I was. "Keep your chin up. Take it slow. I'll be here the entire time."

Ollie's constant wisdom flooded the corners of my heart, lifting my head of its own accord as we slowly walked down the aisle. My smile was forced until my eyes found Von's.

It was only then that I understood the music. I understood the flowers. I understood the white dress, and all that it stood for.

For the first time, I think I started to understand myself. I could be kind, with a bit of a temper when you crossed someone I loved. I was a hard worker who needed my friends to teach me how to rest. I was a friend, a sister, a mama, a daughter, an aunt, a councilmember, and now I would be a wife. Somehow over the past couple years I'd become all those things without losing myself completely, and that was no small feat.

I wasn't perfect, and I'd chosen a man who loved that about me.

Von's anxious smile beamed when his eyes found mine. I couldn't help but wonder why he'd chosen me, of all people, to look on with such unabashed adoration like that. I didn't deserve him, but I wanted to. I forgot that I was supposed to wait for the end of the ceremony to kiss Von. He was too stunning in his perfectly tailored tuxedo. Not letting go of Ollie's hand, I leaned up and kissed Von's lips, knowing I couldn't wait another second. Blue and gold decorated the chapel like a million tiny fairies, blinking their wings at us as they watched the love bloom that created them. I heard the chimes and bells, and gasped at the wedding-like pronouncement they made – and perhaps had always made from the moment of our very first kiss. The music I know I didn't hire started playing a rousing tinkling tune that nearly swept us both away from the church and our friends.

My cheeks flamed pink when I heard catcalls and whistles rise above the wedding bells. I shrank down from my tiptoes, casting an apologetic look up at Von, whose eyes were lidded and dotted with moisture, his hand on his racing heart. "I was probably supposed to wait for the whole vows thing. Sorry about that," I offered to Ezra, who merely chuckled. I'd never been one for huge public displays, but some things just couldn't be helped. Von had worn too stunning a tuxedo, so really, this was all his fault. "I'm sorry I made you wait, Von." It was a simple apology that encompassed all of our many complicated missteps.

My best friend traced the curve of my cheek, his blue and gold eyes sparking with love I still couldn't fathom the depths of. Von ignored our audience completely, and looked deep into my eyes with all the sincerity of a promise. "You were worth every agonized second it took to get here."

"I love you," I whispered, my quiet pledge echoing out like slow-moving thunder through the cozy church, tuning everyone in to our unquenchable addiction to each other.

The corner of Von's sculpted lips tugged upward. "I don't blame you." Leave it to Von to say the perfect thing.

When Ezra asked who gave this woman away to be married, Ollie, Allie and Levi all stood together. "We do." It was too soon for tears, but there they were anyway, streaming down Allie's face.

Ollie moved my hand toward Von's, but clenched it tightly before it touched down in Von's palm, refusing to release me. I thought he was trying to be funny, but when I frowned up at him, his hazel eyes were filled with panic. "I don't think I can let go," he whispered. "I might be having a stroke or something!"

I leaned up on my toes and kissed his cheek, ignoring the adoring coos echoing around us. "Keep your chin up.

Take it slow,'" I whispered to him. "I'll be here the entire time."

Ollie nodded, bringing Von in for a tight one-armed hug that squeezed the emotion out of both of them. He whispered something into Von's ear, and Von nodded solemnly. We were letting the Vandershots into our secretive world, which perhaps was the biggest growth of all. Von held Ollie tight until my brother finally trusted Von enough to release my hand.

Mason breathed a sigh of relief that he hadn't had to intervene. He stood at attention in his tuxedo at Von's side, casting me a wink that we'd truly made it through the most harrowing part of the wedding. Mason had taken his post as Von's best man seriously, studying up on wedding traditions and even throwing him a bachelor party. I'd resisted the idea until Mason explained that he was taking Von and all of our brothers down to Sombi for a little zombie apocalypse adventure.

I hadn't been too thrilled about that, but I guessed a little *Evil Dead* action had to be better than strippers.

Anastasia was cooing from the front row where Danny stood, rocking his daughter while Ms. Vandershot held tight to Penny's hand. I'd caught her sneaking out of Ezra's bedroom this morning before breakfast, and while I'd wanted to shout my glee from the rooftops, I kept my mouth shut to grant one of my many dads his privacy.

Von turned from the intensity of his guy hug, and acted startled when his eyes fell on me again. His hand flew to his chest, as if seeing me for the first time. "Marry me," he breathed, pretending to be stunned by my beauty.

With absolute certainty, I answered Von with an enraptured, "Only you."

From that moment forward, I knew that no matter what mess life hurled at us, Von and I would never again throw away the treasure we found in each other.

The End.

Love the book?
Leave a review.

TENDER

Continue the series and read *Tender*,
book nine in the *Terraway* series.

"I swear, if you make me mess up, I'll sic all the zombies in Sombi on you." It was a useless threat, since we all knew I had no control over the reanimated undead that roamed the icy region of Terraway's least traveled-to nation. This was a game of endurance and concentration—two of my fortes. Plus, it's not as if I could beat my beefy Puller in a round of arm-wrestling. I took my wins where I could get them.

"Is that so?" Mason scoffed, tipping my elbow just to make the entire tower of O-shaped cereal topple off of Allie's bulbous belly.

"You jag! I almost beat my record!" My sister giggled while I chucked the O's at Mason's face. I couldn't help but grin when he mimed falling over at the assault, acting as if anything could harm him. With his larger-than-life Matruculan strength, there wasn't much that could take him out. Still, it was worth a shot. I flicked the cereal at his face, my smile widening with each dramatic groan I dragged out of him as he amped up the theatrics just to entertain Allie and me. "I stacked them twenty high! You're just sore I beat your record."

He combed his fingers through his hair. It finally grew out to just above his shoulders, and I loved the rugged lion-man look to him. Add his burly form to the mix, and I'm a goner, taken under by attraction to rival any teenaged girl with a crush. "I barely nudged you. You know nothing gives me greater joy than letting you win."

My mouth popped open in a scandalized gasp. As if I hadn't earned every obnoxious "I Win, You Suck" dance I'd treated him to. "That's it. Rematch. Allie, I hope you didn't have any plans tonight."

Graham tutted our childish competition when he entered Ezra's spotless living room, his posture erect, like the gentleman he was. His hair was never messy, which I think is sort of an extension of his entire being. Ever since Graham came into Allie's life, the messiness of her childhood was quickly replaced with an orderly, calm adult existence.

Gotta love a man in love.

Graham smiled adoringly at Allie, which made me love him all the more. He winked at her, and the solitary freckle near his left eye granted Allie a flash of playfulness to soften his professional demeanor. "As a matter of fact, she does have plans. I'm taking my wife out for dinner. Might be the only fine dining experience we get this month. We only have a day a week we travel Topside, so I'd like to make the most out of proper civilization."

I clasped my hands under my chin. "Say 'proper' again. You sound so very British when you do."

"You are a proper pain in my arse, October Grace." He said it with a tease on his lips, so I knew he was joking.

Graham was never parted from Allie for more than a handful of minutes. The more obviously pregnant she looked, the more he hovered. She was barely halfway through her pregnancy; I could only imagine how much more of a watchman he'll become toward the end. I loved watching them be sweet to each other. After all Philip put my big sister through, she deserved to be treated like a treasure.

My treasure. And I guess she was Graham's treasure now, too. I hugged her belly as I snuggled in next to her on the pure white couch. Mason came around and scooted in next to me, his bulk sinking the cushion and making my body nearly tip onto his lap, which I'm pretty sure was his plan. He draped his hand over my hip, tracing a lazy circle with his thumb. He was content to watch me fawn over Allie like the queen she's always been to me.

My spine turned to jelly when a swath of relaxation pumped into me via Mason's touch. He always thinks he's being subtle, but I can feel when he's pulling. I cast a stink-eye over my shoulder, but he shrugged it off. I knew he was worried I was going to get worked up over the sight of a pregnant woman, but it's been two years since I lost my baby. I'm not devastated when I see pregnant women who get to keep their little bundles of joy. I don't feel gutted at all.

I don't.

As if he could hear my internal pep-talk, Mason planted a kiss on the back of my shoulder and rubbed lightly up and down on my bicep.

Allie's voice is maybe the best sound in the world. "Honey, I'm not sure I should leave October Grace. Seeing my brother and sister one day a week is hardly healthy. To cut even *that* short?" She shook her head.

Graham narrowed his eyes at my triumphant grin, holding in his comment on what exactly "healthy" should look like. "Whatever you like, dear."

I drew hearts on Allie's belly with my fingertip, sending messages of love to her baby boy. We only just found out last week, and I was still geeked about it. "Sucks that you have to live in Terraway during your pregnancy. I mean, I get that it's healthier for you and the baby, but still. I just got you back, and I have to miss you all over again." My siblings and I had been through enough to where we felt no shame over our separation anxiety, and clung as tight as we needed.

Allie had been woken from her coma for barely over a year and a half, but much of that had been spent in Terraway, due to how quickly her and Graham got married and decided to start a family. It was fascinating to watch them dote and fawn and fall into gooey promises and blush-laced late-night kisses. He was so proper and precious to her, and she was amazed that a man could be so very kind. If I was limited to once-a-week visits for nine months so her baby could stay healthy, then I would deal with the separation (though not gracefully).

I rubbed my sister's belly and leaned into her side. "Lynna is a better cook than any old restaurant. What are you craving lately, Allie-Bear?"

Allie didn't respond but stared vacantly ahead, her eyes going out of focus.

She did that every now and then. She was with us, and then not. No one wanted to admit her brain had been severely messed with when she was violated by Sama, but the hallmarks of lasting damage were there. She'd bathed in the healing waters, which had healed a great many things wrong with her internal organs from years of cutting, anorexia and just plain neglect. The psychological wounds ran deeper, and though the healing waters were miraculous, my Allie still wandered off into the abyss in her mind far too often for it to be considered a cute quirk.

Graham stiffened, and I caught his eye. The tightness

of his mouth told me that her brain-blanks weren't as few and far between as everyone was hoping. "Can I get you some water, sweetheart?" Graham bent at the waist to touch her ankle, bringing her back to the present.

"Hmm?"

"Water, Allison. Are you thirsty?"

"Thirsty?"

He squeezed her ankle that had somehow managed to stay slender through five months of pregnancy. I had looked like an overinflated balloon back when I'd been knocked up, while Allie looked like the picturesque mom-to-be that you see in magazines, shopping for organic produce and insisting on hypoallergenic baby carriers.

Of course, her personality couldn't be more opposite. Every baby gift was a huge celebration, with her waxing poetic about how much easier things would've been if she'd had fancy things like a stroller back when I'd been the baby she'd looked after. And she didn't understand the fuss over organic produce. When she first came to, it was all we could do to remind her not to dig in the trash for discarded scraps of food.

Yes, she'd come a long way, but her brain-blanks were the red flag that she still wasn't quite one-hundred percent. Every time she had one, panic and something maternal choked me around the throat until I could feel pressure building behind my eyes, just waiting for me to blink so my pent-up tears could go cascading down my cheeks.

"You don't have to go to the trouble. I can get myself

some water," Allie replied with a gentle smile that matched Graham's.

Mason and I both moved to get up, as if the mere mention of a want electrocuted the couch to make our bodies act in Allie's favor.

Graham held up his hands to us. "Don't get up. She's my wife."

"She's partly my charge," Mason insisted. Though he was my Reaper, he was also one of Allie's four Pullers, so he felt the draw to watch over us both, down to getting the simplest glass of water. Death Omens had a hard job, reaping souls to keep the suns of Terraway running. If we didn't fulfill our roles, the entire underworld starved and withered. While the job was lightyears easier than it ever had been, with us only having to reap one soul a week to keep things afloat, the life expectancy for Omens wasn't all that long. The entire Vandershot/Manaul/Reese clan was determined Allie and I would be the first Omens to make it to our forties.

Grand ambition, indeed.

Graham waved for Mason and me to sit back down. "Stay just like that." Then to Allie, he mused, "I love to see you so relaxed. Your sister is good for you." Graham reached over and tucked an auburn curl behind her ear, and then flicked me hard on the nose for overruling his restaurant plans before moving to the kitchen.

Whatever. He had her all to himself six days a week in

Terraway, with only Boston as the third wheel. My sister, my turn.

My phone buzzed in my pocket. When I pulled it out, Judge's warning flashed across the screen. *"Stay inside tonight."*

He's been doing that more often these past couple weeks. Staying out of sight for the most part, but texting me warnings to stick close to Mason or stay away from windows. I wish I could say Judge was paranoid, but I know better than that.

I swipe back a quick, *"Will do. Miss your angry face."*

"Promise me, October."

I huffed at the screen. *"I super-duper promise."*

One day Judge will text me an emoji. For now, he's too old and serious for such things. But one day he'll be a goof like the rest of us, I'm sure of it. That'll be after he quits the drug trade he's been married to for the better part of his adult life.

I pulled out my hand sanitizer and wiped my fingers off. You have no idea how many germs lurk on phones, even one that's cleaned as often as mine. I'm just covert enough with my slight movements that I didn't divert Allie's attention from her husband.

Call me a creeper, but I loved watching Allie study Graham. The look of wonder whenever he did anything thoughtful struck me with equal amounts of joy and sadness. I was thrilled to see a man finally appreciate the perfect woman she was and dote on her so lavishly. Then my happiness crested when I realized that kindness and sweetness shouldn't be something that felt foreign to my amazing sister who'd helped raise me. What a terrible journey she'd had to endure to get to this point. She'd confessed that Philip had been sweet in the beginning when he came to her in her dreams, just as he'd been with me. But when she started resisting his advances, he turned violent.

Sama, I scolded myself as I snuggled back into Mason's body heat, stroking Allie's belly. Sama was the Mangkukulam who'd infiltrated her mind, and then mine, seeking out a Death Omen who could carry his offspring. Allie and I hadn't known what he looked like, so it was easy for him slip into our dreams and cozy up to us, pretending to be the perfect guy. He'd been Philip to me— a sexy romantic with a killer beach body and princely white-blond hair. He'd been a good listener, for the most part. That is, until he tried to have his way with me against my will. Then the whole listening part went out the window. Rapists are funny like that.

He'd been Thomas to Allie, coming into her mind before she knew anything about Terraway. He'd left her a comatose shell, giving me ample motivation to track him down for a good old-fashioned murdering.

Only I hadn't dealt the final blow to the man who haunted my dreams and orchestrated too many of my nightmares.

"Hey, are you alright? I felt a downward swing. Steeper

than usual." Mason cozied in closer at my back, sliding the flat of his hand from my arm to my hip. He seemed to like that part of me in particular. He rubbed in slow, soothing circles, knowing exactly how to bring me back to the present.

I kept doing that, even though it had been two years since Finn had killed Philip.

Sama. Not Philip, Sama.

My stomach roiled, as it always did when thoughts of Captain Finn trickled back into my mind, creeping out of the dark closet in my psyche where I kept memories of him stashed. Most people hadn't understood Finn, but I got to see his softer side. I'd spent many nights with him curled around me while we slept. We'd fought together, killed together, listened to each other, and...

I swallowed hard, trying to shove the sight of Finn's smile away. It was too powerful, that cocky brush of happiness that came over his face whenever he saw me. The memory of it could yank me out of any normal moment, plunging me into the despair that comes when someone gives their life to protect yours, and you know it wasn't worth the trade.

I worked up a convincing smile, but knew Mason could feel my melancholy. He always knew how to sense when something was off with me, despite my best bravado and denial. "I'm totally fine. Just glad to have Allie back."

Mason didn't argue but slid his hand toward mine, acknowledging without verbally calling me out on my obvious tell that no, I wasn't actually fine. I hadn't realized I was scratching up the back of my hand until he brought it to my attention. He separated the offending fingers and laced them through his to stop me from hurting myself further. I hadn't realized I was doing it. Old habits die hard, I guess. He labeled it "self-mutilation" which is just about the grossest description. I saw it as pain management. When my insides got backed up with too much sadness, clawing the skin off the backs of my hands dulled the ache I'd never been able to fully escape.

Finn had been my scandalous bliss but now he was my ache. If that was all I had of him, I wasn't ready to give it up.

Mason kissed the nape of my neck before he leaned over and picked the O's up off the floor with his free hand. I shuddered when he popped them in his mouth, grimacing at the floor germs he merely shrugged at.

"Dad, we're staying in tonight," Graham called into the next room. Then he cocked an eyebrow at Allie. "What's that grin for?" He looked down at his khakis and white button-down dress shirt, always the business-dressed professional, especially now that he was a full-fledged Puller for the most amazing woman in the world.

Allie had worn the constant look of wonder from the time she woke up from her coma, learned about Terraway, and was introduced to her handsome Puller, who couldn't get enough of her. "I hope I never get used to your accent.

James Bond never sounded so good. Do you think our son will talk like you?"

Graham blushed in response, which is just about the cutest color on a man. I stinking loved them together.

"We can totally make that happen." I leaned closer to her belly and murmured in a terrible impression of a cockney accent, "Cheerio, bangers and mash, Helen Mirren."

Allie giggled as she kissed my auburn curls.

My phone buzzed with a text from Danny. *"Ana's still sleeping. Should I wake her up from her nap or let her sleep through dinner?"*

I chewed on my lower lip, wondering at what point I should let Danny sink or swim with this whole parenting thing. *"Wake her, or she'll be up all night. I put her down for her nap at one."*

"Can you come up and help me? She's going to throw a fit if you're not there."

I wanted to help. I love Ana, of course. Von and I lived at the mansion two weeks a month to help Danny raise her. The other two weeks were spent at my house with Mason, so I could get a double pull. *"I'm with my sister. You're her father. You can handle a bit of crying."*

Danny doesn't skip a beat with, *"You're her mum."*

I pocketed my phone and busted out my trusty hand sanitizer to expunge any germs from my fingers once more. Every time Anastasia Grace called me "mama," my heart melted for her. I've done everything for that little ballerina with a smile of gratitude on my face. This putting down of my foot was more to get Danny to grow up than Ana. As far as I'm concerned, that sweet girl can stay my little princess forever.

When Ezra moved into the living room, Allie sat up straighter, as if something in her needed to impress the parental figure. "Hello, D-Dad. Is it okay if we have dinner here tonight?"

Though the tired lines that had taken up residence around the edges of Ezra's eyes since Mariang's death didn't ever fade completely, whenever Allie, Ollie or I claimed him as our father, his smile couldn't be helped. His perfect British lilt made me wish my own slightly southern cadence sounded more regal. "Of course, princess. I wouldn't have it any other way. What would you like?"

Allie shrank at being put on the spot. Though it had been over a year and a half she'd known Ezra, she'd lived five months of that time in Terraway, sequestered from his adoration and sweetness. I remembered how often I pushed him away in the beginning, mistrusting any parental figure who claimed they could help me. Allie wasn't quite so visceral as I'd been, though she was often confused and bashful at the perks of her new life. Having Ezra as our dad? It was more than a perk; it was like winning the paternal lottery. "Ollie likes Mexican food, so maybe that for when he gets back?"

Ezra tilted his head to the side, taking in her inability

to ask for anything for herself. So deeply was scarcity engrained in her that even after hefty doses of pure Ezra, she still didn't have the language to ask. "I can get Mexican food for Ollie. But what about you?"

Allie fiddled with the hem of her shirt, unable to look at him when he focused his kindness directly onto her. "Whatever you want is fine. You know I'm not picky."

I gave Ezra a look and he nodded, not saying a word as he kept his eyes on Allie, waiting for a true response. It was a series of baby steps, drawing Allie out of the childhood we often still felt trapped in. Though Bev was long gone, the ripples of her abuse echoed through many of our choices.

Mason reached over me and pulled a portion of anxiety from Allie, knowing her triggers like a good partner should.

Allie fiddled with the hem of her shirt. "I mean, maybe if Lynna had extra pasta in the fridge, that would be nice. But if there isn't, don't go to any trouble. Never mind. I shouldn't have said anything. I'm speaking out of turn."

The corners of Ezra's mouth quirked upward. "As you wish it, Allison Mercy. Do we know when Oliver James is getting back from Sombi? I would've thought he and Levi would be home by now."

I pointed to the ceiling. "Levi's in the shower. He got back half an hour ago. But I didn't see Ollie with him. I don't think my brother went to Sombi. I thought last week before he left Ollie said he was going to hang with Langgam instead."

Ezra frowned. "Well, I know that's not accurate. King Langgam's in Lumipad, sorting through some political mess. Ollie told me he was going to Sombi with Levi."

I sat up straighter. "I thought Lumipad was off-limits to the three of us." I motioned between Allie and myself and the absent Ollie.

"It most certainly is. That country's not nearly stable enough for a family of Omens to walk through. King Langgam knows how I feel about that. Excuse me."

Mason made a "yikes" face. "That's about as cross as I've seen him in ages. If Ollie's really in Lumipad with Langgam, he's in for a stern dose of 'I was worried sick about you, young man.'"

I stood, knowing the only thing that could pry me away from Allie was Ollie. "I'll go check with Levi. Maybe some wires got crossed." Before I could let my imagination run away with me, I scampered out of the flawless living room and up the steps toward my second dad's bedroom. Or, well, my first dad, since Levi was my birth father.

I knocked on the door, not hearing the water running. "Dad? Got a minute?"

Levi opened the door to the bedroom that was in the same hallway as the one I shared with my husband, but far enough down so that he couldn't hear our nighttime hijinks. That's the thing about mansions.

His long auburn and caramel-colored dreads were

bound up in a leather lace, which Lynna had woven into a thick ball that somehow looked like an elegant nest at the base of his neck. He was dressed in simple jeans and a white button-down shirt, which, now that he was on two legs, was what he preferred. "For you? I've got all the time in the world."

"Easy to say when you're immortal." I smirked up at him, wishing I'd gotten even a portion of his height. He looked more like Mason in stature, where I wasn't nearly as sturdy. I leaned up on my toes, pecking his freshly-shaved cheek. "Welcome home. How was Sombi?"

He grinned, showing off his white canines. "Never a dull moment, as usual. Put down two dozen zombies before I came back. Didn't want to miss Allison's visit. You know how I love it when my three kids are under the same roof."

"She'll be happy to see you. Is Ollie in your room? I didn't see him come in with you."

Levi frowned. "I didn't take Oliver to Sombi. He was going to come along but decided to stay here instead."

"That's not what he told us. Ollie hasn't been here since we saw him leave with you." I tried to turn my back on my growing anxiety but the angst was petulant in its insistence that something was very, very wrong. I pulled out my cell phone and dialed my brother, who always picked up when he saw it was me. When the call went to voicemail, my mouth went dry. I held out my phone for Levi to hear the maudlin drone of Ollie's request for the caller to leave a message. My voice was taut with tension when I spoke into the phone. "Ollie, if I find out you ditched us to go somewhere you shouldn't, don't think I won't unleash my inner Bruce Campbell and come find you. Call me so I know you're safe." I ended the call, but didn't feel like the message got me any closer to my brother.

Levi's shoulder's bobbed. "Maybe he's just stepped away from his phone."

I swallowed hard, wishing I wasn't right about something being so very wrong. "I called Ollie during a job interview once. He stopped the interview and answered. The only time he doesn't pick up is if he can't." I spun on my heel and trotted to Ollie's bedroom, which was next to Levi's. "He's got to be in Terraway, where he can't get cell service."

"What are we looking for in here?" Levi inquired, his eyebrows bunched as he took my consternation upon himself, like a good dad does when his daughter's about to go off the deep end.

I shoved open the closet and peered up at the top shelf. "His backpack is missing. Ollie packed a bag and left without telling us the truth about where. He told Ezra he'd be in Sombi with you. He told me he was going to hang with Langgam, but Lang's been in Lumipad, where we're obviously not allowed to go."

"And he told me he was staying here with you all."

My mouth drew to the side. "Would he have told Von where he was actually going?"

"Seems unlikely he would confide in Von something none of us know, especially since Von's still in Europe."

"No stone unturned at this point."

Levi moved around Ollie's bedroom, and then called my name after I thumbed out a text to Von, and then to Danny, for good measure. "Um, you might want to take a look at... Oh, no."

I was by his side in the next breath, our matching hazel eyes widening at the note in Levi's hand. When he read it aloud, the entire world stopped spinning.

"OCTOBER,

I don't want you to worry, but I went to Terraway to pick something up. I'll be back before you know it.

Stay close to Mason, Von and Danny while I'm gone.

Love,

Ollie"

Read *Tender* and finish the Terraway series today!

ABOUT THE AUTHOR

USA Today bestselling author Mary E. Twomey lives in Michigan with her three adorable children. She enjoys reading, writing, vegetarian cooking, and telling her children fantastic stories about wombats.

While she loves writing fantasy, dystopian, and paranormal tales for her readers, Mary also writes romance under the name Tuesday Embers, and cozy mysteries under the name Molly Maple.

Visit her online at www.maryetwomey.com, and sign up for her newsletter, so you never miss a new release.